ONE OF THE YEAR'S
MOST ACCLAIMED NOVELS

UNION STREET

by
PAT BARKER

"A WONDERFUL BOOK...
about heartbreak and
unemployment and the terrible
wounds of family life on the
poverty line; about the things men
do to women out of drink and
unemployment and frustration, and
the way women survive them...while
UNION STREET has subtleties of
thought and language, they are not
its point; the point is life and how rich
and hard it is, and the different ways
people have of toughing it through
the pain without being crushed. For
all the sorrow in it, it leaves you
feeling stronger and more alive."

UNION STREET

Pat Barker

BALLANTINE BOOKS • NEW YORK

First American Edition 1983

Library of Congress Catalog Card Number: 83-9723

ISBN 0-345-31501-4

This edition published by arrangement with G.P. Putnam's Sons

Manufactured in the United States of America

First Ballantine Books Edition: September 1984

Contents

I

Kelly Brown

There was a square of cardboard in the window where the glass had been smashed. During the night one corner had worked loose and scraped against the frame whenever the wind blew.

Kelly Brown, disturbed by the noise, turned over, throwing one arm across her sister's face.

The older girl stirred in her sleep, grumbling a little through dry lips, and then, abruptly, woke.

"I wish you'd watch what you're doing. You nearly had my eye out there."

Kelly opened her eyes, reluctantly. She lay in silence for a moment trying to identify the sound that had disturbed her. "It's that thing," she said, finally. "It's that bloody cardboard. It's come unstuck."

"That wouldn't be there either if you'd watch what you're doing."

"Oh, I see. My fault. I suppose you weren't there when it happened?"

Linda had pulled the bedclothes over her head. Kelly waited a moment, then jabbed her in the kidneys. Hard.

"Time you were up." Outside, a man's boots slurred over the cobbles: the first shift of the day. "You'll be late."

"What's it to you?"

"You'll get the sack."

"No, I won't then, clever. Got the day off, haven't I?"

"I don't know. Have you?"

No reply. Kelly was doubled up under the sheet, her body jack-knifed against the cold. As usual, Linda had pinched most of the blankets and all the eiderdown.

"Well, have you?"

"Cross me heart and hope to die, cut me throat if I tell a lie."

"Jammy bugger!"

"I don't mind turning out."

"Not much!"

"*You've* nothing to turn out to."

"School."

"School!"

"I didn't notice you crying when you had to leave."

Kelly abandoned the attempt to keep warm. She sat on the edge of the bed, sandpapering her arms with the palms of dirty hands. Then ran across the room to the chest of drawers.

As she pulled open the bottom drawer—the only one Linda would let her have—a characteristic smell met her.

"You mucky bloody sod!" The cold forgotten, she ran back to the bed and began dragging the blankets off her sister. "Why can't you burn the buggers?"

"With him sat there? How can I?"

Both girls glanced at the wall that divided their mother's bedroom from their own. For a moment Kelly's anger died down.

Then: "He wasn't there last night."

"There was no fire."

2

"You could've lit one."

"What? At midnight? What do you think she'd say about that?" Linda jerked her head towards the intervening wall.

"Well, you could've wrapped them up and put them in the dustbin then. Only the lowest of the bloody low go on the way you do."

"What would you know about it?"

"I know one thing, I'll take bloody good care I never get like it."

"You will, dear. It's nature."

"I don't mean that."

Though she did, perhaps. She looked at the hair in Linda's armpits, at the breasts that shook and wobbled when she ran, and no, she didn't want to get like that. And she certainly didn't want to drip foul-smelling, brown blood out of her fanny every month. "Next one I find I'll rub your bloody mucky face in."

"You and who else?"

"It won't need anybugger else."

"You! You're not the size of twopenn'orth of copper."

"See if that stops me."

There was a yell from the next bedroom. "For God's sake, you two, shut up! There's some of us still trying to sleep."

"No bloody wonder. On the hump all night."

"Linda!"

"Notice she blames me. You're getting to be a right cheeky little sod, you are."

"Did you hear me, Linda?"

"Just watch it, that's all."

"Linda!"

"I'll tell Kevin about you," Kelly said. "He wouldn't be so keen getting his hand up if he knew what you were really like."

"Have I to come in there?"

The threat silenced both girls. With a final glare Kelly picked up her clothes and went downstairs to get dressed. On the landing she paused to look into her mother's bedroom.

There was a dark, bearded man zipping up his trousers. When he saw her his face twitched as if he wanted to smile. It wasn't Wilf. It was a man she had never seen before.

She ran all the way downstairs, remembering, though only just in time, to jump over the hole in the passage where the floorboards had given way.

Dressed, she turned her attention to the fire. Since there were no sticks, she would have to try to light it on paper alone, a long and not always successful job. Muttering to herself, she reached up and pulled one of her mother's sweaters from the airing line. There were sweaters of her own and Linda's there but she liked her mother's better. They were warmer, somehow, and she liked the smell.

She picked up the first sheet of newspaper. The face of a young soldier killed in Belfast disappeared beneath her scrumpling fingers. Then her mother came in, barefoot, wearing only a skirt and bra. The bunions on the sides of her feet were red with cold.

She was still angry. Or on the defensive. Kelly could tell at once by the way she moved.

"I see you've nicked another of me sweaters. Beats me why you can't wear your own. You'd think you had nowt to put on."

She searched along the line and pulled down her old working jumper that had gone white under the armpits from deodorants and sweat. After a moment's thought she rejected it in favor of a blue blouse, the sort of thing she would never normally have worn at work. It was because of him, the man upstairs.

Kelly sniffed hungrily at the sweater she was wearing, which held all the mingled smells of her mother's body. Though the face she raised to her mother afterwards could not have been more hostile.

"You got started on the fire, then? Good lass."

"I'd've had it lit if there'd been owt to light it with."

"Yes, well, I forgot the sticks."

She perched on the edge of the armchair and began pulling

4

on her tights. Kelly watched. She went on twisting rolls of newspaper, the twists becoming more vicious as the silence continued.

At last she said, "Well, come on, then. Don't keep us in suspense. Who is it?"

"Who?"

Kelly drew a deep breath. "Him. Upstairs. The woolly-faced bugger with the squint."

"His name's Arthur. And he doesn't squint."

"He was just now when he looked at me."

"Oh, you'd make any bugger squint, you would!"

"Does that mean Wilf's had his chips?"

"You could put it that way."

"I just did."

"It isn't as if you were fond of Wilf. You weren't. Anything but."

"You can get used to anything."

"Kelly. . . ." Mrs. Brown's voice wavered. She didn't know whether to try persuasion first, or threats. Both had so often failed. "Kelly, I hope you'll be all right with . . . with Uncle Arthur. I mean I hope . . ."

"What do you mean 'all right'?"

"You know what I mean." Her voice had hardened. "I mean *all right*."

"Why shouldn't I be all right with him?"

"You tell me. I couldn't see why you couldn't get on with Wilf. He was good to you."

"He had no need to be."

"Kelly . . ."

There was a yell from the passage. Arthur, still unfamiliar with the geography of the house, had gone through the hole in the floor.

He came in smiling nervously, anxious to appear at ease.

"I'll have to see if I can't get that fixed for you, love."

"Arthur, this is my youngest, Kelly."

He managed a smile. "Hello, flower."

"I don't know what she'd better call you. Uncle Arthur?"

5

Kelly was twisting a roll of newspaper into a long rope. With a final wrench she got it finished and knotted the ends together to form a noose. Only when it was completed to her satisfaction did she smile and say, "Hello, *Uncle* Arthur."

"Well," said Mrs. Brown, her voice edging upwards, "I'd better see what there is for breakfast."

"I can tell you now," said Kelly. "There's nowt."

Mrs. Brown licked her lips. Then, in a refined voice, she said, "Oh, there's sure to be something. Unless our Linda's eat the lot."

"Our Linda's eat nothing. She's still in bed."

"Still in bed? What's wrong with her?"

"Day off. She says."

"Day off, my arse!" The shock had restored Mrs. Brown to her normal accent. "Linda!" Her voice rose to a shriek. She ran upstairs. They could still hear her in the bedroom. Screaming fit to break the glass. If there'd been any left to break.

"That'll roust her!" Arthur said, chuckling. He looked nice when he laughed. Kelly turned back to the fire, guarding herself from the temptation of liking him.

"You've done a grand job," he said. "It's not easy, is it, without sticks?"

"I think it'll go."

After a few minutes Mrs. Brown reappeared in the doorway. "I'm sorry about that, Arthur." She'd got her posh voice back on the way downstairs. "But if you didn't keep on at them they'd be in bed all morning."

She could talk!

"Anyway, she'll be down in a minute. Then you'll have met both of them." She was trying to make it sound like a treat. Arthur didn't look convinced. "While we're waiting Kelly can go round the shop for a bit of bacon. Can't you, love?"

"I'm doing the fire," Kelly pointed out in a voice that held no hope of compromise.

"Don't go getting stuff in just for me."

"Oh, it's no bother. I can't think how we've got so short."
Sucking up again. Pretending to be what she wasn't. And for
what? He was nowt. "Anyway, we can't have you going out
with nothing on your stomach. You've got to keep your
strength up." There was a secret, grown-up joke in her voice.
Kelly heard it, and bristled.

"She won't let you have owt anyway," she said. "There's
over much on the slate as it is."

Her mother rounded on her. "That's right, Kelly, go on,
stir the shit."

"I'm not stirring the shit. I'm just saying there's too much
on the slate."

"I'm paying for this, aren't I?"

"I dunno. Are you?"

Mrs. Brown's face was tight with rage and shame. Arthur
had begun fumbling in his pockets for money. "Put that
away, Arthur," she said quickly. "I'm paying."

The door opened and Linda came in. "I can't find me
jumper," she said. She was naked except for a bra and pants.

"It'll be where you took it off."

Linda shrugged. She wasn't bothered. She turned her attention to the man. "Hello!"

"My eldest. Linda."

Arthur, his eyes glued to Linda's nipples, opened and shut
his mouth twice.

"I think he's trying to say 'Hello'," Kelly said.

"Thank you, Kelly. When we need an interpreter we'll let
you know." Mrs. Brown was signaling to Linda to get
dressed. Linda ignored her.

"Is there a cup of tea?" she asked.

Arthur's hand caressed the warm curve of the pot.

"There's some in," he said. "I don't know if it's hot
enough."

"Doesn't matter. I can make fresh." She put one hand
inside her bra and adjusted the position of her breast. Then
she did the same for the other, taking her time about it. "Do
you fancy a cup?" she asked.

"No, he doesn't," said her mother. "He's just had some upstairs."

Mrs. Brown looked suddenly older, rat-like, as her eyes darted between Arthur and the girl.

Kelly, watching, said, "I don't know what you're on about tea for, our Linda. If you're late again you're for the chop. And I don't know who you'd get to give you another job. 'T'isn't everybody fancies a filthy sod like you pawing at their food."

"Language!" said Mrs. Brown, automatically. She had almost given up trying to keep this situation under control. She would have liked to cry but from long habit held the tears back. "Kelly, outside in the passage. Now! Linda, get dressed."

As soon as the living room door was closed, Mrs. Brown whispered, "Now look, tell her half a pound of bacon, a loaf of bread—oh, and we'd better have a bottle of milk, and tell her here's ten bob off the bill and I'll give her the rest on Friday, *without fail*. Right?"

"She won't wear it."

"Well, do the best you can. Get the bacon anyway."

Now that they were alone their voices were serious, almost friendly. Mrs. Brown watched her daughter pulling on her anorak. "And, Kelly," she said, "when you come back . . ."

"Yes?"

"Try and be nice."

The girl tossed her long hair out of her eyes like a Shetland pony. "Nice?" she said. "I'm bloody marvelous!"

She went out, slamming the door.

". . . and a bar of chocolate, please." Kelly craned to see the sweets at the back of the counter. "I'll have that one."

"Eightpence, mind."

"Doesn't matter."

"Does to me! Forty pence off the bill and eightpence for a bar of chocolate. I suppose you want the tuppence change?"

"Yes, please."

8

Kelly Brown

Grumbling to herself, Doris slapped the bar of chocolate down on the counter. "Sure there's nowt else you fancy?"

"I get hungry at school."

"Get that lot inside you, you won't be." Doris indicated the bacon, milk and bread.

"Oh, that's not for me. That's for her and her fancy man."

"But they'll give you some?"

"No they won't."

"Eeeeee!" Doris raised her eyes to the washing powder on the top shelf. "Dear God. You can tell your Mam if she's not here by six o'clock Friday I'll be up your street looking for her. And I won't care who I show up neither."

"I'll tell her. Thanks, Missus."

After the child had gone Doris stationed herself on the doorstep hoping for somebody to share the outrage with. Her and her fancy man! Dear God!

A few minutes later her patience was rewarded. Iris King came round the corner, bare legs white and spotlessly clean, blonde hair bristling with rollers, obviously on her way to Mrs. Bell's.

She listened avidly.

"Well," she said, "I wish I could say I'm surprised, but if I did it'd be a lie. I saw her the other week sat around the Buffs with what Wilf Rogerson. I say nowt against him, it's not his bairn—mind you, he's rubbish—but her! They were there till past midnight and that bairn left to God and Providence. I know one thing, Missus, when my bairns were little they were never let roam the streets. And as for leave them on their own while I was pubbing it with a fella—no! By hell would I, not if his arse was decked with diamonds."

"And they don't come like that, do they?"

"They do not!"

Kelly, meanwhile, was eating a bacon butty.

"Time you were thinking about school, our Kell."

Kelly twisted around to look at the clock.

"No use looking at that. It's slow."

"Now she tells me!"

"You knew. It's always slow."

Kelly wiped her mouth on the back of her hand and started to get up. "I'll get the stick if I'm late again."

"They don't give lasses the stick."

"They do, you know."

"Well, they didn't when I was at school."

"Well, they do now."

Kelly was really worried. She tried twice to zip up her anorak and each time failed.

"And you can give your bloody mucky face a wipe. You're not going out looking like that, showing me up."

"Oh, Mam, there isn't time!"

"You've time to give it a rub." She went into the kitchen and returned with a face flannel and tea towel. "Here, you'll have to use this, I can't find a proper towel."

All this was Arthur's fault. She'd never have bothered with breakfast or face-washing if he hadn't been there. Kelly dabbed at the corners of her mouth, cautiously.

"Go on, give it a scrub!" Mrs. Brown piled the breakfast dishes together and took them into the kitchen.

"I'll give you a hand," said Arthur.

"No, it's all right, love, I can manage. It won't take a minute."

It had been known to take days.

Arthur sat down, glancing nervously at Kelly. He was afraid of being alone with her. Kelly, looking at her reflection in the mirror, thought, how sensible of him.

"Uncle Arthur?" she said.

He looked up, relieved by the friendliness of her tone.

"I was just wondering, are you and me Mam off around the Buffs tonight?" As if she needed to ask!

"I hadn't really thought about it, flower. I daresay we might have a look in."

"It's just there's a film on at the Odeon: 'Brides of Dracula'."

"Oh, I don't think your Mam'ld fancy that."

Why not? She'd fancied worse.

"It wasn't me Mam I was thinking of."

"Oh." He started searching in his pockets for money. Slower on the uptake than Wilf had been, but he got there in the end. He produced a couple of tenpenny pieces.

"Cheapest seats are 50p."

"I thought it was kids half price?"

"Not on Mondays. It's Old Age Pensioners' night."

"Oh, I see. They're all sat there, are they, watching 'Dracula'?"

"Yeah, well. Gives 'em a thrill, don't it?"

He wasn't as thick as he looked.

"Here's a coupla quid. And get yourself summat to eat."

"Kelly! Are you still here?"

"Just going, Mam." At the door she turned. "Will you be in when I get back?"

"Don't be daft. Arthur's meeting me from work. Aren't you, love?" She smiled at him. Then became aware of the child watching her. "I don't *know* when I'll be in."

"Doesn't matter."

"There's plenty to go at if you're hungry. There's that bit of bacon left. And you're old enough to get yourself to bed."

"I said, it doesn't matter."

The door slammed.

Kelly stared across the blackening school yard. The windows of the school were encased in wire cages: the children threw bricks. Behind the wire the glass had misted over, become a sweaty blur through which the lights of the Assembly Hall shone dimly.

There was a ragged sound of singing.

> "New every morning is the love
> Our wakening and uprising prove . . ."

11

If she went in as late as this she might well get the stick. Safer, really, to give school a miss. She could easily write a note tomorrow in her mother's handwriting. She had done it before.

There was a fair on, too, on the patch of waste ground behind the park. She hesitated, felt the crisp pound notes in her pocket, and made up her mind.

She ran into the railway tunnel, her footsteps echoing dismally behind her.

She wandered down a long avenue of trees, scuffling through the dead leaves. Horse chestnut leaves, she realized, like hands with spread fingers. Immediately she began to look at the ground more closely, alert for the gleam of conkers in the grass.

It was too early though—only the beginning of September. They would not have ripened yet.

The early excitement of nicking off from school was gone. She was lonely. The afternoon had dragged. There was a smell of decay, of life ending. Limp rags of mist hung from the furthest trees.

As always when she was most unhappy, she started thinking about her father, imagining what it would be like when he came back home. She was always looking for him, expecting to meet him, though sometimes, in moments of panic and despair, she doubted if she would recognize him if she did.

There was only one memory she was sure of. Firelight. The smells of roast beef and gravy and the *News of the World,* and her father with nothing on but his vest and pants, throwing her up into the air again and again. If she closed her eyes she could see his warm and slightly oily brown skin and the snake on his arm that wriggled when he clenched the muscle underneath.

She was sure of that. Though the last time she had tried to talk to Linda about it, Linda had said . . . had said . . . Well, it didn't matter what Linda said.

Absorbed in her daydreams, she had almost missed it. But

there it lay, half-hidden in the grass. It wasn't open, though. She bent down, liking the feel of the cool, green, spiky ball in her hand.

She had heard nothing, and yet there in front of her were the feet, shoes black and highly polished, menacingly elegant against the shabbiness of leaves and grass.

Slowly she looked up. He was tall and thin with a long head, so that she seemed from her present position to be looking up at a high tower.

"You found one then?"

She knew from the way he said it that he had been watching her a long time.

"Yes," she said, standing up. "But it's not ready yet."

"Oh, I don't know. Sometimes they are. You can't always tell from the outside."

He took it from her. She watched his long fingers with their curved nails probe the green skin, searching for the place where it would most easily open and admit them.

"Though everything's a bit late this year. I think it must be all the rain we've been having."

She didn't want to watch. Instead she glanced rapidly from side to side, wishing she'd stayed near the railings where at least there might have been people walking past on the pavement outside.

There was nobody in sight.

When she looked back he had got the conker open. Through the gash in the green skin she could see the white seed.

"No, you were right," he said. "It's not ready yet."

He threw it away and wiped his fingers very carefully and fastidiously on his handkerchief, as if they were more soiled than they could possibly have been.

"I've got some more," he said, suddenly. "You can have them to take home if you like." He reached into his pockets and produced a mass of conkers, a dozen or more, and held them out to her on the palms of his cupped hands. She looked at them doubtfully. "Go on, take them," he said.

His voice shook with excitement.

13

Kelly took them, hoping that if she did as he said he would go away. But he showed no sign of wanting to go.

"What's your name?" he asked. He had a precise, slightly sibilant way of speaking that might've been funny, but wasn't.

"Kelly," she said.

"Kelly. That's an unusual name."

Kelly shrugged. It wasn't particularly unusual where she came from.

"And does your mother know you're here, Kelly? I mean, shouldn't you be at school?"

"I've had the flu. She said, Go and get some fresh air."

Normally she was a very convincing liar. But uncertainty had robbed her of the skill and her words clattered down, as unmistakably empty as tin cans.

He smiled. "I see. How sensible of her to let you come out. Much better than staying indoors."

He had accepted the lie without believing it. Kelly shivered and looked longingly towards the road. She would have liked to turn and walk away from him, just like that, without explanation, without leave-taking. But she could not. He had done nothing, said nothing, wrong; and there was something in the softness of his voice that compelled her to stay.

"I've been ill too," he said. "That's why I'm not at work."

And perhaps he had. He looked pale enough for anything. "Well, I think I'd . . ." She didn't bother to finish the sentence.

"I come here every day," he said abruptly. "I come to feed the ducks." He had been looking away from her towards the lake. Now, heavily—almost, it seemed, reluctantly—he bent his head to her again. "You could come with me, if you liked," he said.

And stood breathing.

"I don't think . . ."

"It's near the road." He smiled faintly, holding out reassurance on an open palm.

He looked at her so intently. Other people—her mother,

14

Linda, the teachers at school—merely glanced at her and then with indifference or haste, passed on. But this man stared at her as if every pore in her skin mattered. His eyes created her. And so she had to go with him. She could not help herself. She had to go.

When they got to the lake she relaxed. It was, as he had said, quite close to the road though screened from it by a long line of willow trees that hung over their own reflections in the water. And there were people going past. You could hear their voices, the sound of their footsteps. There were even people at the lake itself: a youngish man with two small girls. They, too, had come to feed the ducks. Kelly watched enviously as the younger of the two girls leaned out over the water to scatter crumbs while her father held on to her skirt.

"I've got the bread here somewhere. And cake. They like cake." He produced a greaseproof bag from an inside pocket. "Only you have to watch the geese don't get the lot. They're very greedy."

Already, from every corner of the lake, ducks and geese and swans were taking to the water, cleaving its smooth surface, while in their wake the willow-tree reflections rippled and re-formed.

The bread was still in slices. Kelly began tearing it into smaller pieces, scraping the really stale crusts with her fingernails so that the crumbs showered down. She was happy. She had put her fears to one side. The birds began to arrive. Some showed signs of wanting to clamber out of the water on to the path, but Kelly clung to the trunk of an overhanging tree and leaned far out to scatter the crumbs. With the surface of her mind she watched the long thick necks bend and sway as the birds squabbled over the bread, but deeper down she had begun telling herself stories again, fantasies whose warmth eased away the last ache of doubt. Her father had come back. It was her father behind her on the path. When she leaned still further out and felt the man's hand holding on to her skirt it was so much part of the dream that she did not bother to turn around.

15

But the bag was empty. Kelly shook out the last crumbs and straightened up. The man standing on the path behind her was not her father. The family on the other side of the lake had gone. She started to say something and then stopped, for the geese would not accept that there was no more food. They came hissing and swaying from the water, long necks outstretched, wetting the path with their cracked orange feet. Kelly stepped back but they followed, thick necks thrust out, yellow beaks jabbing at her hands and thighs. She pushed them away, sickened by the feel of wet plumage over bone.

"It's all right. They won't hurt. They're more frightened of you than you are of them."

He stamped his feet and clapped his hands. The geese swayed and rocked away, heads upraised in a long, sibilant hiss of protest.

"There, you're all right now."

But she was not. She looked down at the mottled flesh of her thighs and remembered how the yellow beaks had jabbed. Then up at him. All her original distrust had returned.

"I've got to be going now," she said.

"Oh, dear. I was hoping we might . . ."

"No, I've got to go. Me Mam'll be wondering where I am."

There was a sudden blast of music that went on for a few bars, got stuck, started up again. Kelly's face lit up.

"Well," said the man, "It's been very nice. I've enjoyed it."

He smiled at her and she smiled back. Now that she was going, now that he was making no attempt to keep her there, she felt again that yes, it had been nice.

Yet, as she walked away, the sense of oppression grew. It was so dark near the pond. The light filtered down through the leaves, staining everything green. Even her skin was green.

She walked more quickly, not daring to look back, while the muscles at the back of her neck tightened. And tightened.

Suddenly she came out on to a field of brilliant, white light.

There were seagulls there, hundreds of them, standing motionless in pools of reflected cloud. Kelly watched for a moment, while her knotted muscles relaxed and dissolved into streams of water or light. Then, with a shout of joy, she ran towards them.

One by one with the clapping of wings, and then in a whole flock, they rose up and burst like spray in the air above her head.

By the main gate she turned to look back but could see nothing. She stood, scanning the trees, for a full minute before she could bring herself to leave.

There was a moment of complete stillness. Then in the shadow of the trees, a shadow moved. He was no longer looking towards the gate. He had turned to stare in the direction of the music. The music that had seemed to interest her so much.

At the entrance to the Hall of Mirrors Kelly paused. There was somebody there she knew: Joanne Wilson, who lived only a few doors down. But it didn't matter. Joanne was with her boyfriend and too wrapped up in him to notice anybody else.

She stood with his arms around her waist and looked at their reflections in the glass. Hag and goblin, witch and toad, vampire and crow, and every face their own. They giggled and pointed, and fell silent. Joanne hid her face in the young man's neck.

"Don't reckon this is worth ten p," Kelly said.

"Oh, I don't know." Her friend, Sharon Scaife, who was plump and suffered for it, had found a mirror that showed her long and stringy as a bean. "I quite like it."

"Well, I don't." Kelly was watching the young man's reflection in the glass. "I think it's crap."

"O.K. We'll go somewhere else. There's no need to stop here if you don't want."

"What about the Ghost Train?"

"Yeah. All right."

They stood in the queue for the Ghost Train, eating chips so saturated in vinegar that it leaked out and trickled down their wrists. When the last chip was gone Kelly licked the paper, relishing the grittiness of salt on her tongue, worrying at the corners of the bag to get out the last crumb of burnt and crispy batter.

Ahead of them the Ghost Train rumbled and clanked. A girl's scream sliced the air.

Kelly felt that she was being watched. She looked around, but it was almost impossible to recognize anybody. People's faces were purple under the lights and a lot of the men wore funny glasses with big red noses stuck on to them. They were for sale just inside the gate. They hid so much of the face, you couldn't tell what was behind them.

"What you looking for?" Sharon asked.

"Teachers. Don't forget I nicked off today."

"I dunno how you have the nerve." Sharon, a well-behaved little girl, was breathless with admiration.

The Ghost Train burst through its swing doors.

"Try and get up front," Sharon said. "It's better there."

But Kelly was still looking behind her. Even when they were in the front car—Sharon gripping the rail until her knuckles showed white—Kelly still looked back. The train began to vibrate and shudder beneath them. The last carriages filled quickly and there—yes, she was almost sure—there he was, dressed all in black as he had been in the park, standing out, thin and dark as an exclamation mark, against the colored shirts and funny hats, the laughter and joking of the other men.

The train sprang into life, burst through the swing doors into hot and quivering darkness. Girls screamed as skulls and skeletons and vampires leaped down on them from the ramparts of cardboard castles.

"I thought you were going to pass out in there," Sharon said, looking at her curiously, without the usual admiration.

"It was too hot."

Kelly was watching the people leave the train. He was not

among them. Perhaps he had slipped out before, or perhaps
. . . perhaps she had just imagined it.

"I'll have to be going," Sharon said awkwardly. Kelly
was no fun at all tonight.

"It's only ten o'clock."

"I'm meant to be in bed at nine. Me Mam'll go hairless."

"Tell her you couldn't get on the bus."

Sharon hesitated, afraid of seeming soft. "She's got me
Dad bad again."

"Oh, your Dad. He's always bad."

"It's not his fault, is it? Anyway, you can talk. Where's
your Dad?"

If she stayed any longer they would quarrel. It was better to
let her go.

At the gate Sharon said, "Why don't you come with us?"
Kelly thought. "No," she said. "I'll stop."

She watched Sharon walk away. She felt a moment's fear
as Sharon reached the gate, and called out to her. But the
moment passed. When Sharon turned around, Kelly said
only, "No, it's O.K. Go on. I'll see you tomorrow."

Slowly Kelly walked back into the swirl and dazzle of the
fairground. She was beginning to feel sick, and as she pushed
and jostled her way through the crowds the feeling grew. She
was not sure now that she liked the fair. All that screaming,
and the smells of oil and sweat and stale beer, and people
unrecognizable under funny hats. That woman in the booth,
who had looked so fat and jolly before, looked rapacious
now as she poured her cascade of pennies from palm to palm,
and shouted for people to come up; and the goldfish she
handed out—they were only too clearly dying inside their tiny
polythene prisons.

Kelly made herself keep going. There was a roundabout,
and she stopped to watch. The revolving animals twinkled,
blurred, and finally stopped. She looked over their heads and
there he was, watching her, a patch of darkness against the
lurid brightness of the fair.

She started to run. The buffeting of the crowds and her

own gasping breaths increased her fear. She did not dare look back, because she was afraid that he was following. She ran faster across the purple grass until at last she came out into the silence and darkness of the vans where there was only the throbbing of an engine to disturb the stillness.

There were long black passages between the vans. She started to walk down one of them but stopped when she heard a man cough close at hand. She started to run again, tripped over a coil of rope and fell, not into emptyness, but into hands that caught and held her.

"Hey up!" a voice said. "You're not meant to be around here, you know. I only come here for a pee."

He was fat and shiny with a black moustache. So much she could see in the glow from a caravan window. Nothing that she had feared, nothing that she had imagined, could have been more terrifying than this entirely ordinary face.

When he stood aside to let her pass she ran and did not stop running until she had reached the gate.

Her stomach was heaving. She hung on to the railings and hoped it would settle down. But it didn't. It got worse.

The pub opposite was just coming out. As Kelly watched, a woman turned suddenly and swung her handbag into a man's face. He backed off, swearing viciously. She thought of her mother sitting in the Buffs with Arthur.

She was so near to being sick that she daren't move. And in spite of her fear of what might lie behind her in the fairground she was in no hurry to move away from the lighted area near the gate. For beyond that was total darkness. And the Moor, by day a sour, brick-strewn stretch of waste land covered with dog shit, newspaper and beer cans, acquired at night a mysterious and threatening immensity. But it had to be crossed if she was to go home through the park.

So she hesitated. Until eventually her stomach took the decision for her. She staggered through the main gate and doubled up in the gutter.

When eventually she was able to look up he was there. Again she had the feeling that he had been there a long time.

20

But he wasn't wearing black: he couldn't've been the man on the Ghost Train. Or the man near the roundabout.

Perhaps there hadn't been a man at all.

She said, slowly, "It wasn't you."

He looked surprised. When no explanation came he said, "I've only just got here. In fact . . ." He looked out over the darkness of the Moor, "I was in two minds whether to come at all."

She couldn't reply. A second spasm of vomiting had her squatting in the gutter. When she straightened up again he said, "But now I'm glad I did."

He had not been the man in the fairground. That ought to have been reassuring, but somehow it wasn't.

"Do you think that's all?" he asked. "Or is there more to come?" He was staring at her with a kind of disgusted fascination.

"No, I think that's the finish."

"I should hope so."

He was wearing a light-colored jacket, and fawn trousers. Casual clothes like all the men at the fairground wore. Only on him they looked like fancy dress.

"What have you been eating?"

As he spoke, he drew her towards him and began wiping her mouth with his handkerchief, which he first dampened with his spit. She was too surprised to resist and after a while she found it pleasant to be taken care of.

"Chips. Lolly." She thought further back. "Sherbet bomb, candyfloss, ice cream."

"You *have* been having a good time." He sounded jealous as another child would have done. But he wasn't a child.

"Do you always come to the fair?"

None of the other men had come alone.

"I usually look in."

It wasn't the answer she wanted.

"Here," he went on. "You'd better hang on to my handkerchief. Just in case."

"No, I'm all right now." And she was. She could empty

her stomach and be well again in seconds. Only she was shivering with cold.

A fat woman in a flowery dress had stopped to stare at them.

"Been sick, has she?"

"Yes." His eyes when he looked at the woman were small and frightened.

"Poor bairn. Eyes bigger'n your belly, love?" She looked again at the man. "Best place for her is bed."

"We won't be long out of it."

The fat woman ambled off to join her husband. The man stared after her.

Then he looked at Kelly again, and smiled. "I suppose we *had* better think about getting you home."

But there was something Kelly needed to get straight. "That woman. She thought you were me father."

"And I didn't say I wasn't?"

She stared at him.

"Perhaps I wish I was."

Kelly drew in her breath. At first she wasn't even sure she'd heard properly.

"I don't even know your name," she said. Nobody was going to con her.

"Lewis," he said. And stopped, abruptly. He didn't say if it was his first or his last name. It didn't matter. At least he'd told her who he was. She relaxed a little. He didn't seem so much of a stranger now. In fact, when she looked around her at the people streaming in and out of the gate, his was the only familiar face.

"Where do you live?" he asked.

"Union Street," she said.

"Where's that?"

"You go down Light Pipe Hall Road, past the steelworks, and then under the railway tunnel."

"The steelworks. . . ."

The way he said it, in that light, precise, slightly sibilant voice, it sounded as remote as the Pyramids.

"It's quite a long way then. I don't suppose you've kept the money for the bus fare?"

She hadn't, of course.

"I can go home across the Moor. Through the park."

"It's shut."

"There's holes in the railings."

"You'd go in there? After dark?" He sounded almost frightened.

"I can run, can't I?"

She was scornful, as if he were indeed another child. At the same time it was reassuring. He was saying exactly what any grown-up would have said. It might have been her own mother talking to her.

He said, "But you mightn't be able to run fast enough."

He was staring at her intently. For him at that moment she was not one child but hundreds of children, rough, noisy dirty children, the kind his mother dragged him past at bus stops, the kind he leant against the window pane to watch during the long afternoons of his childhood, those window panes that seemed in retrospect to have been always mizzled with rain. Children who played hard, fast, ruthless games, the girls as tough as the boys and always more humiliating because you were supposed to be able to beat them.

If only we didn't have to live here, his mother said. And sighed. It had been the refrain of his childhood: *if only we didn't have to live here.*

Now he said, "I don't think you ought to walk all that way by yourself. I'll see you to the bus stop."

So they set off together, the tall man and the child, while behind them the lights of the fairground shriveled into darkness. And,

"You'll be safe with me," he says, the quiet, precise man whom people set their clocks by, and avoid.

"I know a short cut," he says, the small, pale boy, taking the girl by the hand.

"Will your parents be worried about you?"

"No."

23

It was the first time he had spoken. At first the silence hadn't bothered her at all: she was tired, and she didn't want to talk. But then, as street succeeded street, as his footsteps continued to ring out over the cobbles, she felt the quality of the silence change. It had become deeper, tense, finally a vortex sucking them both under. She was afraid. She was afraid that if she tried to leave him he might not let her go.

"It's me Mam's night for the club," she made herself say.

"Oh, I see."

No words could have broken this silence. They were like dead leaves that floated across the surface for a second or two and then were sucked under out of sight.

By now they had left the Moor behind and were walking through an area of mixed factories and housing. Here and there a window glowed the color of its curtains: green, or yellow or red. But the streets themselves were ashen. More than once they had passed a row of houses that was boarded up and waiting for demolition.

"Here we are." He was standing at the entrance to an alley. On one side was a tall factory. It had no windows at all on the ground floor and the single window in the upper storey seemed to be boarded up. "You can cut through here. It brings you out into Wellington Street." When she hesitated he said, "You can get the bus from there."

She could have got a bus from where they'd started from.

"Aren't you coming?"

"No, it's late. I'd better be getting back. But I'll stay a few minutes. Just to make sure you're all right." He felt about in his pockets. "How much do you think you'll need for the fare?"

"I don't know."

"Here's a pound."

It was far too much.

There was a street lamp at the entrance to the alley, but its light did not carry far. The light shone directly on to his head so that his eyes looked like black holes in the shadow of his brows. She was glad he wasn't coming with her. The sense of oppression she had felt in the dark was back, only worse. She was aware of the movement of her lungs, sucking in and expelling air.

"Go on, then. And mind you get the right bus."

She started to walk forward into the darkness. His shadow cast by the street lamp stretched many yards in front of her as he followed her to the entrance of the alley. She was walking on his shadow.

She looked back and realized with a jolt of fear that not only the factory windows but those of the houses on either side were boarded up. The whole place was derelict.

Which meant they must be somewhere down by the river. Wharfe Street. Moat Street. Somewhere like that.

Nowhere near where she wanted to go.

She stopped.

At once the voice called after her, "Are you all right?"

She turned around. He was still standing at the entrance to the alley, a tall, thin man casting an immense shadow.

"Are you all right?" he asked again.

His voice had changed. It was coarser, thicker. She turned back to stare into the darkness. It terrified her, but she would rather go on than go back and meet the owner of that voice.

"Yeah, I'm all right."

Soon the alley way opened out on to a yard: the factory yard. She stopped again. There seemed to be no way out. But at least she could see. The moonlight streamed down. The yard look very white and blank, though there was darkness again on the other side, shadows, where the exit must be.

Slowly she stepped out into the yard. She felt herself crawling across that vast expanse of whiteness like an insect over an eyeball. A lifetime seemed to go by before she reached the other side.

But there *was* a way out. Only now when there was no

more need for fear could she admit how frightened she had been. She had thought the yard was a trap.

She ran into the alley, her heart pounding with relief after dread. She had gone perhaps thirty feet when she saw the wall. At first her brain simply refused to accept it. She felt all over it with her hands, looking for the opening that must be there, although there was light enough for her to see that there was none.

The bricks were new. Perhaps the wall had been built quite recently. When the factory closed down. Perhaps he hadn't known it was there. Perhaps it was all a mistake.

Then she heard his footsteps crossing the yard. There had been no mistake.

She pressed herself against the wall, until she could feel every knob of her backbone against the brick. She looked around for a way of escape as her heart hammered blow after blow against her ribs. Climb the walls? Too high. Get into the yard and dodge around him there? Yes. She darted forward, but already it was too late. He came around the corner and stopped for a moment, watching her. She backed away until she felt the wall behind her again.

He started to walk towards her. His shirt front shone in the moonlight. Above it his face looked gray. She tried to think of something to say. Incoherent memories of other confrontations, with teachers or policemen, jostled together in her mind. If you thought of the right thing to say and said it quickly enough, sometimes they would let you off. But she couldn't think of anything. Her tongue felt big and furry against the roof of her mouth.

Then, as he closed in on her, deeper memories of childhood punishments choked her so that she cried out, "Don't, please. I won't do it again. Oh, please."

He was beyond hearing her. She looked into his eyes and there was nothing there that she could reach.

"Mam!" she screamed, then, with the full force of her lungs, "Mam!"

His shadow towered over her, cutting off the light.

Don't be afraid, he had said. The words thick, terrifying. *Don't be afraid. I'm not going to hurt you.*

But he had hurt. He was hurting now.

She closed her eyes, because his glazed eyes and hanging face were too terrible to look at.

After the first shock of fear she had not cried out. There was no point: nobody could hear her. He had chosen the place well. And she was afraid that if she screamed again he might kill her.

At first he had just wanted her to touch him. "Go on," he whispered. A single mucoid eye leered at her from under the partially-retracted foreskin. "Touch me," he said again, more urgently. "Go on."

But even when he had succeeded in forcing her hand to close around the smelly purple toadstool, it wasn't enough. He forced her down and spread himself over her, his breath smelling strongly of peppermint and decay. At first her tight skin resisted him, and he swore at her until he found the way in.

She stiffened against the pain, but even then did not cry out, but lay still while he heaved and sweated. Then, with a final agonized convulsion, it was all over and he was looking at her as if he hated her more than anything else on earth. He stood up and turned aside modestly until he got his trousers fastened. After a while, since there was no point in lying there, she stood up too. There was a pain between her legs, a mess of blood and slime on her thighs, but she hardly noticed that. She was watching to see what he would do.

And he *was* tempted to kill her. She watched the thought form in his eyes like a cloud and then slowly dissolve.

They stood and stared at each other. He seemed to sag and shrivel as she watched, like a balloon that before Christmas is big and shiny and full of air and afterwards, when you take it down, is just a sticky, wrinkled bag. His eyes flickered. In another minute he would be gone.

"Don't leave me here," she said.

"It's in the next street," he said. "The bus stop. It's in the next street."

He was panting with fear.

"Don't leave me here."

For a moment she thought that he might break away and run. Then, with an odd, wincing, ducking motion of his head, he gave in. "I'll show you," he said.

But as they came out on to Wellington Street he stopped as though the roar of the traffic startled him.

"You'll be all right now," he said. He had got his normal voice back. His upper lip was working overtime as if he was in some sort of competition for speaking properly. "If you go down here, the bus stop's past the second set of traffic lights. If you keep to the main road you'll be all right."

The balloon had blown up again.

As she watched he pulled one cuff clear of his jacket sleeve. He was waiting for her to go.

"No," she said. *"No."*

"What do you mean, 'No'?" He sounded frightened. Her voice had been loud enough to attract the attention of passers-by.

"I mean I don't want to go home yet." There were no words for what she meant. "I'm thirsty. I want something to drink."

"Well, you can't," he said savagely. "There's nowhere open."

There were beads of sweat on his upper lip. She saw them with pleasure.

"They're open, aren't they?" She nodded at the fish and chip bar across the road.

"But . . ."

"There's a place at the back."

Still he hesitated, wiping sweaty hands on his thighs.

"Or would you rather I yelled?"

"Oh, all right." Again the odd, wincing, ducking movement of his head. "But you'll have to be quick."

They crossed the street together. She thought, I don't have to be quick. I don't have to be anything I don't want. Though

28

in spite of his words he lagged behind until she turned and hauled him on to the pavement. The more he hesitated, the more obviously afraid he became, the greater was her rage, until in the end she seemed to be borne along on a huge wave of anger that curved and foamed and never broke. She pushed him into the shop in front of her.

The woman behind the counter looked up as they entered, but without interest. While he spoke she went on fingering the back of her neck, enjoying a pimple or a boil. When he'd finished she stopped long enough to say "You can't have a cup of tea this time of night, not without something to eat as well."

He looked at Kelly. "You're not hungry, are you?" For the woman's sake he managed a watery smile.

"I'm famished."

Their eyes met for a moment, and again he admitted defeat. He was too easily defeated. Kelly's anger was turning to contempt: she had to fight to keep it alive. And always there was this dreadful intimacy of knowledge, so that when he blinked she knew how his eyeballs pricked and burned, from the weight of the lids dragging across them. Because her own were doing the same.

They sat down opposite each other at the table in the center of the room. A single light, harsh and glaring, hung from a cord in the ceiling, so low down that it left the upper part of the room in shadow. The cord swung in the draught from the open door, pulling the shadows after it, until the whole room dipped and swung like a silent bell.

She tried to make the man look at her. She needed him. He was all she had. But he did not want to look. His eyes, small and reddish-brown, skittered about like ants in a disturbed nest.

The woman came in to wipe and lay the table.

Suppose I told her? Kelly thought.

There were red burn-marks on the woman's arms where the fat from the chip pan had splashed them.

She would never tell anybody. Nobody else would understand.

29

It wasn't like falling down, or getting run over by a car. She *was* what had just happened to her. It was between the man and her.

And he was . . . nothing!

She had started to think about what had happened, to try to place it in the context of her life. Half-understood jokes—"Got to keep your strength up, Arthur!"—drawings on lavatory walls, the time she had gone into her mother's room and seen Wilf having a fit on the bed: all these pieces started to fall into position, began to make sense, though not yet a sense she could use.

This was deep and wordless. On the surface she felt . . . a revulsion from surfaces. The dishcloth had left slimy smears all over the table. The slipperiness disgusted her. Everything disgusted her. Her skin seemed to have flared up into an intense and irritable life of its own. Plastic was too plastic, wool too woolly, and the grains of salt and sugar left behind on the table felt like rocks beneath her wincing fingertips. Most of all she hated the remembered texture of his jacket, the moist, lard-whiteness of his skin. She found herself wiping her hands on her thighs in a gesture that was the mirror-image of his.

She looked away from him again. But it was no use: the room was lined with mirror-tiles. Wherever she looked, their eyes met.

The fish and chips arrived. From sheer force of habit Kelly picked up her knife and fork and started to eat. One mouthful was enough. She said, "I don't think I'm hungry after all."

He didn't say anything. He was making no attempt to eat. The fish and chips, steaming up into his face, had opened the pores on his nose: he look coarser than she had seen him look before. But still unlined. There were no laughter or frown lines on his face. It wasn't a grown-up face at all, she thought.

Then, as she continued to stare, she saw a slight movement, a crumbling almost, at the corners of the lids. Something was happening to his face. It was beginning to split, to crack, to disintegrate from within, like an egg when the time for hatching has come. She wanted to run. She didn't want to stay there and see what would hatch out of this egg. But horror kept her pinned to her chair. And the face went on cracking. And now moisture of some kind was oozing out of the corners of his eyes, running into cracks that had not been there a minute before, dripping, finally, into the open, the agonized mouth. She watched, afraid. And looked away. But that was no use.

From every side his reflection leapt back at her, as the mirror-tiles filled with the fragments of his shattered face.

Kelly looked around for help. But the woman had gone. She stood up. It seemed necessary to say something but the words would not come. He went on and on and on crying as if he had forgotten how to stop.

Kelly turned and ran.

Mrs. Brown stood in the kitchen, and waited for the kettle to boil. She kept her hand on the handle and couldn't tell whether it was the vibration of the metal or her own distress that made her hand shake. She leaned forward, she was parched for a cup of tea, and her reflection loomed up, ox-jawed and brutal, in the curve of the teapot.

It was past schooltime and Kelly was still in bed. But on this day it didn't matter. On this day there would be no nagging. Linda, pink and moist-eyed, had crept out to work early. Arthur was still asleep.

And Kelly, was she asleep? Or was she lying awake, staring at the ceiling? Mrs. Brown didn't know and was afraid to go upstairs and find out. The sight of her daughter's misery would bring her own gushing to the surface again, and it had taken most of the night for her to get it under control. She had asked the doctor to give Kelly a sleeping pill, but he had said, no, let her shout and scream if she wants to. It was better for her to do that than go on bottling it up. Better for who? Mrs. Brown had wanted to ask, though of course she didn't. She had wanted Kelly unconscious as fast as possible, as much for her own sake as the child's.

The kettle boiled. She made the tea, but when she tried to lift the tray her hand shook so much that some slopped over the sides of the cups. She dabbed at the mess with a dishcloth, ineffectually, and heard herself start to whimper. The whimpering frightened her; it sounded so lost, so out of control, so unlike her normal self. For she thought of herself as a hard, tough, realistic woman, able to cope with most things. She had had to be, bringing up two children on her own.

She felt a spasm of hatred for her husband whom she had not thought of for years but who was now, momentarily, identified in her mind with The Man. It had been so easy for him to walk out, and he didn't give a bugger, he never even sent them something for Christmas, not even a bloody card; not that she wanted him to, mind, she wouldn't've thanked him for it if he had; they could do without him. Then there was Arthur, who, in spite of his big talk last night, had fallen asleep as soon as his head touched the pillow, and was still asleep now, his cheeks juddering with every breath. God, what a useless lot!

She needed a woman to talk to, but in all this sodding street there wasn't one of 'em you could trust. They'd all turned against her, because since Tom left there'd been other men in the house. Jealous cows. And how they'd talk! Coo and sympathize, oh, yes. But talk. She could hear them now, "Well, what can you expect, leaving the bairn alone half the bloody night? You know where *she'd* be, don't you? Out boozing at the Buffs with that Arthur Robson. Eeeee!"

Trouble was, none of them knew what Kelly was like. You'd need eyes in your arse to keep track of her.

She was crying as she carried the tray upstairs. She'd got up because she couldn't stand the warmth of Arthur's body a second longer. He never wore owt in bed and whenever in the night he'd turn over she could feel the fuzz of gingery-pink hairs on his backside. The first night that hair had excited her, though it made her shudder now. The hard, hairy, male bum clenching and unclenching . . . She twitched her thoughts away.

As she put the tray down Arthur started to wake up, bringing his lips together with little contented smacking sounds. It was intolerable. She could not bear to stay and watch it, or see the memory of what had happened in his eyes.

She left her own tea beside his on the table and ran downstairs. On the doorstep she hesitated, but only for a second. Muriel Scaife would be safest but she worked as a cleaner in the mornings and might not be back yet. Iris King, then. Iris, built like the side of a house, seemed to offer the same assurance of shelter.

She knocked on Iris's door and waited, hugging herself, protecting herself as much from the memory of last night as from the wind that whipped whirls of dust along the street. There was nobody about. The men were already at work. The women had not yet got ready to go shopping. Long and gray, the street stretched away into the distance. She shivered, knowing it too well to hate it.

Iris King's eyes widened when she saw who was on her doorstep, but only momentarily. She had seen the police car parked outside the Browns' last night as she was coming home from the Bingo, and had even made a special trip up to the fish and chip shop hoping for news. She had never thought that Mrs. Brown would come to her, for she was apt to play her mouth on the subject of women who neglected their children and she didn't care who heard her. Iris saw that Mrs. Brown was close to tears. She led her along the passage and into the living room, resting one massive freckled arm on the other woman's thin shoulders, for she was a woman who needed to touch people.

For a long time Mrs. Brown could only sob and choke and when she did manage to speak it was only the single word "Kelly", and then, "My bairn."

Iris stood with her back to the fire and waited. She was a formidable sight with her bare arms and massive breasts. Her frizzy blonde hair was in rollers: pink spikes stuck out aggressively at all angles, except where a headscarf pressed them uncomfortably close to her scalp. Her bairn indeed! Pity she hadn't thought of that a bit sooner.

Gradually, Iris got the full story out of her. My God, she thought, unwilling to believe it. She knew Kelly well. When Kelly's own house was empty—which, let's face it, was more often than not—she would go across to watch Iris's telly. She was no bother and the bit of food that bairn ate'd never be missed.

"They should flog 'em," she said when Mrs. Brown's sobs had died down. "It's no good mucking around with probation and all that. They should bring the birch back in."

"I wouldn't flog 'em," said Mrs. Brown. "I'd get a blowtorch and burn the bugger off. And I wouldn't care how they screamed. It's not even as if she was old-looking for her age. She's not. He could see she was a bairn."

"No hope of them catching him?"

"No. Well, it's three weeks, he could be anywhere now. If only she'd come straight out with it!" This thought, arousing as it did all Mrs. Brown's doubts about her daughter's story, reduced her to silence for a while. But her voice, cracked and bleating with distress, went on echoing all over the room. Both women heard the echoes and were made uncomfortable by them.

Mrs. Brown said, "You know she even tried to wash her own pants out? She was just going to put them away and not tell anybody. Then when she couldn't get the blood out she wrapped them up and put them in the bin. I knew a pair had gone missing, mind." For a moment she hugged herself and rocked.

"We were just sat there," she said. "And suddenly she set on screaming. You know all I could think of was she must be ill. And then it all come out."

They had been watching *Crossroads*. Even as Kelly screamed there had been a moment of resentment that she should have chosen that time of the day to get appendicitis or whatever it was she had.

"I wonder why she waited that long?"

"I don't know. I've thought and thought and I just don't know."

"She's mebbe been too frightened, eh?"

"But she must've known he couldn't do anything to her."

"Aye. But bairns don't think like that."

It was a comforting line of thought, though Mrs. Brown knew her daughter too well to believe it entirely. "Yes, I suppose that must be it. She's been too scared. But that was what the police said, you know. If only she'd spoke up a bit sooner. Oh, and then there was the doctor messing her about. I mean, I know they have to, but you can't help thinking if they're not going to get him anyway . . . what's the point? And that upset her."

"What you need is a good strong cup of tea."

Iris went into the kitchen to make it. Now she was no longer faced by the sight of Mrs. Brown's misery she was more inclined to withhold her sympathy and make judgments. Her bairn! Where had she been when it happened?

And Mrs. Brown, looking uneasily around the fanatically clean and tidy living room, wondered what on earth had possessed her to come. Iris wouldn't keep any of this to herself—well, you couldn't expect her to. But the version that went the rounds wouldn't be fair on her. And it had been late, and she had been at the club. But then what was Kelly doing wandering around at that time of night when she'd been told to come home? The police had blamed *her* for it. They hadn't said much but you could tell. The one with the moustache had been looking right down his nose . . .

Nobody understood. It was her child, her daughter, and in this extremity so utterly hers that she felt her own flesh torn.

"He didn't just muck around with her, you know," she burst out as soon as Iris came back. She wanted them all to understand the enormity of what had happened. "He stuck it right the way in."

The words felt solid and sticky in her mouth like phlegm,

and after she had said them there was nothing else that she wanted to say. She huddled over the cup of tea and rocked herself for comfort.

Iris looked at her closely. Say what you like about her, she was feeling it. In fact, she was bloody knackered. "Howay," she said, when Mrs. Brown had finished her tea, "I'll take you back home."

She led her across the street and saw her settled on to the sofa in the living room, sparing no more than a single glance of disapproval for the messy room and the unwashed hearth.

"I haven't had time . . ." said Mrs. Brown.

"No, of course you haven't, love," Iris replied. There was six months' muck in the room if there was a day's. "Tell you what, I'll put the fire on. You'll feel a lot better when you're warmed through." She knelt down and started to rake out the ash. "Still in bed, is she?"

"Yes," said Mrs. Brown.

"Best place."

Iris had the fire alight in no time despite the lack of sticks. She waited until the paper she was holding over the fireplace turned bright orange and began to char, then whipped it away in a cloud of acrid smoke. "There. That should go."

She was remembering that she'd shown Kelly how to light a fire without sticks. Hanging was too good for the sods.

Arthur shambled in. He stopped abruptly when he saw Iris, for he was wary of her, as many men were.

"Now then," she said.

"Now then."

Arthur sat down in the armchair to demonstrate his right to be there and immediately wished he hadn't, because she towered over him.

"Well," she said, "I'll be away now. If there's owt you need you know where I am. Or Ted. He's on two till ten so he'll be in the house all morning."

"Right, thanks, Missus," Arthur said, taking over the role of man of the house. He went to the front door with her and Mrs. Brown could hear their voices on the step.

He came back looking furtive. Of course it was difficult for him, not being one of the family. He could neither take part in what was happening nor decently go away. But his creeping about, his attempts to obliterate himself, irritated her more than the most insensitive intervention could have done.

"Have I to stop home?" he asked.

"Oh no, you go to work. Keep everything normal."

"Right."

It was the answer she had wanted and yet she resented it. He needn't've sounded so relieved. He stood there looking helpless and the sight of him increased her own feeling of helplessness. She wanted to cry again but she couldn't.

As if reading her thoughts, he said, "You know, you'd be better if you could let yourself go. It's no use bottling things up."

"Crying won't help."

If he thought it might it was not his place to say so.

They sat in silence. She wanted to say something nasty to him but could find no justification. Instead she said, "Iris doesn't miss much, does she? I saw her looking at the hearth." Bending down, she started picking up cigarette butts.

"Oh, don't bother with that now," he said.

One of the cigarette ends had pink smears around it. They always brought a woman with them, they said: to talk to the child.

Her eyes prickled. She might have cried after all if the sound of Kelly's footsteps on the landing had not stopped her.

"She's awake," Arthur said, looking more than ever as though he would like to bolt for the door. She wished he would. Then was glad he was there. She was afraid of Kelly. Then, again, she wanted him out of the way.

"Pop out and see if I've opened the yard door, love. The bin men won't be able to get in and it's practically overflowing."

But he sat on, frozen, as she was, by the sound of bare feet slapping across the lino overhead.

37

"Have you told the school?" he asked. "I mean, that she's not going in today?"

She shook her head. "No. They'll know soon enough."

Kelly was on the stairs now. Mrs. Brown tried to think of something to say, but her mind was blank. She half expected the child to look different; but she looked the same, only heavier perhaps, with something clay-like in the color of her skin. She gave them one glance, cool, almost hostile, and hurried past them into the kitchen. It was hard to believe in the extreme distress of the previous night; but then it had vanished by the time the police arrived. She had been mulish, obstinate by then: not obviously disturbed at all.

She wore a skimpy nightdress. Mrs. Brown noticed for the first time that she had outgrown it. It was almost up to her bottom at the back.

"Hadn't you better put something on? A cardigan?"

Mrs. Brown reached up and pulled one down from the airing line.

"I'm not cold."

"I'll get you something to eat."

"I'm not hungry."

"Oh, you must be."

"I see the milk's off."

By this time Mrs. Brown had followed her daughter into the kitchen. Kelly, one eye closed, was squinting down the neck of a milk bottle.

"Oh, it's still usable. I'll put the kettle on."

Kelly stood aside to let her get to the sink. Her skin, Mrs. Brown could not help thinking, was exactly the same shade as the milk: blue-white, slightly "off"-looking.

"I wish you'd put something on," she said again.

"I've told you. I'm not cold." Though the October morning outside the kitchen window looked like the dead of winter.

Mrs. Brown had to endure those white, smooth, childlike and yet not sufficiently childlike shoulders. For something to do, she started to butter bread. Arthur hovered uncertainly in the passage between the living room and the kitchen. Every-

body seemed to feel that if they moved too suddenly something might break. Mrs. Brown found herself taking long,
shallow, noiseless breaths.

"Who's all that for?" Kelly asked.

Mrs. Brown looked down and realized that she had but-
tered enough bread for a family of six. Blushing, she pushed
the plate aside. She felt a spasm of dislike for her daughter.
She said, "You know, you should make the effort to eat
something. You didn't have anything last night."

Kelly shrugged. She seemed so normal. Her hair fell in a
greasy tangle over her face, but even that was usual. She was
adept at using her hair to hide her thoughts. Mrs. Brown was
disappointed. She felt as if she was being cheated of a drama
that she had the right to expect. Kelly couldn't scream like
that and have police all over the house, and then go back to
being normal.

"Did you sleep all right?" she asked.

"Not bad."

The nightdress was slightly transparent. Although Kelly
had nothing that you could call a bust, hardly as much as
many men, her nipples seemed to demand attention. Like eyes
in her chest. You couldn't avoid seeing them.

Arthur decided he would check that the yard door was open
for the bin men. When he came back into the kitchen, Kelly
was leaning against the larder with both hands round a cup of
tea. He felt shy with her. He said, gruffly, he might have a
walk down the town if nobody wanted him for anything?
Nobody did. He hunched his shoulders, as if expecting a
blow, and hurried out of the house.

Normally when Arthur left the relationship between mother
and daughter became easier. Today of all days Mrs. Brown
needed that slackening of tension. It didn't come. Kelly had
started picking at a slice of bread. Mrs. Brown tried to catch
her eye but her hair was all over her face. Kelly was determined not to look.

"If I was you I'd have a good wash and brush me hair. It'd
make you feel better."

When had soap and water made Kelly feel better? But her grubbiness in this altered situation was no longer childish dirt. It looked sluttish.

"Later," mumbled Kelly, through a mouthful of bread.

"I'm only trying to think what's best for you," said Mrs. Brown, her voice quivering. "A nice bowl of water in front of the fire? I'll bring your clothes down."

"No, thanks. I'm going back up in a minute." She paused. "Why aren't you at work?"

The question took Mrs. Brown's breath away.

"You will have to go back, won't you?" Kelly sounded indifferent, if not cheeky.

"But not today!"

"Mam, it happened three weeks ago. You've been out every night since then."

The remark chafed a raw edge in Mrs. Brown's mind. "Well, what do you expect? If you don't tell people anything. What are we meant to do? You know bloody well if you'd told us you wouldn't't've been left on your own for one night. And there might have been some chance of catching the bugger then . . ."

"They won't catch him."

"No, thanks to you, they won't! He could be anywhere. Mucking about with some other little lass. I don't know, Kelly, I just don't understand. He mightn't let the next one go. Have you thought of that? He could have strangled you. That's what they do, you know. Why didn't you run away?"

Kelly screwed up her face with the effort of not listening. She was off. There was no stopping her now.

For Mrs. Brown it was a relief. The questions chased each other out. Why go with him? Why didn't you run away? And afterwards, why did you stay with him? Why did you go into the café? If he made you go, why didn't you tell the woman. Why didn't you tell me? Why wait three weeks? And after waiting three weeks and nearly screaming the house down, why say so little to the police? Why?

Kelly waited for it to be over.

When her mother seemed to have finished, she put down the half-eaten slice of bread and made towards the door. She had to pass her mother to get to it. They looked at each other. Each at that moment expected, and perhaps wanted, an embrace.

Mrs. Brown could smell her daughter. Was it her imagination or was there, mixed in with the smell of unwashed child, another smell, yeasty and acrid? There couldn't be. After all, three weeks! And yet the smell repelled her.

If only she could have reached out and held her daughter. The childish bones jutting through the off-white skin might have reassured her that what she felt was merely sympathy and outraged love, not a more complex mixture of fascination and distaste for this immature, and yet no longer innocent, flesh.

Kelly looked at her mother. If she longed for love she did not know it. She felt only a renewed and more savage pride in her ability to survive alone.

Mrs. Brown stood aside to let her pass.

As Mrs. Brown had foreseen it was not long before everybody knew, though they were not told by Iris King, who was quite capable of relishing that last refinement of power: to know what others do not know and yet say nothing.

Nobody knew how to react. They all knew and liked Kelly. You couldn't very well ignore it. And yet to come right out with it. . . . In the end they behaved as if the child had been ill. They asked after her, they gave comics and sweets, they clucked, they fussed; they even offered to do the shopping.

The women were more open in their sympathy than the men, who felt the outrage if anything more deeply but sidled past the subject, wincing.

The children were told to play with Kelly as usual and not ask any questions. They did play with her, dutifully, for a while, but they knew by instinct what their parents preferred to ignore: she was no longer a child. After a decent interval they left her alone. Which seemed to suit her very well.

41

Behind the family's back they talked, grown-ups and children alike. The whispering never stopped. Behind closed doors voices spoke out more freely. Mr. Broadbent, sparse hair standing up with excitement, spit flying, strode up and down the bedroom floor telling Mrs. Broadbent at great length and in some detail how he would punish sexual offenders. Finally, in a burst of civic zeal, he mounted that heap of white and defeated flesh and gave it such a pounding as it had not enjoyed, or endured, for many a long year.

Gradually the excitement died down. Most people in the street regretted that and made sporadic attempts to revive the topic. Only Mrs. Broadbent was pleased.

But though the talk died away, Kelly remained alone. The other children avoided her—or she them. Mrs. Brown, after the first shock was over, went out every night as she had always done. And Kelly roamed the streets till all hours, as *she* had always done, but alone.

Of course she was not the same. For one thing her appearance changed. People were used to the mane of coarse, dark hair. They were used to the way she hid behind it to avoid awkward questions. Suddenly, it was gone. She cut it off. You could tell she'd done it herself because it stood up all over her head in jagged spikes and chunks. Give the woman her due, Mrs. Brown had her around to the hairdresser's the next day, and by the time they'd finished it didn't look too bad, not bad at all.

And yet it was shocking. She could have shaved her head, the effect it had. People took it for what it was: an act of rebellion, at once self-mutilating and aggressive. And they drew back from her because of it. In the past she had avoided their eyes. Now they found themselves avoiding hers, for the short hair revealed eyes of a curious naked amber: an animal's eyes.

The trouble was, she was not enough of a child. Her nipples were bigger than they had been. It was difficult to avoid seeing them. Even the scruffy boy's tee-shirts she'd taken to wearing didn't hide them, but rather made them, by contrast, more painfully apparent. You looked. You couldn't help yourself. And raised your eyes. And when you floundered, not knowing how to express, or hide, your thoughts she didn't help at all: she let you flounder. And always there were those eyes. Cool. Amused. Hostile. Controlled.

They were affronted. They had offered sympathy and been rejected. What they could not know was that in their own eyes when they looked at her she saw not sympathy but an unadmitted speculation.

In the end they let her alone.

Whatever else she was, she was no longer the child they had known. Dimly they sensed an inner transformation that paralleled the one they saw. But they did not try, or hope, to understand it. She was accepted in Union Street as her mother was not. But for the moment at least, she had moved beyond the range of understanding.

*　　*　　*

It was a cold night. Frost glinted on the surface of the cobbles as Kelly ran the few yards from the fish and chip shop to her house. Sometimes she regretted the loss of her hair: it had kept her neck warm better than any scarf. She burst into the house, too cold to feel frightened. She *was* still frightened sometimes, though only of the darkness, and only in the house, when she was alone.

The telly kept her company on the nights her Mam and Linda were out.She watched anything rather than switch it off. Tonight, there was a program about Northern Ireland. She settled down, expecting to be bored. But then there was this young man, this soldier, and he was lying in a sort of cot, a bed with sides to it, and he was shouting out, great bellows of rage, as he looked out through the bars at the ward where nobody came. What caught her attention was: they'd shaved all his hair off. You could see the scars where they'd dug the bullets out. His head was like a turnip. That was what they'd done to him. They'd turned him into a turnip, a violent turnip, when they shot the bullets into his brain.

The cameras switched to gangs of youths throwing stones. But his eyes went on watching her.

She finished the fish and chips and pressed the bundle of greasy newspaper down on to the fire. Blue flames licked around it, reluctantly, then blazed up. She wiped her mouth on the back of her hand, switched the telly off, and felt her way along the passage to the front door. It was pitch black at first, but then the landing window gave a glimmering of light. She could almost feel her pupils dilate.

The street was her home now. Once over the step she was more herself. She picked her way along the cracked pavements as delicately as the cat that, seeing her, whisked itself into the gutter. There was a square of light cast by the fish and chip shop window. She hurried across it. Outside, in the street, it was not darkness that frightened her, but light.

After a few minutes she passed a woman walking home, alone, in the middle of the road, as Kelly had been taught to do. The idea was that if somebody—a man—leaped out at you, you would have more time to run away. Her lips curled. It was a bit late for that! She looked at the woman with contempt. The real defense was to be one of those who leapt.

Inside the boy's tee-shirt and jeans her skin felt cool and muscular. She was glad it was cold. Cold was clean.

Only once since that night had something happened that might reasonably have made her afraid. There had been a man standing in the shadow of a doorway, his face screened from the light. He had beckoned her to approach. She had stopped at once and gone towards him, cautious, but not afraid.

"Hello," he had said. "And what's your name?"

She had smiled. If he could have seen her smile he might have been afraid. But she was standing in shadow. She was part of the shadow.

"Kelly," she said.

And stood breathing.

"Come here, Kelly. I've got summat to show you. Summat you'll like."

She went, but without hope. This man's voice was coarse.

"There," he said. "That enough for yer?"

She looked with her unblinking eyes. She watched the purple flesh-flower bloom, and wilt. He backed away from her, swearing, his hands clawed together over a shriveling of flesh.

It didn't surprise her. She knew she had the power.

But tonight no voice accosted her as she slipped silently across the road. She knew what she was going to do because she had done it before. And tonight there was the same sensation of pressure, the same feeling of blood squeezing through narrowed veins.

The school this time.

The gate was easy. She climbed it, hung for a moment poised between pavement and sky, then dropped lightly into the playground on the other side. There was a huge pile of coke against the far wall. It would have made a marvellous slide but you were not allowed to play on it. Now, feeling that anything was permitted, she ran a little way up the slope and slid down again. Pieces of coke peppered down after her. But it was no fun playing that game by herself. And she wanted to get inside.

The window shattered, not at the first, but at the second blow. Despising herself for the timidity of her first attempt, she slipped her hand in through jagged glass and found the bolt. She opened the door and went in. There were the long, silent, forbidden corridors and she passed along them stealthily, noiselessly: the intruder.

But in the end it was disappointing. There was a smell of chalk—an impersonal smell—and the cool sound of water gushing in the boys' toilets. All the cupboards were locked and when you found the keys and opened them it was still no use because the things inside didn't belong to anybody. Nobody cared about this place. There were no private smells.

She went into the Headmaster's study, but even that was impersonal despite the photographs of his wife and children. She was bolder now. She put the light on. There wasn't much danger of its being seen because the window overlooked the playground.

She sat down in his chair. Her bottom slid easily across the black leather which, on closer examination, was not leather at all, but plastic. It creaked, though, when she shifted her weight. He liked the way it creaked. If he was telling you off and it didn't creak enough to satisfy him he would wiggle his bum around until it did.

On top of the cupboard behind the door was the cane. She'd only had that once. Girls didn't get the cane very often. Girls did as they were told.

She wetted her fingers and rubbed them across the plastic, but she couldn't make it squeak as leather squeaks. She swivelled the chair experimentally from side to side. All the time anger and courage were draining away from her. It had been a mistake to come here.

The house. Oh, yes, the house had been better. . . .

She had gone to the park. It must have been about the middle of October. A month ago now. It had been her first trip outside since that dreadful day when she had started to scream and the police had come. She had gone to the park. To the exact place. To the same tree . . .

She thought she was being defiant. She thought she was proving to herself that she was not afraid. But in fact when the park was empty, when no shadow moved within the shadow of the trees, she felt . . . What did she feel? Abandoned? Though she told herself that she was glad, and began making up what would have happened if he had been there—what she would have done, or said. Perhaps she would just have run home and told the police and then he would have been caught and put in prison.

She stood alone under the tree, feeling the blood squeeze through her veins. Her whole skin felt tight like a boil which you know is going to burst soon. She started to walk towards the lake.

The area bordering on the park was one of the wealthiest in

town; the houses big, substantial Victorian houses that had preserved their air of smug assurance into a more violent and chaotic age. She wondered if The Man lived in one of those houses. He had sounded as if he might.

There was a lane between their long back gardens and the park, muddy and overgrown, a strip of the countryside, expensive in a steel town. One of the houses stood out from the rest, in Kelly's eyes, because it had a slide, a swing and a sandpit in the garden. She was too old for such things but they still caught her eye sometimes, just as she found herself looking at the toy pages in her mother's catalogue.

She felt a sudden need to be inside the peaceful, green enclosure of that garden. A month earlier she would have repressed it. Now she wriggled through a gap in the hedge almost before the thought was fully formed. If anybody caught her she could say she'd lost a ball. Or something. It didn't much matter. The fear of being caught was part of the thrill.

She approached the house, telling herself with every step that she would turn back now. The French windows were open. She stood outside and sniffed. Her nose told her at once that the house was empty. But they could not have gone far. On a long trip they would have remembered to shut the windows.

She stepped inside. When she closed the door behind her and stood in the big hall, everything seemed to stir around her, as if resenting the intrusion. Motes of dust seethed together in a beam of sunlight. She began to go from room to room very quietly, her gym shoes squeaking slightly on the polished wood of the floors. There was a smell of lavender. The living room was gold and white and pink, cool after the sunlight in the hall. There was a bowl of roses on top of the open piano, and a photograph of a girl on a pony. At first she touched things gently, feeling her rough skin catch on the silk of furniture and cushions, reluctant to disturb this peace, though she knew she would have to destroy it in the end.

She went upstairs. Her feet padded on soft carpets, fingernails—or claws—clicked on polished wood. She snuffled her way around like some small, predatory animal. She wanted to touch everything, but she was cautious too: her nerves quivered just beneath the surface of her skin. She could hear the dust settle in empty rooms.

The girl's bedroom bored her in the end. Photographs of school—imagine wanting to be reminded of that! Books about ballet, and ponies; lipstick in a drawer. She looked into the garden, so green, so enclosed, so sheltered. She might have pitied or despised the girl who lived in this room, but she would not have known how to envy her.

The bathroom next. She fingered the towels, she selected a bottle from the rows of bottles on a shelf and squirted aftershave on to her skin. It brought goosepimples up all over her arms. Hidden away in a little cupboard were the nastier necessities: hair remover, acne cream, a long steel thing with a little hole in the end that you used for squeezing blackheads out. Linda had one.

She pulled handfuls of clothes out of the dirty linen basket, shirts and underwear mainly. She could tell whether the pants belonged to a man or a woman with her eyes shut, by the smell alone. She snuffled into armpits and stained crotches, then sniffed her own armpits.

The parents' bedroom was best, though at first she could hardly take it in, it was so different from anywhere else she had been. She looked casually at the big, plump, satiny bed, sniffed the smells of perfume and powder, stood on tiptoe to reach the top of the wardrobe because that was where Uncle Arthur kept the things he put on to go with her mother. There was nothing there.

She turned her attention to the bed, rubbing her hands across the flesh-colored satin until a roughened flap of skin from a healing blister snagged on one of the threads and tore. There was a pile of cushions at the head of the bed: big, soft, delicately-scented, plump, pink, flabby cushions, like the breasts and buttocks of the woman who slept in the bed. A man slept there too, of course, but you could not imagine him. It was a woman's room, a temple to femininity. And the altar was the dressing-table.

There were so many creams: moisturizer, night cream, throat cream, hand cream, special tissue cream for round the eyes. And so much make-up! Little jars and pots of eyeshadow: green, blue, mauve, gold, silver, opal, amethyst. Even yellow and pink. She opened one of them and rubbed a little on the back of her hand, then thrust her finger deep inside the pot for the pleasure of feeling the cream squirm.

She wanted something else, something more. She felt her skin tighten as if at any moment it might split open and deposit her, a new seed, on the earth. She began clawing at the satin skin of the bed dragging her nails across the dressing-table hard enough to leave scratches, claw marks, in the polished wood. Was this what she wanted? She thought of all the things she could do—pour powder and nail polish all over the carpet, daub dressing-table and mirror with lipstick. She did none of them. Something was stopping her. She looked around. It was the mirror. It was her own reflection in the glass that caught and held her, and drained her anger away.

She looked as wild and unkempt as an ape, as savage as a wolf. Only her hair, glinting with bronze and gold threads, was beautiful. She dragged it down to frame her face; then lifted it high above her head and let it escape, strand by strand, until it was swinging, coarse and heavy, around her shoulders again. But she looked bad. She peered more closely in the glass and saw that the pores of her nose were bigger than they had been, and plugged with black. When Linda used the blackhead remover little worms of white stuff came wiggling out of the unblocked pores. Suddenly, Kelly hated the mirror. On the man's side of the bed was a heavy ashtray. She picked it up and threw it, hurling her whole body against the glass.

It smashed, as a sheet of ice explodes when you drop a stone on it. Lines and cracks radiated out, trapping, at the center of the web, her shattered face.

She rocked herself, and moaned, thrusting her fingers deep

into her mouth and biting on them to stop the groans. She got up. In a manicure case in the dressing-table drawer she found a pair of scissors, and began hacking at her hair. But the scissors were too small. She remembered a spare bedroom across the landing, with a sewing machine, and ran across to it. The dressmaking scissors she brought back bit into her hair with thick, satisfying crunches. In no time at all big loops and coils were slipping to the floor. When she was shorn, she looked back in the glass and was comforted a little by the sight of her ugliness.

She listened. In every room of the house there was the sound of clocks ticking, curtains breathing, the minute squeaks and rustles of an empty house. But her ears had caught something. There it was again. A quickening of the silence. They were coming back. A second later, she heard a car turning into the road.

She slipped out through the French windows as they came in the front door, though not before she had felt the house begin to heal itself, to close like water, seamlessly, over the disruption of her presence. From the end of the lawn she looked back resentfully at the smug, bland windows, and wished she had done all the things she had thought of doing. She wished she had written all over the house, in bright red lipstick, the worst words that she knew. She wished she had torn and scattered and smashed, because then nobody could have pretended that nothing had happened.

Now, remembering that day, she twisted and turned in the Headmaster's chair, willing that tiny, impersonal box of a room to be vulnerable, to expose itself to her as those other more intimate rooms had done. She picked up the photograph of the Headmaster's wife and children and smashed it on a corner of the desk. She reached out for the paper knife and held it a second, poised above his chair. She expected the blow to jar her wrist but the knife slid in easily, through unresisting plastic. She ripped and tore at the soft, smooth, phoney skin while little white balls of polystyrene escaped from the cuts and trickled down on to the floor. She was sobbing, her excitement mounting on every breath.

There was nothing bad enough to do.

Yes, there was. She went into a corner of the room, pulled her jeans and pants down, and squatted. A lifetime of training was against her and at first she could do nothing but grunt and strain. But finally there it was: a smooth, gleaming, satiny turd. She picked it up and raised it to her face, smelling her own hot, animal stink. It reminded her of The Man's cock, its shape, its weight. She clenched her fist.

She began to daub shit all over the Headmaster's chair and desk, smearing it over papers, wood and plastic. When there was no more left, except a bit between her fingers, she scraped it off carefully on the sides of a Register.

She careered down the corridor to her own classroom, the smell of her shit hot above the usual smells of gymshoes and custard. She almost ran at the blackboard, and wrote, sobbing, PISS, SHIT, FUCK. Then, scoring the board so hard that the chalk screamed, the worst word she knew: CUNT. The chalk broke on the final letter and her nails, dragging across the board, were torn down to the quick. She stood, panting, with her back to the board and sucked her fingers, glad of the pain and the taste of blood that soothed in some small measure the aching of her tight, her unappeased flesh.

The night she was raped Kelly had gone home across the park after all. As she stood on the pavement outside the fish and chip shop there had seemed to be nothing else to do but retrace her steps. As though in going back the past could be undone.

She did not look back, though if she had done so she would have seen him, there, in his mirror-tiled cell, moisture still oozing out of his eyes and dripping down his face. She did not need to look back. She would carry him with her always, wherever she went, a homunculus, coiled inside her brain.

It was her first experience of the street at night. Not just late: that she was used to. Real night.

At first she was afraid. She started away from every shadow.

She had good reason for fear. And yet, as she walked, the empty streets with their pools of greasy, orange light grew on her. She no longer envied the life that still went on here and there, behind colored curtains. It was better outside. She walked past the drunks and other late-night stragglers without fear, for tonight her glance could kill; and her skin, where the moonlight fell on it, was as white and corrosive as salt.

She slid through a gap in the railings. Generations of children had made it. Next year she would be too big, next year she would have to use the gate. It was a tight fit even now and she scraped her knee on a jagged edge of metal. Normally she would have bent to examine the cut, even in this moonlight that made all blood look black, but tonight it hardly seemed worthwhile.

She went back to the tree. His face pursued her. In a gesture of defiance she pulled all the conkers from her pocket and threw them on the ground. The action looked, and was, futile. His face remained. And would be there always, trailing behind it, not the cardboard terrors of the fairground, those you buy for a few pennies and forget, but the real terror of the adult world, in which grown men open their mouths and howl like babies, where nothing that you feel, whether love or hate, is pure enough to withstand the contamination of pity.

She had said nothing to anybody that night, though next morning when she woke up the feeling of invulnerability was gone. For three weeks she was afraid. For three weeks she sweated in darkness while his face pursued her in and out of dreams and down the howling corridors of nightmares. Then, with a sensation of splitting open, of pissing on the floor, she started to scream.

They came. They sat over her. But the feeling of numbness was back. She tried to tell them about his face. She tried to tell them about that moment in the fish and chip shop when the grown-up man had started to cry. But they weren't interested in that. They wanted her to tell them what had happened in the alley behind the boarded-up factory. And they wanted her to tell it again and again and again.

In the end they went away.

But she was not the same. Thank God, she was not the same. She could step out into the street now and become as quick and unfeeling as a cat. She moved through the empty streets with unnamed purposes at work inside her, and her body, inside its boy's clothing, was as cold and inviolate as ice.

Only she was afraid of herself. Increasingly, she was afraid of herself. And she was afraid of what she might do.

One night in early December Kelly came home to find her mother on her knees cleaning the fireplace. It was an odd time of night for the job and her mother was oddly dressed for doing it: she was wearing her best dress.

Kelly watched in silence. Her mother always turned to housework when she was especially distressed. It was a tribute to her stoicism that so little got done.

Eventually her mother looked around, a question in her eyes that she was too frightened to ask. Kelly found no difficulty in ignoring it. Then, as her mother looked down, she thought, We're alike. It had never struck her before, but it was true. There, in the lines of nose and chin, was her own face, glimpsed in a distorting mirror.

The brief realization of kinship made her ask, "Where's Arthur?"

"Arthur didn't fancy the club tonight. I went with Madge."

So that was it. He'd packed her in.

"All right, was it?"

"Oh, yeah. There was a smashing turn on at the finish. Bloke dressed up as a woman. We howled and laughed. He ended up sticking pins in his tits." Her voice shook. "They were . . . balloons!" The word "balloons" burst out of her mouth like a cork, ugly sounds and cries came glugging after it. Her red, greasy mouth was square with anguish like an abandoned baby's. Her breasts, only too obviously flesh, shook as she cried. Kelly looked away to avoid seeing them.

"Arthur's not coming back. Is that it?"

"Yes." She bowed her head, so that at least now you did not have to look at that ravaged face. Though the downcast cheeks had tears on them, ruthlessly revealing seams and cracks that make-up had tried in vain to hide.

Kelly looked around, half-expecting to see the ugly little scene reflected in mirrors. But there was only the familiar, untidy room. A bottle of milk going sour on the table.

"I'm going to stand that milk in water," she said. "That way we might get a decent cup of tea in the morning."

On her way back from the kitchen she looked at her mother again. She was still kneeling by the half-washed hearth, but not crying now. She knew there was no point.

Kelly wanted to speak, but was afraid that sympathy would set her mother off again. And anyway she felt no sympathy. She felt, rather, distaste for this woman whose hard exterior had cracked to reveal an inner corruption. Her mother had been the one solid feature in the landscape of her mind, not much attended to, perhaps, but there, a presence on the skyline that you felt even when your back was turned. Now that was gone. Her mother's face, crumbling, reminded her of The Man. She could not allow herself to feel pity.

Kelly now turned her back altogether upon the spurious safety of home. More than ever she haunted the streets by night. She liked particularly the decaying, boarded-up streets by the river. There a whole community had been cleared away: the houses waited for the bulldozers and the demolition men to move in, but they never came.

Grass grew between the cobbles, rosebay willowherb thronged the empty spaces, always threatening to encroach, but still the houses stood. Officially empty, but not in reality. You had only to walk down these streets at night to realize that life, life of a kind, still went on.

Kelly went cautiously. But however carefully you trod sooner or later glass crunched under your feet or a sagging floorboard creaked and threatened to give way, and instantly that hidden life revealed itself, if only by a quickening of the silence. Tramps. Drunks. As she became more skillful she saw them. These were not the drunks you meet wending a careful path home to the safety of hearth and bed. These were the hopeless, the abandoned, the derelict.

. It shocked her at first to find a woman among them: a woman who bulged and waddled as if she were pregnant. Though when she took her coat off, it was to reveal only wads of newspaper fastened to her body with string. For the nights were cold now. An old woman could easily freeze to death.

She had the bluest, most muculent eyes Kelly had ever seen. They seemed to have melted and flowed over on to her cheeks, which were furrowed and cracked almost beyond belief. These were not laughter-lines, frown-lines, worry-lines. They seemed to occur at random, like the cracks in parched earth, the outward and visible signs of an inner and spiritual collapse.

Parched in any other sense she was not. Her conversations with Kelly were punctuated by frequent swigs from a bottle whose neck she wiped fastidiously on the palm of an inde-scribably filthy hand. Her name, she said, was Joan. As a younger woman she had worked at the cake bakery. She produced this fact with some surprise, as if it referred to a time in her life she could hardly now recall.

"They used to think I was mad," she said, her blue eyes less than ever confined to their sockets. "But I wasn't mad. It was them buggers was mad, skivvying away for their three-piece suites. They wanted looking at it."

She muttered to herself and became suddenly alert, glancing rapidly from side to side, though her surroundings could not have been more bleak or empty in their desolation.

"They're listening, you know. They think I don't know, they think I can't tell. The buggers is always listening."

She strained to hear. Eventually, somewhere down the street, a door banged in the wind.

"There," she said, satisfied, lips pleated over empty gums. "There. They'll have that nailed down tomorrow."

She lapsed into silence. Kelly, thinking the conversation was over, got up to go, but Joan was suddenly convulsed with laughter, and caught her arm. "I used to spit in it, you know. I did! I never let a batch get past without."

Seeing Kelly look blank, she added, sulkily, "The cake mixture."

"You spat in the cake mixture?"

"Aye!"

"What you do that for?"

"Because I couldn't reach to piss in it." She rocked herself with laughter or anguish or cold. "It had years of my life, that place."

But this was too near reality. Easier to raise the bottle and glug. Kelly watched the wasted throat working as she drank.

The men, Kelly avoided. Not out of fear, but because they became maudlin very easily, wanting to touch her arms or stroke her hair. There was nothing sexual in this. They were too far gone for that. No. She was the daughter they had wanted and never had, or had had and lost. And she could not follow them along that road. She felt no pity. At times her mind seemed to slice through them like a knife through rotten meat. And in those odd flashes of total clarity that occur in alcoholics on the verge of stupor, they were aware of it, and shrank from her as if they had burned their hands on frozen steel.

She went back to Union Street. And there was Blonde Dinah staggering home, her hair daffodil yellow under the drooping light. Earlier that night, under that same lamp, a group of girls had been playing. Hands linked together to form a circle, they had turned slowly through the misty radiance; and their voices, chanting the half-understood words, were passionate and shrill. One of the girls was Sharon Scaife, who had been Kelly's friend and would be so again if Kelly would allow it. But Kelly had gone away. The circle in the lamplight was closed to her forever. She knew it, and she was afraid.

On another night, playing in the rubble of a partially-demolished street near her home, she found a baby buried under a heap of broken bricks, a baby as red and translucent as a ruby. She looked at him, at his sealed eyes and veined head, and put the rubble back carefully, brick by brick, guarding this secret as jealously as if it had been her own.

She haunted the park, too. She walked up and down, searching, perhaps, though if she was she did not know it. He never came.

Others came. Even in this weather people came to the park to make love. She watched a couple once. He had actually taken his trousers down. She shivered for him, watching his small hard buttocks bob up and down like golf balls. At first it was funny. Then something mechanical in his movements, a piston-like power and regularity, began to make it seem not ridiculous, but terrible. When he lifted his head, his glazed eyes and hanging face revealed the existence of a private ritual, a compulsion of which he was both frightened and ashamed. The girl who lay beneath him was as much an intruder on it as Kelly would have been, had she chosen to step out of the shadow of the trees.

Christmas came and went. Kelly was given more presents than usual: a doll that wet itself, a hairdressing set, a matching necklace and brooch. She did not play with them or wear them, but arranged them carefully in her room, where they acquired, over the ensuing weeks, an extraordinary strangeness like the abandoned apparatus of a lunar probe.

It was a hard winter; the weather after Christmas was particularly cold. The miners were on strike. That didn't affect Kelly much, except that she was sometimes sent around all the corner shops to look for paper bags full of coal. You could still get those after the coalmen had stopped delivering. The cold weather did not keep her indoors. She still spent her evenings in the streets by the river, where she was expert now at stalking her shambling and shabby prey.

Her mother came in very late and often drunk. There was nobody to take Arthur's place, and if she went on like this there never would be. Linda was going steady. She solved her problems by spending more time at her boyfriend's house than she did at her own. Kelly cut herself off from both of them; but underneath the fear increased. She was more than ever alone. Ther were days now when she felt trapped inside her own skull.

One morning in late February she went out into the back yard to open the door for the bin men. The center of the yard was so badly drained that in winter it became a sheet of ice. She had to pick her way across it. And there by the dustbin was a bird, its feathers fluffed out, too far gone to fly away or even struggle in her hand. She felt the thinness, the lightness of its bones; she felt the heart flutter. Its neck rested between her forefinger and her thumb, and she thought. Suppose I squeezed? She could so easily let her fingers tighten. She could watch its eyes glaze, feel the final fluttering of its heart. And why not? Why should there be life rather than death? Then her mother came to the kitchen door to tell her to be quick, she was late for school again; and she put the bird down on the ground where she had found it.

When she came home at tea-time it was dead anyway.

In the end even her nights in the derelict streets lost their savor. She seemed to be drying up, to be turning into a machine. Her legs, pumping up and down the cold street, had the regularity and power of pistons. And her hands, dangling out of the sleeves of her anorak, were as heavy and lifeless as tools.

One dank afternoon at the very end of winter, she left the house. It was too early to go to the streets by the river, so she went to the park instead. It had been raining for days. The ground was covered with sheets of water that trapped the last light of the sky and reflected it back again. As Kelly walked on she was aware of the steely blue radiance gathering all around her. It was disorientating: the leaden, lifeless sky and the radiance of light beating up from the earth. She felt dizzy and had to stop.

The mist that had hung about all day had begun to clear, except for a few small pockets above the surface of the lake. Beyond the chemical works in the far distance the sun was setting, obscured by columns of drifting brown and yellow smoke. A brutal, bloody disc, scored by factory chimneys, it seemed to swell up until it filled half the western sky.

With a sensation of moving outside time, Kelly started to walk forward again. At first, there was total silence except for the squeak of her gym shoes in the wet grass. Then a murmuring began and mixed in with it sharp, electric clicks, like the sound of women talking and brushing their hair at once. The noise became louder. She climbed to a ridge of higher ground and there at the center was the tree, its branches fanned out, black and delicate, against the red furnace of sky. By now the murmur had become a fierce, ecstatic trilling, and when she looked more closely she saw that the tree was covered in birds that clustered along its branches as thick and bright as leaves, so that from a distance you might almost have thought that the tree was singing.

The singing went on. The tree pulsed and gleamed with light. But she could not break out of that room inside her head where she and The Man sat and stared at each other's reflections in the mirror tiles. She would have liked to scream and beat the air but lacked strength to raise her hands.

She fell back, and found herself standing on a patch of muddy ground.

She wandered on, not knowing or caring where her footsteps were leading her. She was hungry and had nothing to eat except a few crumbs of chocolate biscuit that she dug out of the deepest corners of her pockets. But she would not give in and go home.

In the hollow ground around the lake darkness came early. White birds shone through the dusk, heads tucked in, wings furled, feather upon feather furled. But on the open ground the light had become an electric, tingling gold. You did not walk through it: you waded or glided or swam.

In the big houses around the park lights were already being switched on. Homecomings. She turned into the main avenue of trees and began to walk along it, hoping for nothing.

But there on a bench at the far end was a dark figure, sharply etched against the outpouring of gold. She began to hurry; she broke into a run; she arrived at the bench panting for breath, and alive with hope.

At first there seemed to be nothing there but a heap of old rags. Then the old woman lifted her head. Her face was an ivory carving etched in trembling gold. She peered at Kelly, evidently unable to see her properly. Her eyes, magnified by the thick lenses of her glasses, were milky with cataract. Her clothes were covered with egg and cereal stains where she had aimed for, and missed, her mouth.

"What are you doing here?" Kelly asked. Normally she would not have bothered with the old woman. Only the sharpness of her disappointment made her speak.

"Picking me nose with me elbow."

Her speech was slurred. Kelly moved closer. The old woman's coat, or dressing gown, was open. Her dress had a lowish neck.

"Why don't you fasten the buttons?" Kelly asked. "You'll catch your death."

For the flood of warm gold was deceptive: it was cold enough to make your fingers ache.

"I'll fasten them if I want them fastened."

Kelly was silent for a while. After a struggle, she said, "Won't anybody be expecting you back home?"

She felt concern for the old woman: an ordinary, unfamiliar feeling. They had had a talk in Assembly about old people: how the cold could kill.

"Not a living soul." It ought to have sounded bitter or self-pitying, but it didn't. There was another silence, then the old woman went on slowly. "They're going to put me in a Home." She laughed. "*Think* they are! I've got other ideas."

She paused, then added reluctantly, "They say I can't see to meself."

Even to Kelly's eyes this was obviously true. The old woman's skin was stretched tight over the bones of her skull.

"They say I'm not getting me proper food."

"Well, perhaps you're not." The front of her dress seemed to have got most of it. "At least in the Home you'd get your meals." She paused. Then burst out, "And they'd see you were warm. They'd see you had a fire."

"Is not the life more than meat and the body than raiment?"

She wasn't quoting. She had lived long enough to make the words her own.

Again silence. The old woman's hands were like birds' claws clasped in her lap.

Kelly said, "I could take you home."

"No thanks. You bugger-off home yourself! I suppose you have got one?"

"Yes. I suppose I have."

They sat in silence. The light increased.

"I used to come here when I was a little lass, aye, younger than you." The old woman looked with dim eyes around the park. Kelly followed her gaze and, for the first time in her life, found it possible to believe that an old woman had once been a child. At the same moment, and also for the first time, she found it possible to believe in her own death. There was terror in this, but no sadness. She stared at the old woman as if she held, and might communicate, the secret of life.

"There used to be a band then," the old woman said, nodding towards the bandstand that the dead leaves rattled through. "You used to sit and listen to them on a Sunday afternoon."

With renewed energy she looked at the child, who, sitting there with the sun behind her, seemed almost to be a gift of the light. "Don't tell anybody I'm here," she said. It was the closest she had come to pleading.

"You're crying," Kelly said. She stared at the tears that were streaming down into the cracks and furrows of the old woman's face. She looked at the throat that in its nakedness was as vulnerable as a bird's. "There must be another way," she almost pleaded in her turn.

"There's no other way. They're trying to take everything away from me. Everything." She smiled. "Well, this way they can't. That's all."

In spite of the smile she was still crying. Kelly reached out and touched her hand.

"I won't tell anybody," she said.

She looked down at their hands: the old woman's cracked and shiny from a lifetime of scrubbing floors, her own grubby, with scabs on two of the knuckles.

They sat together for a long time.

"I feel warmer now," the old woman said, "I think I'll have a little sleep."

Kelly went on watching her. The old woman's tears had dried to a crust of white scurf at the corners of her lids. Which were closed now, in sleep, or unconsciousness, or death.

At any rate, it was time to go. Kelly slipped home through the growing darkness.

There was a sound ahead of her, a sound like the starlings had made. And there, coming out of the cake bakery, was a crowd of women, talking together. She stopped to watch them.

Most of them began to run as soon as they were released, with the peculiar stiff-legged gait that women adopt as they grow up, though it is not natural to them. They were anxious to get home, to cook the dinner, to make a start on the housework. A few lingered. Their hair, which might have caught in the machines or contaminated the food, was bound back under scarves or nets. Their voices as they talked together were shrill and discordant from a day of shouting over the noise of the conveyor belt.

Then a young girl came to the factory gates alone. She hesitated. On the other side of the street a boy dropped the newspaper he was reading, and waved. They ran to meet each other and, oblivious of the crowds around them, kissed.

Kelly stared after them, hungrily. Then she bent her head and followed in their footsteps. She was going home.

II

Joanne Wilson

The Wilsons lived a few doors down from the Browns on the other side of Union Street, but there was a time at the end of October when Joanne did not go home. Instead, she woke up in a strange bed and sweated, remembering the previous night.

She had gone to the Buffs and got drunk and, watched by several people from the street, including two girls who worked at the cake bakery, she had allowed herself to be seen going home with a midget. Even as she thought the word she felt disloyal, for the midget in question was Joss, who had always fancied her, and never got anywhere, and went on being kind.

He still hadn't got anywhere, but who would believe that now?

She could just imagine the jokes. Step-ladders. Everybody the same size in bed. All that. Even her own mother had had a bloody good laugh, but she wouldn't be laughing when she heard about last night.

It was her fault, really, thought Jo. If only she'd leave me alone.

The alarm sprang into hideous life. Jo sat up, her eyes tight shut, and groped for the clock. It skittered away from her across the lino.

Footsteps in the passage. The sound of the door opening.

"Jo?"

No reply.

"Alarm's gone."

"Never! You should send that bugger around the morgue. Wherever did you get it?"

"Oh, I've had that years. Never fails."

Joss came further into the room. When he stood at the foot of the bed his head was no higher than the rail. "Howay, then!"

"I can't get up with you stood there, can I?" She struggled to sit up, dragging the sheet with her. "I've got nowt on."

He stepped back. "Well, how was I supposed to know that? Decent folks wear summat in bed."

"Is that right?"

"You know it is. You could've had a lend of something, you only had to ask."

"Oh, I never wear owt."

The flesh of her shoulders gleamed where the light from the street lamp fell on them. He stepped back again, baffled. "I'll go and get breakfast started. I don't suppose you've ever boiled an egg in your life."

As soon as the door closed behind him she got out of bed, too quickly, forgetting that any sudden movement made her sick. She grabbed an ashtray from the dressing-table and retched, but only a little bile came up, tasting bitter. She wiped her mouth on the back of her hand.

Through the open door she could hear Joss, still moving around in the next bedroom.

"Anyway, how come you're up so early? I thought you said you were two till ten?"

"I am."

So he had got up specially to see her off. She felt a stab of guilt and uneasiness, then forgot it as her stomach clenched. She wouldn't've cared if anything ever come up, but it never did. There was just this painful retching on an empty stomach. She straightened up for the second time.

"This is bloody ridiculous, this is," she muttered, and, turning, caught a glimpse of her reflection in the mirror.

She stood, pressing her hands fearfully against the still flat belly. No sign there at least. But her shoulders, her arms, her breasts! Blue veins showed up all over them, as intricately linked as the branches of a tree; all leading down to the nipples which themselves were bigger and browner than they had been a month ago. Some yellowish stuff had dried to form a crust over the skin. She picked at it with her fingernails.

Her body, from childhood so familiar, had become frightening. It occurred to her that it looked like another face, with nipples instead of eyes, a powerful, barely-human face. By comparison, her real face seemed childish and unformed.

She was afraid. "What the hell am I going to do?" she asked that other, inhuman face, which was aware of no problem.

"Breakfast's ready!"

"Coming!"

With a sense of relief, she turned her back on her reflection and began to dress.

Joss was at the kitchen sink when she got downstairs. The kitchen itself was immaculately, old-maidishly tidy. Of course he hadn't much else to occupy himself with.

"There was no need for *you* to get up, you know," she said. "You could've had a lie-in."

"I never lie in. I can't. Soon as I'm awake, I'm up."

Joanne sat down at the table, and pulled the plate towards her. Bacon and fried bread. Dear God! Her stomach heaved at the sight of it.

"It was a good night, though, wasn't it?"

"You were knocking it back a bit, weren't you?"

"Only halves."

"No point in drinking halves if all you do is get through them twice as fast."

"Oh, shurrup, man. You sound like me Mam."

"Somebody's got to . . ." He stopped abruptly and turned back to the sink. For a while he concentrated on sweeping breadcrumbs into the sink tidy with the side of his hand. His shoulders were on a level with the draining board. Yet the face above them was handsome—even beautiful, if you could call a man beautiful. He seemed to carry his good looks around with him, like a special form of crucifixion.

Pity made Jo aggressive.

"Somebody's got to what?" she demanded.

He spun around. "*Care* about you!"

She was taken aback by the passion in his voice. There was a brief, uncomfortable silence. Then she said, trying to lighten the atmosphere, "You promised you'd tell what Joss is short for, but you didn't."

"I said I'd tell you if you made that drink your last."

"And I didn't?"

"Not by a long shot. But I'll tell you anyway. It's short for Joyce."

"That's a girl's name."

"No, it's not. There were a few lads called Joyce down our way. All about my age. A fella gassed himself. His wife had left him. He just come home from work and found everything gone, all the furniture, everything. Except the gas cooker. So he put his head in it."

"And that was the end of him. You're sure it wasn't 'cause he was called Joyce?"

"No, it wasn't—it was his wife. And after that all the kids were called Joyce, for a bit."

He saw her look blank. "It's lucky, isn't it? Calling a kid after somebody what's gassed themselves."

"I never heard that."

"Oh, they used to do it a lot down our way. Wharfe Street."

Wharfe Street was the worst street in the town, or had been until a couple of years ago, when the people were rehoused. Now the houses were empty and boarded up, though not yet demolished. In the hierarchy of streets it came almost as far below Union Street as Union Street came below Buchanan Street, with its bay windows and strips of garden outside the front doors.

Something of what Jo was feeling must have shown on her face.

"Plenty of decent folks down Wharfe Street," Joss said.

"Gassing themselves to get away from the rest."

It was true. Suicide, mental illness, crime, incest had flourished there, as though inhaled with noxious fumes from the river. Those who had lived there, whether they had loved or hated the street, did not find it easy to forget.

"Anyway," Jo went on, "you live here now. There's worse places. And you've got the house very nice."

"It gets lonely. Sometimes."

They were on dangerous ground again. She remembered last night, how stupidly, sloppily affectionate she had been. She remembered him hauling her upstairs and half-pushing, half-throwing her on to the bed. He could have had her then. But he hadn't. He'd been kind. Responsible. It was like everybody said. He'd be a husband in a million, if only his arms and legs were the normal length. What had made them like that? she wondered.

"Still, if you get fed up you can always have a walk around the Buffs. I've seen you in there many a night with Iris King. And Ted." Not always with Ted, she remembered.

"Oh, me and Iris are old friends. I've known her since she was a bairn."

"In Wharfe Street?"

"Yes."

"Perhaps if I gassed meself they might start naming bairns after me."

"Well, Jo's better than Joyce anyway. Crack or spout, it'd do."

He was messing about with the sink tidy again. She watched him for a few minutes then said, impatiently, "I wish you'd stop fart-arsing about. You're as bad as a woman. Worse."

"I like things tidy. Anyway, what sort of talk is that? Gas ovens, at your age."

"Oh, don't worry. I'm a long way off that yet."

Was she? She thought again about the baby, and her stomach clenched with fear. She pushed the plate away.

"What's the matter with that bacon? Is it too salty?"

"No. It's all right. I'm just not hungry." She roused herself to lie. "I never eat much breakfast."

He set the bacon aside without comment.

"I can't seem to stomach the fat."

"It's O.K. I'll have it for me bait."

Silence.

"Oh, what's the use? You've guessed anyway. I'm pregnant."

He didn't reply at all for a long time. Then, "There's some digestive biscuits up in that cupboard behind you. You can't go to the bakery on an empty stomach. You shouldn't be going at all."

"Don't say you hadn't guessed."

"I wondered." He watched her nibble the biscuit. "You should make it up with your Mam."

"It's gone too far for that."

"You'll need her."

"No, I won't. She had no right to carry on the way she did. Moaning and groaning all over the house. You'd've thought she was having it. And questions. . . . 'Who is he? I'll kill him when I get my hands on him.' "

"She's got a right to know."

"She's no right at all. Good God, she hasn't told me who my father was yet."

"She's bound to be worried."

"Aye. Worried in case she might have to do summat! But I'll take good care she never has."

"You're talking through the back of your head. If you're

not going back to your Mam's, where are you going to go?''

Joanne looked around the kitchen. "You wanting rid of me, are you?''

"You know I'm not. You can stay here as long as you like. Only . . . people'll talk.'' He paused. "You don't want folks taking a tape measure to its legs, do you?''

She lowered her head while the silence widened and engulfed them.

"So,'' he went on, expressionlessly, "what are you going to do?''

She swallowed. "I might be getting married.''

He looked at her doubtfully. "Have you told him yet?''

"No. Well, I couldn't. He's been away on a course. You can't say summat like that over the phone—I can't anyway. And before he went . . . I wasn't all that late. I thought I'd come all right.'' She stared at him, defiantly. "It does come all right sometimes. People can be late without it being . . . that.''

"And when are you going to tell him?''

"Tonight. He's back today. That's one of the reasons I couldn't face going home last night. I felt I just had to have a bit of peace. Get me wits together.''

"Instead of which you've got a hangover.''

"I'm still glad I'm here and not there.''

"You'll have to tell your Mam where you are. You can't just leave her to fret.''

"Oh, I wouldn't worry about that. By ten o'clock, it'll be in every house in the street. You know it will. You'll have it to face when you get to work.''

"So will you.''

"Oh, they mightn't come right out with it. And if they do, I'm ready for 'em.''

She went out the back way, more for Joss's sake than her own, and set off down the alley, picking her path between piles of dog muck.

Further down she came upon a black-clad backside bending

over immediately in front of her. Old Mother Harrison. The old lady straightened up. "Now then."

"Now then."

"Your Gran keeping all right?"

"Well . . . her chest's bad."

"Everybody's is this weather." She looked around at the dank, soot-laden mist. "I'm wheezing a bit meself." Phlegm rattled in her chest as she spoke.

"You should go to the doctor."

"What? With bronchitis? No!"

It was said that Mrs. Harrison had been a very beautiful girl. It was still there. You could see it, even though her cheeks were now red-veined and hung loosely from the bone. Her eyes were startlingly, almost incredibly, blue. "Keeping all right yourself?" The blue eyes were now fixed on Joanne's coat, which she wore unfastened in spite of the weather.

"Yeah. I'm fine."

"I'll have a walk as far as the end."

As they walked, Mrs. Harrison scanned the ground closely. After every few steps she swooped down and picked up a french letter with a pair of silver sugar tongs. These were all transferred to a maroon canvas bag. She muttered something under her breath.

"I'm sorry, I didn't . . ."

"I said it's a good day. For them."

"Oh."

Further along, and another treasure carefully transferred to the bag.

"I expect you wonder why I do this."

Bugger-all use denying it. "Yes."

"You'd be surprised. They come in very handy. . . ." A woman poked her head out of her back-yard door. "Morning, Mrs. Bulmer."

"Morning, Mrs. Harrison."

They walked past. "You know, sometimes I wonder why I lower myself to speak to her—she's as common as muck." A quick glance over her shoulder. "No, I use 'em to get a good

71

blaze on the Mission fire. We meet at ten, you know, for the Breaking of Bread, but I always go up early to give the place a sweep around, and get the fire going. Only the other Sunday, the Pastor come in a bit early, and there he was, stood over the fire, warming his hands. 'Oh, Mrs. Harrison,' he said, (he talks posh, you know—tries to), 'Oh, Mrs. Harrison, I don't know how you do it. I don't know how you do it in the time.' 'Why,' I said, 'it's man's energy. It's man's energy goes onto that fire!' '' She chuckled wickedly. ''It doesn't half make me laugh, seeing 'em all sat around, praying and singing hymns. Not that I'm not a God-fearing woman. I am.''

''But doesn't it worry you?''

She stopped, while another condom was retrieved and put into the bag. Mrs. Harrison shivered: ''Imagine it, this weather. All them cold bums clagged up against some bugger's back-yard door.''

''Aren't you afraid of catching something?''

''The Bad Disorder? No. The Lord looks after his own. Anyway, I never touch them.'' She held up the tongs, and smiled. ''George is the one for sugar in our house.''

They walked on in silence for a while. Then, ''I see you're going around with Joss. Not that it's any of my business.''

''No.''

''You want to watch out for Iris King. He's her fancy man, you know.''

''I don't believe it.''

''She's always going around with him though, isn't she?''

''Well, so what? People can be friends, can't they?''

''She doesn't go around with her husband.''

''You don't go around with yours.''

''And she sticks up for him like a tiger. I was stood outside the Bluebell one night''—a favorite collecting-ground—''and two young lasses come out, sniggering. One says to him, 'What's it like down there?' And mind you, that was all she said. Next thing anybody knew she was sat on her arse in a puddle, and Iris was stood over her. 'Right, dear,' she says. 'Now you know'.''

"If it was who I think it was it served her right."

Mrs. Harrison lowered her voice. "You know what they say, don't you? His mother had him to her father and that's why his legs are so short."

"The whole family's like it."

"Aye, but he got a double dose."

"It amazes me how things like that get out. How the hell could anybody know she had him to her father? She's not going to invite the buggers around to watch, is she?"

"Well, no. But if it wasn't to her father I don't know who it was to, because he never let her over the threshold. He was jealous to death of her, and she was only fourteen. Then after, when she was married, he was brought up by his father's sister. He used to go around to see his Mam but his stepfather'ld never let him eat with the others. He allus had to stop in the kitchen." She paused. "Course she had to do as she was told."

"Why?"

"Well, you did in them days."

"I wouldn't shove my bairn in the back kitchen for any man."

Mrs. Harrison looked taken aback by the sudden passion of this outburst. "You don't know married life."

"It's different nowadays."

"Aye, is it? You'll find out it's not as different as you think."

Mrs. Harrison parted from her just outside the Bluebell. It was seldom she ventured further than this. The Bluebell on one side and the Mission on the other were the limits of her range. Jo turned to wave, but the old woman had already scuttled back into the shelter of the alley. She had been glad of her company, though the prying irritated her. But anything was better than to be left alone with her thoughts.

Jo crossed the bakery yard. A few young men, waiting around

to start loading up the vans, whistled and called out after her. Even this didn't cheer her up. There were none of them she fancied, and anyway in a few months' time they wouldn't fancy her.

She went down the steps to the basement. There was the usual line of women, pushing and jostling to get to the clock.

"Worst one-armed bandit I ever saw," a woman said, as she pulled the lever. "Bastard never pays out."

"Gerraway, one of these mornings there'll be three lemons up there, and we'll all be bloody rich."

Everybody laughed more loudly than the joke was worth.

In the cloakroom they put on nylon overalls. There was always a smell of sweat in this room. The younger girls peered in the mirror at greasy morning skins and pink eyes, arranging scarves over the rollers they would wear all day. Doris, who was nearly sixty, sucked on a cigarette end. Her scarlet lipstick had bled into the wrinkles around her mouth. When she had finished she ground the butt under her foot and said, "Well, howay then. Bugger won't go away. We'd best get stuck in."

The women were lined up facing each other at either side of the conveyor belt. A few women who had been to the Essoldo the previous night continued to talk.

"I was sweating on all the twos. All the threes come up. Then all the eights. Then bugger me, all the fives! At the finish, a woman behind me shouted on eighty-one."

"Well, at least you had a sweat on. I always think you don't begrudge the money if you get a sweat on. It's when you're twiddling y' thumbs all night."

At Jo's end of the line, there was silence.

There were four women working together: Lilian, Big Bertha—a West Indian woman, older than the rest—Elaine Watson, and Jo. Lilian's job was to line the cakes up before they went into the slicing machine. Big Bertha and Elaine had to restack the layers of sliced and creamed sponge as they came out of the machine. Jo's job—an easy one by comparison with Elaine's and Bertha's—was to slide a card under the reconstituted cake as it slid past her on its way to the packers.

The trouble had started when Bertha first came to work at the factory. Nobody liked it. She was the first colored worker there. But Elaine had gone on louder and longer than most: there was "nigger stink" in the cloakroom; why was she being allowed to use the same toilets when everybody knew what mucky buggers they were; and anyway if she had to be there at all, why sponges? There was chocolate cake upstairs; why not there?

As Bertha continued impassive, Elaine's remarks became ever louder and more outrageous until many of the women who had at first supported her became uneasy. There was a general feeling that Elaine was going too far, a revulsion against the constant persecution of a woman who seemed at least reasonably quiet, anxious to pass unnoticed. Doris gave this movement added impetus. One day as they were all sitting in the tea-room she nodded towards Elaine, who was sitting in the far corner, out of earshot.

"You know what's eating her, don't you?" She lowered her voice. "It's their Barbara. Her eldest sister. She had three to a nigger."

"No!"

"She did. As true as I sit here. What's more, he buggered off and left her, and now she's bringing them up on social security, so we're all paying for that little caper."

"I don't believe it. I know their mother."

"So do I," Doris said promptly. "And God knows why it had to happen to her, for a nicer or a cleaner woman you couldn't wish to meet. But it did happen. And they're living in Bradford."

"No wonder she's agin 'em."

"Still, whatever-her-name-is, Bertha, *she's* not to blame for it, is she?"

"No," Doris said, deliberately. "She's not. Now you all

know me," she leaned forward, "nobody's more against the colored people than what I am. That's right, isn't it?"

There was a general murmur of agreement.

"But the way she's been going on this past week—Elaine Watson—it's been scandalous. You make your own minds up, but I'm having nowt to do with it."

By the end of that week, Elaine was almost as completely isolated as Bertha, though there were two very young girls who followed her around in the tea and dinner breaks. If you were young and defenseless, it paid to be on Elaine's side.

Then one day, it happened. Elaine, taking off her overall at the end of the week, complained as usual about the smell. It was neither more nor less than she had said at the end of every other day, but Bertha's patience was at an end. She was sitting on a bench at the other side of the cloakroom, changing into her outdoor shoes. Her eyes fastened on Elaine. She lowered her head and thrust it forward, bull-like. Elaine grinned, nervously, and started to say something else, but the words died on her lips as the other woman got up and lumbered towards her.

"Hey, now then . . ."

But it was too late for anybody to intervene. The black woman's fist shot out and struck Elaine full in the mouth. She fell back against the wall, half-stunned, the impact squeezing an odd farting sound out of her chest. She opened her eyes and saw Bertha hanging over her, fist drawn back for the next blow. She raised her hands, clawing at the air in front of her face. Her mouth hung open with fear, but no sound came out of it. Not for a second did she try to hit back. Another blow crashed down, and then another. Blood and mucus streamed from Elaine's nose.

The other women, stupefied until then, roused themselves to take a hand. One of them took Elaine's arm and hauled her away into a corner. Nobody dared touch Bertha, but somebody said, "You'll get the sack, you know, if they see you carrying on like that." Bertha stared at her blankly for a moment and then slowly nodded her head. Her eyes were bloodshot, giving her a look of bridled ferocity. She went back to the bench and started to put her indoor shoes into a polythene bag. Elaine, sobbing and slobbering in the corner, was in no state to hear what anybody said.

This happened on a Friday night. None of the women seriously expected to see both Bertha and Elaine back in their places on Monday morning. It did not seem possible that normal life should continue after such an event. But they turned up, if anything, earlier than usual, facing each other across the conveyor belt like gladiators.

"You want to get yourself shifted," several of the older women had said to Jo. "There'll be trouble up your end before long."

Nobody had any sympathy for Elaine. Even the two young girls who followed her around had wavered in their allegiance, until brought back firmly into line. But neither was there any feeling that Bertha's action had been justified. Many of the women were horrified by it. Men fought, sometimes man and wife fought, but violence between women was unthinkable. Occasionally it happened: usually in Bute Street, usually on a Saturday night. But even then it was a modest affair: a little scratching, a little hair-pulling, accompanied by a great deal of abuse. Bertha's use of her fists, the silent ferocity of her attack, was something quite foreign to their experience. And they hated it. More even than the color of her skin, it confirmed that she was an outsider amongst them.

So today, a few weeks later, while jokes and laughter flew across other parts of the line, the little group around the slicing machine stood and faced each other in silence.

Then Lilian stepped back and, ignoring Bertha and Elaine, said, "Jo, I've got some new shoes." Like all Lilian's remarks it was oddly abrupt and disjointed. Difficult to answer. Fortunately, just at that moment, the machines started up and spared Jo the need to reply. She pointed at Lilian's feet and mimed appreciation. Then she drew the stock of cardboard discs closer to her side and prepared to start work.

The noise was horrific as usual. There was no possibility of conversation. Even the supervisor's orders had to be yelled at the top of her voice and repeated many times before anybody heard. At intervals, there were snatches of music. It was being played continuously but only the odd phrase triumphed over the roar of the machines. Some of the women moved their mouths silently, singing or talking to themselves: it was hard to tell. Others merely looked blank. After a while not only speech but thought became impossible.

The first sponge cake reached Jo. She began the sequence of actions that she would perform hundreds of times that day. It took little effort once you were used to it and, provided the cakes continued to arrive in a steady stream, it could be done almost automatically.

Almost. But not quite. Now that she was alone—for in this roaring cavern of sound each woman *was* alone—she wanted to think about Ken, she wanted to plan the evening, to work out exactly how she was going to tell him about the baby. She couldn't do it. Each half-formed thought was aborted by the arrival of another cake. She was left with a picture of his face floating against a backcloth of sponges: dark-haired and sallow-skinned, the rather prominent Adam's apple jerking when he laughed.

The brief break in concentration had allowed a sponge cake to escape without its card. She chased it down the belt and, by working rather faster than usual, gradually made her way back to her starting place.

When Jo was able to look up she saw the supervisor shouting at Lilian. Perhaps she had been feeding the sponge cakes into the slicing machine too slowly. Or too fast. Or not lining them up properly before they went in. More probably there was nothing wrong and the supervisor just wanted somebody to shout at. If that was it, Lilian was by far the safest choice.

"Soppy Lil", as she was called, had worked there longer than anybody else, except Doris. Always, as far as Jo could recall, on the same job, which was by far the easiest on the line. Anything else would have been beyond her.

She was now about thirty, unmarried, and distinctly girlish in appearance. She still wore her hair in two greasy bunches on either side of her head. She had worn it like that at school. She had gone on wearing it like that when she started work and spent her dinner-hour hanging around the men on a nearby building site. Perhaps her mother had hoped that the childish hairstyle and the dresses that went with it would help postpone the inevitable. Perhaps they did, but not for long. At twenty, she was pregnant.

Her mother, a respectable, chapel-going woman, had stormed and raged throughout the pregnancy, always insisting that the child must be adopted. She changed her mind abruptly when she saw it and became equally insistent that it be brought home. Nobody asked "Soppy Lil" for her opinion and probably she didn't have one. Her frantic desire to placate her mother seemed to have robbed her of what little wits she had.

It had been decided that the child should be brought up to regard its grandmother as its mother, and its mother as its sister. At first this seemed to work well. Lilian went to the cake factory to work. Her mother, with no apparent reluctance, stayed at home to take care of the child. It was a little girl, very pretty—unlike Lilian who had never been attractive, even as a child, and who now became increasingly slovenly. The grandmother doted on the child. The three of them could often be seen walking down Union Street together: an elderly woman with hair crimped into neat, stiff waves like corrugated iron; the child skipping on ahead, her hair worn, as Lilian still wore hers, in little bunches at either side of her head; and Lilian herself, bringing up the rear.

This situation dragged on for some years. It was obvious to everybody that there was no longer a place for Lilian in the home—to everybody, that is, except Lilian herself. She hung on, desperately, fawningly, trying to ingratiate herself. Then, suddenly, she was pregnant again. Nobody knew who by.

This time her mother's attitude was entirely different. She refused even to look at the baby. When it became clear that this time she would not accept the child, Lilian gave it up for adoption, almost casually it seemed, and returned home alone. But now her exclusion from the family group became more obvious. The child, without understanding anything of what had happened, knew nevertheless that her "big sister" was in disgrace. Her little voice could be heard, piping censoriously, whenever Lilian did something wrong, which was certainly not seldom. From the moment that she returned from hospital without the second child, Lilian began to deteriorate.

At work, too, she had exhausted most people's patience. One illegitimate child was accepted easily enough; two was evidence of stupidity or worse. She became, though always in a mild way, the butt for jokes. The younger women, in particular, despised her. The older ones were more tolerant.

So she went on, aging a little, but always retaining the too-girlish dresses, and the bunches of hair. On Saturday nights, she was said to go around the Buffs, letting men take her out the back, for a port and lemon if they were flush, for nothing if they were skint. There was a rumor that she had been sterilized. At any rate no more babies appeared.

Jo had been familiar with this story for many years, though she had hardly thought about it, merely absorbed it unconsciously as she had absorbed so many others during the years of her growing up. She hardly knew why, suddenly, it seemed important. Lilian herself she did not much like: there was too much of the spiteful child in her, she was too obviously delighted to see somebody else in trouble. When Elaine had just begun to persecute Bertha, and seemed to be getting away with it, Lilian had been beside herself with glee. The violence when it came had shocked her almost as badly as it had shocked Elaine. She had crept about quietly for days after it.

Meanwhile, the trouble so long forecast seemed to have started. Elaine was leaning across the belt to shout at Bertha, who merely shrugged her shoulders and turned aside. The sponges no longer arrived in front of Jo in a steady stream, but two or three at a time. This difference, hardly perceptible to a casual observer, altered the whole nature of the job. Now, instead of merely lifting each cake with one hand and slipping the card underneath it with the other—an economical movement that used only muscles hardened to it by long practice—she had to lean sideways and forwards over the belt, working, moreover, at many times the normal speed in order to regulate the flow of cakes before they reached the packers at the end of the line. This altered movement, repeated, as it would have to be, hundreds and hundreds of times, would amount by the end of the morning to agonizing pain.

When the next pause came she looked at Elaine. She was screaming at Bertha again, screaming until the veins stood out on her head. The lights beat down hard on her, revealing a moustache of sweat on her upper lip.

Bertha's task was to put the upper layer of cake on top of the middle layer as it left the slicing and creaming machine; Elaine's to lift the two layers and put them on the bottom layer. By holding on to the upper layer a fraction too long, or releasing several in quick succession, Bertha could treble the amount of effort Elaine had to put into her job if she were to keep pace with the flow of cakes. She had been doing this for some time, though so imperceptible was the alteration, that even a close observer, unfamiliar with conveyor-belt work, might not have detected the change.

Elaine had to chase the cakes down the line. She jostled against Jo, who yelled at her and was herself forced back. Gradually, Elaine inched back to her normal position, working like lightning, reaching far out over the belt.

If you had to lean out like that to pick them up, the cakes were surprisingly heavy. Jo could see the pain and desperation on Elaine's face as she panted and sweated to keep up. Speed made the job messier too. Jam and synthetic cream oozed out over Elaine's hands until they were coated up to the wrist. Inevitably, Jo found herself trying to do Elaine's job as

81

well as her own, straightening out lopsided cakes before she slipped the cardboard underneath. Even so, some very odd-looking sponges found their way down to the packing department.

This went on until the morning tea-break. Bertha looked blank, Lilian gawped, Jo and Elaine sweated and winced with pain. Once the supervisor walked past, puzzled by the apparent break in rhythm at that end of the line. But while she was there Bertha worked normally, so that after a few minutes she wandered off again. Jo, sweat pouring from her armpits, thighs trembling from the strain, simply prayed for it all to stop.

Yet when the machines were finally switched off the four of them simply stood and stared at each other for a second, all antagonism forgotten in the shock of silence. Gradually conversations started and rose quickly to a babble as the women moved towards the door.

As they all climbed the three flights of stairs to the tea-room, Jo could feel aggression simmering in the air. Elaine had been joined by her two friends from the packing department and marched up the stairs between them, keeping up an unmistakeably vituperative monologue. Jo crawled up, hanging on to the banister for support. She felt terrible. Then, suddenly, as they reached the top, hope flashed into her mind. Backache, belly ache, thigh ache. Stickyness? With all the clarity of an hallucination she saw her pants stained with blood. Glorious, marvellous, wonderful blood. Oh please, God, yes yes. . . .

"Where's *she* gone?"

"Taken short by the looks of it."

"I don't wonder. I'm damn sure these breaks are getting later."

There were three long trestle tables in the tea-room, with a fourth table to the right of the door on which were dozens of cups, the tea already poured out, gray and steaming. The women collected their tea and sat down. They sat in much the same order as they worked on the conveyor belt. A woman might move up or down a few places to be near a friend, but in general the order did not change much. If any of them had been asked what they thought of this arrangement, the answer would probably have been "Terrible." Yet they continued to abide by it. It was easy; it required no thought. So that when Jo returned it was to sit next to Elaine, and almost opposite Bertha. Lilian sat by herself at the end of the table, because her place was occupied by the two girls from packing. Elaine continued to mutter and to dart vicious glances at Bertha, who smiled and blew out smoke, slowly, knowing that she had nothing to fear. Elaine got out a little manicure set and began jabbing at her cuticles.

The supervisor passed, holding a cup of tea in her hand. Like everybody else, she kept to the routine and seldom sat down from beginning to end of the breaks. The women disliked her for it.

"What's the matter with you?" she asked, stopping opposite Jo. "You look as if you'd lost a bob and found a tanner."

"Me back aches," Jo said, as disagreeably as she could. "I've been working."

"Your back aches? My heart aches."

Aye, and your arse'd ache 'n' all if I got near it.

"If she was doing her job," Elaine muttered, "there'd be none of this carry-on."

Bertha blew out smoke. It drifted across the table and got into Elaine's eyes.

"I saw you around the Buffs last night," Elaine said, squinting to avoid the smoke.

Lilian gave the odd little wriggle of embarrassment and pleasure that she always gave when somebody noticed her.

"You were with that Wilf Rogerson. Weren't yer?"

Lilian produced a fawning grimace like a dog that doesn't know whether the upraised stick means a beating or a game. "Yeah, I was there. I didn't see you but . . ."

"Oh, we were over in the lounge part." Elaine flicked the

chewing gum to the other side of her mouth. "Saw you, though."

The two girls from packing looked at each other, excited and nervous. They knew Elaine in this mood.

"Smashing dress you had on. It was." Here Elaine turned to her underlings as if daring them to dispute it. "It was, it was smashing. Only one thing let yer down and that was yer hair. Can't you do summat with it? She doesn't suit it like that, does she?" Again she consulted the younger girls.

"No, it makes her face look too fat."

"And anyway, she's too old for it."

Their names were Barbara and Karen but Jo never succeeded in remembering which was which for long. When Elaine was present, they might just as well have been called Giggle and Squeak.

"You want a good bit of it off," Elaine concluded.

The three of them stared at Lilian, who grinned nervously, overwhelmed by so much attention.

"Either off or up. One or the other." Elaine was smiling pleasantly, but there was a tremor of excitement in her voice. She reached across and pulled the two bunches together on top of Lilian's head. Then she craned her head back and pretended to examine the effect.

"My God, Elaine, rather you than me," Squeak said.

Elaine ignored her. "Shows yer dirty neck, mind," she said to Lilian. "You'll have to get that washed. Here, give us me scissors."

Lilian wriggled again, not daring to protest.

"Keep still, will yer?"

Instantly, Lilian froze.

"My God, she is 'n' all!"

Lilian's failure to stand up for herself took away what little self-control Elaine had. She stabbed at the hair, sawing and hacking away almost at random. Lilian sat still, a fixed monkey-grin of terror and incomprehension on her face, as first locks of hair and then whole chunks of it slid down her shoulders and on to the table.

"There you are. Give that lot a bit trim and you'll be all right." Elaine's voice shook with laughter. "No, hold on, there's a bit here." Elaine nearly choked. "I'll finish it off."

"What about the top, Elaine?" Giggle suggested.

"I think it's gone far enough," Jo said.

Elaine stopped what she was doing and looked at Jo.

"What's it to do with you?"

"Nowt. But I think it's gone far enough. Don't you?"

"You want to make something of it?"

"No. But I will if I have to."

Elaine looked around for support. There was none. Some of the older women at the head of the table were getting reluctantly to their feet.

"She's better off without it."

"I'm not denying that. But you might've let her make up her own mind."

"*Mind?* She hasn't got a bloody mind!"

"No reason to pick on her. We all know what's eating you. If you haven't got the guts to speak out you'd best shut up altogether."

"Come on, girls. Come on." It was the manager. He stood in the open doorway, angrily consulting his watch. "These tea-breaks are meant to be fifteen minutes, you know. Fifteen. Not thirty."

He watched them file past. Looking for trouble, he noticed one of the girls walking along without a hairnet on.

"You," he said. "Whatever your name is."

"Lil—"

He wasn't interested. "Get your hair under that net. And don't ever let me catch you walking around like that again."

He watched them down the corridor and out of sight, noticing how many slipped into the cloakroom, although they were already late back for work. That's right, he thought, angrily. Always pee in the firm's time, never in your own.

That was the motto with some of these girls. "Girls" he said, and they were girls. Would never be anything else though some of them were forty, fifty, even sixty years old. You only had to listen to them: nothing but gossip and giggle and rubbish.

He took one final look around and marched out, banging the door.

On the table where Elaine and Lilian had sat were little coils and crescent moons of hair, lying unregarded among the ashtrays and the dirty cups.

By dinner-time, Joe was exhausted. Instead of going across to the canteen she went back to the tea-room, where at least it would be quiet.

She sat down on one of the benches and let the silence wash over her.

The only other woman in the room, Maureen Sullivan, was over by the cake stands, choosing something to eat. Slices of sponge and chocolate cake were available, free, every dinner-time. "I wouldn't eat that muck if I was starving," was the common reaction. Maureen, although not starving, ate it every day.

There were varicose veins on the backs of her legs, standing out thickly like worm-casts on the beach: she wore no stockings. Jo found herself staring at them. She watched as Maureen sat down and started to eat the cake. Her top teeth were missing so that the flesh was pleated over bare gums, making it difficult to manage the cream. She sat, licking it humbly off her lips; after every few mouthfuls, she washed it down with a sip of weak tea.

God, I'd like to tell them where to shove their bloody cake, Jo thought. She would, too, one day.

Maureen couldn't. She had a houseful of kids and no husband. But still she struggled on and thanked no one for their pity. Her kids went to school well shod though she herself wore the same pair of plimsolls winter and summer.

She was respected, respected but avoided. Luck like hers might be catching.

Maureen chewed her cake. Jo became aware that she had been staring at her too long, and looked away. Everybody she met today she seemed to be seeing for the first time. Perhaps it was because her own life was about to change so radically: every older woman became an image of the future, a reason for hope or fear.

Now, looking at Maureen Sullivan and thinking what her life had been, Jo felt a sense of oppression. And then there was Lisa Goddard, whom she often saw in the supermarket, weighed down with kids and shopping, pushing her belly in front of her like another self. To Joanne, she looked ready to pop: she couldn't imagine a belly bigger than that. But Iris King said, No, she was still a good way off.

Jo turned towards the window. Autumn sunlight filtered down, hazy with smoke and soot. The grime on the glass almost defeated it, but enough got through to gild her face and hair. She gave herself up to it completely, lying back in her chair, her eyes screwed up against the brilliance of the light.

"It's been a long time."

"It has that."

"Well, let's not waste any more of it, then."

He pushed her back on to the coat, and kissed her, pressing the whole length of his body against her own. The tree they were lying under moved a little in the wind, casting its net of branches at the stars which swam through unharmed in bright and glimmering shoals. It made her feel dizzy to look at them.

He pressed his weight down and instantly she felt something sticking into her back. She twisted around and found first one conker and then another,—green, unopened cases.

"Some kid must've dropped them," Ken said. "It isn't even a conker tree."

She lay back. His mouth moved all over her face, blindly,

like some weird, sucking creature of the sea-bed that lives by touch alone; hovered, and burrowed down to stifle the lonely cry that welled up from her throat.

He left her at once and began zipping up his trousers.

"You know what you were saying earlier? About those women fighting? I hope you don't join in with that sort of thing, because there's nothing worse than to see two women fight, nothing more common. It's real low-life, is that." His mouth puckered with distaste, as he hurried his shriveled flesh out of sight.

"Sometimes you've no choice."

"There's always a choice. Decent women don't fight."

Jo thought of Iris King, and wondered.

Meanwhile he had finished fastening his trousers.

It was always like this: after it was over she wanted to cuddle, to talk, to feel close. But he wanted to be on the move at once. There were times when she suspected that he wanted to get away from her, from what they had done together. Their lovemaking never brought them closer. In fact, sometimes, things she'd said earlier in the evening, things that had made him laugh, then, were brought up and held against her.

She lay looking up at the tree. At first its branches hardly stirred, but then a gust of wind shook them, loosening more leaves.

The tree had been green the first time they lay down beneath it. Now almost all its leaves were gone.

And in the wintertime? What would they do then? Where would they go?

"Aren't you cold?" Ken asked. The words were torn out of him. It shocked him that she should just lie there like that, not even trying to cover herself up. Lying there with her legs apart, she challenged his hatred of what his body had made him do. He resented her, even despised her a little. But since he was basically a kind-hearted man, a man who wanted more from a woman than he knew how to take, he was unhappy despising her. He could not do it without despising himself.

And so he wanted to escape, from the situation, from her, most of all from himself. "You must be cold," he went on. "I'm freezing."

Jo lay and looked up at him, not speaking.

"Come on," he said. "We'll have a walk around the Vane Arms, shall we? They'll have a fire on there."

She could not speak. Fear had sharpened her perceptions. She saw every gesture, registered every inflection of his voice that told of his anxiety to be gone.

The silence tightened.

"You all right?"

"No."

"What's wrong? I mean, it was all right for you, wasn't it? You seemed . . ."

"It was fine."

". . . to be enjoying it."

"It was fine."

"Well, then."

Silence.

"Well, then. What's wrong?"

She felt that he already knew. Or guessed.

"I'm pregnant."

But she was wrong. She watched him take the full force of the blow. Disbelief, fear, anger, disbelief, fear chased each other across his face.

"Don't be daft. You can't be. I haven't been near you . . ."

"For six weeks? I've missed twice."

She watched hope die.

"Well. Well, then. . . . You must've known before I left."

"I was a few days late. That's all. I didn't see the point of two people worrying themselves sick. And anyway, I've been that late before."

"You should've told me."

"There was no point."

He stared around him helplessly. Looked down at the shape their bodies had left in the grass and said violently, "Come on, let's get away from here."

"We've got to talk about it, Ken."

"We can talk in the pub."

"It's all very well for you. You haven't had the weeks and weeks of worry that I've had."

"Well, it's not my fault I haven't, is it? You rang me up. Why the bloody hell didn't you mention it then?"

"Oh, have a heart, man. How could I? On the *phone*?"

She was struggling to her feet. He put out a hand:—too late to help.

"I suppose you *are* sure? I mean if you've been late before?"

"I've never been this late. And anyway, I've started being sick in the mornings as well now."

"Oh, my God."

There were little pinpricks of sweat just below his hairline. He was sweating with fear, fear of having to marry her. She saw all that. But there was a certain detachment in her bitterness. She was not going to nag him into it. She would wait and see what he did.

"Did you try anything?"

"Like what?"

"I don't know! Pills."

"Where from? You might know where to get things like that—I don't. And if you're thinking of hot baths and gin, well, for a kickoff it doesn't work. If it did I wouldn't be here for one. And in the second place, we haven't *got* a bath, you daft bugger. If I started boiling meself to death in front of the fire don't you think me Mam'd notice? Don't you think she'd want to know why?"

"You haven't told her then?"

There was so much relief in his voice she could have throttled him.

"No, I haven't told her. Because I didn't have to. The way we live she knows I'm late before I do."

"What did she say?"

"Oh, what do you think she said?"

For a moment he almost got the full story, Joss included. But she stopped herself in time.

They began walking towards the park gate. By the lake they stopped. Geese and swans immediately took to the water and began sailing towards them in search of food.

She said, "Ken, I'm frightened."

"You've no need to be. We're in it together."

"Are we?"

"Oh, yes." She heard him catch and hold his breath to stop it becoming a sigh. "Only you'll have to give me a bit of time. I mean, back home . . . they don't even know your name. . . ."

Because you never thought it important enough to mention. Until now.

Suddenly he was laughing: an ugly sound. "Do you know, my sister and her husband've been trying for a bairn for three year. Three bloody year."

He cut the laugh off quickly.

"What do you think your Mam'll say?"

"A barrowful."

They stood in silence under the trees. A dead leaf rattled along the path towards them. Jo thought, I'll remember this for the rest of my life: the relief. The despair.

She shivered. "You're right. It is cold. Let's go for a drink."

But even about this they couldn't agree. As they left the park he began walking very quickly with his head lowered and his hands thrust deep into his pockets, leaving Jo to follow as best she could. She was so preoccupied with her own thoughts and with the difficulty of keeping up with him that at first she did not realize where he was taking her. When she did it was already too late. They were outside the Bluebell.

"I can't go in there," she said, panting for breath.

It was a steelworkers' pub. There was a strict men-only rule in the bar.

"There's a snug at the back," he said, not looking at her. "Women go in there."

"Yes, and what women?"

"It's not to say you're one of them, is it?"

They stood together under the street lamp. Then the swing doors opened just behind them and Blonde Dinah came out.

"If it's all the same to you I think I'd rather go home."

Evidently it *was* all the same to him, for he turned towards the railway tunnel without another word.

But in the darkness of the tunnel he hesitated. This was their last chance to talk. Heavily, almost reluctantly, he took her in his arms. She stood with her back against the white-washed wall. She could not see his face. He loomed over her like a shadow.

"We've got to talk," she said. But she had no faith in their ability to talk to each other. She thought of the girls she knew who had got married with a child on the way. She had thought it would never happen to her; her marriage would be different.

"I don't want to start raking it all over now. I can't take any more tonight."

He made it sound as if it were her fault. But at least he did not move away. He looked at her, and kissed her. And then—something he had never done before, though they had often stopped in this tunnel to say goodnight—he lifted her skirt, and began to thrust into her.

"Ken," she said. In the distance, a goods train rumbled. It panted towards them, sounding at first rather out of breath and ineffectual. Then it was roaring and crashing above their heads. Flakes of plaster drifted down and landed in her hair.

Ken was panting, and thrusting into her as though he hated her, grinding and screwing and banging hard enough to hurt. She was afraid for the baby and immediately knew what he was trying to do: he was trying to screw it out of her. She went cold, pressing herself back against the wall, but he fastened on to her with a terrible, monotonous power.

There was something exciting in being used like this, in

giving way to this impersonal, machine-like passion. For a moment she let herself relax, and his flesh bit into her like steel.

The goods train clanked and rumbled overhead, no longer roaring, but deadly and monotonous. She could see in her mind's eye the oiled pistons moving around. And around. Almost matching the thrusts of Ken's bum. With deadly corrosive hatred she began to move against him, imposing upon him the rhythm of the train, which was at first exciting, and then terrible and then, abruptly, ridiculous, so that he lost his erection and slid ignobly out of her.

She watched him shield himself and turn aside. There was nothing that either of them could say.

The silence sounded very loud after the train had finally pulled away.

"I'll be in touch before Sunday," Ken said

"All right."

"And don't worry about it. She's not that bad."

"I wasn't going to."

Further along the tunnel they came across Blonde Dinah with the man who had followed her out of the pub. They passed with lowered eyes as the custom was: at this time of night you didn't notice other users of the tunnel. But out of the corner of her eye Jo glimpsed the white thighs and raised skirt of the other woman and a darkness rushed over her so that she stumbled and almost fell.

"What's wrong?" Ken asked. Then with sudden awkward concern, "Are you feeling faint?"

"No. No. I don't know what's wrong." She looked back and shuddered. "A ghost walking over my grave."

He put his arm around her, and together they walked on.

On the way home she bought fish and chips for herself and Joss, and put them in the oven to await his arrival. He would stop for a drink on his way back. In fact he had probably been in the Bluebell.

Another good reason for staying out of the snug.

She sat in the darkness and watched gangs of youths throwing stones on the streets of Belfast. Then turned the volume up for a story about petrol price increases. She wasn't interested, but Joss would be. His car was his god. Iris King, who knew him as well as anybody, used to say that was the real reason he'd never got married: he couldn't afford to run a wife and a car.

Joss came in as the news finished.

"You're back early. I thought you'd've gone for a drink."

"Brought it back with me, didn't I?" He produced three bottles of Newcastle Brown and two of Guinness. "The Guinness is for you," he said. "It's supposed to be good for the milk."

"I haven't had it yet, man."

"You need building up."

"I'll be big enough without any building. There's fish and chips in the oven. Do you want them off a plate?"

"Paper'll do me."

"They don't taste the same off a plate, do they? Have I to bring 'em through there?"

"Aye. And I'll build up the fire." He looked at the telly. "Petrol's up again."

"I saw 'em queueing." He turned off the set. They looked at each other, exposed and vulnerable now that the other presence in the room was gone.

"Well, I'll get the fish and chips."

Ten minutes later Jo was wiping her mouth on the back of her hand.

"My God, you didn't half knock that lot back."

"I was hungry. That's the first I've had today."

"Not my fault. It was offered."

"Takes me stomach time to settle."

The fire roared, clots and flakes of burning soot sparked up the chimney. "I don't know what you're sat back there for," said Jo. "Come down here and get warm."

"This is close enough. Over much like work, is that."

"I suppose it is." She had just remembered: he was a blast-furnace man. "Bit like telling me to bake a cake."

"How did it go tonight? With your boyfriend."

"Oh, all right, I suppose. I'm going to meet his Mam and Dad next weekend. That is, if his Mam's willing."

She pulled a face.

"And then?"

"Then we'll get married, I suppose."

"You suppose?"

"I mean we will."

Silence.

"Well, aren't you going to congratulate me? That's what people usually do, you know."

"Sounds more like a funeral than a wedding."

"You're dead right it does." She piled the fish and chip papers on to the fire and held them down with the poker while they burned. More flakes of soot caught fire and leapt up the chimney. "It's time you had this lot swept." She scoured the back of the chimney with the poker, so that a cloud of soot billowed out into the room and for a minute the fire burned black and chill.

"Yes, well, there's no need for you to do it. You'll have the whole lot down."

Jo stared into the deadened fire. "The trouble is, I know he doesn't want to. Not really."

"How old is he?"

"Eighteen. Same as me. Younger in fact. He's just turned eighteen."

"Dear God."

"He's not the only one who's trapped, you know. Though you'd think he was the way he carries on . . . I'm the one who's got to walk around with me belly swelling, being sick and all that. Then in the end get the poor little bugger out of me. I'm trapped! Worse than he'll ever be. But I'm supposed to be grateful because he's doing the right thing, not leaving me to carry the can by meself. . . . He started it! I didn't do it single-handed!"

"You must love him."

"Must I? Why?"

"Well, you know you must."

"Because I get on me back for him, you mean?"

"There's no need for that."

"It wasn't love. . . . I suppose I must've thought it was. And I'll tell you summat else: it was no bloody pleasure. A sparrow couldn't't've farted quicker."

"It's no use going on like this. If you're going to marry him you've got to try and make a go of it."

"What do you know about it? You've never been married, have you?"

"No."

"Well? Do you think you're missing owt?"

"No." He considered a minute. "Sometimes I think I am. But not when I look around."

"Some folks make a go of it."

"Aye."

"They're not all going at it hammer and tongs."

"I never said they were."

"Well, then. . . ."

"Only there's not many you could say were really happy. You know, more than jogging along."

Silence. Then, "Oh, don't worry. I know what you mean."

"Ted and Iris. You couldn't call them happy."

"Happy! There's many a night we think they're coming through the wall. There's not much we don't hear, you know."

"Same with these two next door to me. . . ."

They both stared into the fire. Then Joss said slowly,

"Well, I hope he knows what he's getting, your young man."

"Oh, what is he getting?" She was prepared to be aggressive.

"Why, best little lass for miles around." He paused. "Anyway, that's what I think."

Their eyes met. Her heart was thumping. She could neither

speak nor look away. She could do nothing to guard either of them from this sudden danger.

"But there, I expect he knows that better than me." Joss looked down at his legs as if for once in his life he needed to be reminded of their length, and caught a sigh. "Anyway."

When he spoke again his voice had changed. "You'll need to make it up with your Mam. You can't very well get married from here."

But Jo was not thinking of the practicalities of a wedding.

"I never feel as if I can talk to him. I'm not his class. No, it's true. . . ." She waved Joss's protests aside.

"Who's he when he's all at home?"

"Well, they've got a furniture shop and a nice house. I don't suppose they know where Union Street is. And he goes to the Poly." She gestured, helplessly. "You can see why he's afraid of telling his Mam, can't you? She's not going to be overjoyed."

"It's him you're marrying, not her."

"Oh, I don't know so much. I've a feeling it might be her."

Silence. Then, "Howay, lass. Get stuck in at your beer."

Jo leant back against the sofa and closed her eyes. She saw Soppy Lil's face, grinning with terror. It was "Soppy Jo" now. God, she needed her head looking at. The face faded, and was replaced by a long line of cakes. That was the worst of the job. You could be away from it for hours, you could think you'd forgotten it, but the minute you closed your eyes: there were the cakes. It was only after a good night's sleep that you got rid of them.

But she'd be leaving the bakery now. Three or four months and she'd be finished. Mebbe sooner. He mightn't let her work there after they were married. Wouldn't suit his ideas a bit. Nor his mother's.

Instead there'd be a house. Somewhere. Housework. And, eventually, a baby.

Well, that was what she wanted. Wasn't it?

She looked around the room. Firelight flickered over mirrors and furniture.

"I like it here. I wish I didn't have to go."

Even the baby, which all day long she had "felt" as a hard nodule of fear, seemed to melt away inside her, to float and merge with her into the peace and safety of this room.

She said, more wistfully now, "I wish I didn't have to go."

III

Lisa Goddard

It was late-night shopping at the supermarket. The shelves were piled high with tins, packets, fruit and vegetables ready for the weekend rush. And everywhere there was the cheerfulness of money to spend at last, after the scrimping of Wednesday and Thursday night. It was fish-and-chip night, too, for many of the families, so the women were able to shop without thinking of the meal they would have to cook when they got back.

Lisa Goddard walked down one of the aisles, wheeling a pushchair with a stout protesting little boy, about eighteen months old, strapped into it. He was fastened in too tightly. There was a shopping bag on his lap which tilted precariously whenever he struggled. Which was often. He was tired of the bright lights, and people's knees, and the sharp edges of shopping baskets banging him in the face. There was another, heavier shopping basket slung over the handle of his pushchair.

His mother walked behind, carrying a wire basket and

hauling along a slightly older boy, who was pulling away from her and screaming. Most of the time she moved the pushchair along with little vicious jerks of her belly. Tiredness and desperation were written all over her face. And still the child hauled on her arm, trying to pull her back the way they had come.

"I wanta . . ."

He didn't say what he wanted, and probably no longer knew. He had reached the stage where he could not have given in even if he had wanted to. His rage possessed him completely. When his mother reached up to get a packet from the shelves, he seized the opportunity and wrenched himself out of her grasp. He didn't go far: the bond with her was too strong; but he backed away, and stood pressed against the deep-freeze counter, screaming now with fear of what his anger had made him do. For he had seen the expression on his mother's face.

She let go of the pushchair and swung around on him, her arm raised to strike. But the pushchair, top-heavy now because of the shopping basket on the back, began to topple over. She had to jump back, and succeeded in catching it only just in time. The baby screamed and struggled harder. The shopping basket on his knee overturned, and tins of peas and carrots rolled out on to the floor.

It was breaking point. Very deliberately, Lisa took off the heavy shopping basket, so that the pushchair would be stable, and went after the older child. He screamed with terror, but she was beyond hearing.

"I warned you, didn't I? I warned you. . . ." She hit the child hard across the face. He gasped and then howled again, louder, but still he hung back. He was incapable of getting himself out of the situation. "Come on!" his mother said, trying to drag him back to the pushchair and the squealing baby. He clung to the deep-freeze counter, and she hit him again and again, stinging, hard slaps, her face distorted by hatred as she looked at him. Yet, inside, another woman was watching, and that woman felt nothing but horror and shame.

"Oh, all right, have your sweets. Have them! And I hope you choke."

The child clutched the packet of sweets, not even bothering to look at it. His little reddened face was raised hopelessly to his mother, mouth wide and screaming, upper lip smeared with snot.

"Oh, my God, and now look at you." She groped about her for a handkerchief, and couldn't find one. She could have sat down beside her son on the supermarket floor and cried as miserably as he was crying.

But there was still the shopping to be done. She took his hand and he allowed it to be taken, stumbling along after her blindly, sometimes tripping and being saved from falling only because she carried him along bodily for a few strides.

"Pick your feet up, can't you?" she said, bending down to whisper her threat. "If you don't pull yourself together and start behaving yourself, I'll knock the living daylights out of you when I get you back."

She raised her eyes and found a young girl staring at her. She was standing just by the tights counter and must have seen everything. Lisa walked more quickly, glaring at the girl as she walked past, daring her to say anything, to interfere. But she wouldn't, of course; people never did. Only looked. And despised what they saw.

The girl was familiar. Lisa looked back at her, taking in the dress, the shoes, the make-up. She looked down at herself, at the shapeless smock left over from her last pregnancy, and at the shapeless body beneath it—also left over from her last pregnancy. The baby's hands reached out towards the brightly-colored sweets that were placed so temptingly within reach. Lisa was too tired to stop him. Just let the assistant say anything, that was all. Just let her start. . . .

Back at home, she dropped the shopping down and almost fell into the armchair. The house was empty, but she had expected that. She lay back in the chair, while Kevin stuffed himself with sweets and spoilt his appetite for supper, and the baby, still imprisoned in the pushchair, yelled to be let out.

101

Her ankles were swollen. Quite badly. They'd have something to say about that when she went to the clinic.

Are you getting enough rest, Mrs. Goddard?

Her blood pressure was up. She had guessed that, though the nurse's face remained carefully expressionless as she wrote the figures down on the card.

Oh, yes, she said, eagerly. *I'm taking things very easy.*

She was afraid they would take her into hospital, as they had threatened to do once before. Not that it mattered much now: she was due anyway. But then, it would have meant weeks away from the children and she did not know what would have happened to them. She looked at them now, and softened.

"Howay, Kevin, come and give your Mam a cuddle. Then we'll get his lordship sorted out, and see what there is for tea. Hey, shall we?" He came into her arms, his face still stained with tears, chocolate mixed in with the snot around his mouth. She had hit him too hard. And not for the first time. When he cuddled in close to her she could hear the tremor in his breath, the shudder where the sobs had been.

God forgive me, she thought. She held him close and rocked him. It wasn't that she didn't love him. It was only that she got so desperate. She loved him all right: this rocking gave her as much peace as it gave him.

Only there was still the baby. There was still Darren to be seen to.

"Howay, let's see if we've got something nice. What would you like?" She mentioned fish fingers, beefburgers, chips, trying to inject some enthusiasm into her voice, and was rewarded, at last, by a shaky smile. Why can't it be like this all the time? she thought. Why am I so bad-tempered with them? It isn't their fault.

She must try to be better. The resolution carried her through the last few hours of the day, until, having seen both children asleep in their cots, she came down to face the evening alone. Then, suddenly depressed, she sat down at the kitchen table. She was remembering the girl who had stared at her in the supermarket. She knew now who it was: Joanne Wilson. They'd gone to the same school, but never really known each other. Joanne had arrived the same year that Lisa left.

But she couldn't be much younger. Three years. Perhaps four. Lisa leaned forward, her arms folded on the table. Her breasts slumped forward, too, and rested on the bulge. She couldn't afford a proper maternity brassiere and the others no longer fitted. She remembered Joanne's dress, her shoes, her hair. She had looked at Lisa so contemptuously.

What right had she to look like that? What did she know about it? What did she know about anything?

As much as I knew at her age.

Lisa hid her face in her hands and wept.

After a little while she sat up and dried her eyes. She was alone in the house, but she was used to that. There were only the two children asleep upstairs.

She rinsed out the nappies that were waiting for her in a bucket under the sink, then built up the living room fire and put the clothes horse in front of it. She could never dry the clothes while Brian was in the house because he liked to sit huddled over the fire. The room was warm, fire-lit. She left the main light off and went to lie on the sofa. From behind the clothes horse came the roar of flames and the smell of wool drying.

The scene was peaceful enough. But inside her the baby boiled and heaved. It always seemed to be restless at this time of night, perhaps because she herself was so tense. Did it know pub throwing-out time already? Before it was born?

The baby kicked hard. Sometimes you could see a foot or a hand quite clearly, or even the whole sweep of an arm moving across beneath the surface of the skin. It had filled her with wonder in the weeks before Kevin was born.

Not any more.

She did not want this baby. They could not afford it: Brian had been out of work for the best part of a year. But even if there had been all the money in the world, she would not have wanted it. Brian was out drinking. As always. She did not want to have his child. The two she had already were as much as she could manage. More. There were times when she doubted whether Brian would ever work again. Oh, he said he was still looking. But she didn't believe him. He had given up.

And of course it wasn't his fault: the redundancy. It wasn't hers either. And yet so often she seemed to bear the brunt of his despair.

Been up to his tricks again, has he? Well, you know what your father said.

And what good would that do?

It might do him a power of good. It'd show him you've still got a family.

It's not often he hits me.

He shouldn't hit you at all! You should've left him when you only had the one. We'd've managed.

It's only when he's had a drink, Mam.

I'm glad he can afford to drink. Many a man in work can't afford to spend what he spends.

He has to have something. Ever since he lost that job . . . It seems to've knocked the stuffing out of him. Completely.

And has he any need to take it out on you?

"There's nobody else."

She realized that she had said the words aloud, and was startled. You get taken away if you do things like that. It's supposed to be the first sign.

She stood up and moved the clothes horse away from the fire. Then she went into the kitchen and started getting his supper ready. He always wanted a hot meal whenever he came in: there was a row if he didn't get it. Yet when he was in work he hadn't minded if she was a bit late. He would even sit and play with the bairns for a bit while she finished getting it ready.

She sighed, and went on scraping the carrots. She seemed to be so far away from her own childhood, from her youth. It seemed hardly possible that this heavy woman lumbering around the kitchen of a poky house should be the same person as that girl who had worked all day at the cake bakery and still found the energy to dance at night. Still less possible that she should be that child who had run shouting through the park.

It was almost closing time. God alone knew where he was finding the money from. Only last night he had complained of being broke. Perhaps he was sponging on his friends? But no, he wouldn't do that. She wasn't even sure that he had any friends. The ties formed at work were beginning to dissolve now.

The dinner was prepared and in the oven. Still he didn't come. She settled herself into an armchair and got out her knitting. If he didn't come soon she would go to bed. She was tired, and it was a mug's game waiting up for somebody who never seemed to notice whether you were there or not.

In spite of herself the fear grew. Where *was* he finding the money from? She went back into the kitchen, telling herself that she was only going to check that she had turned the gas on.

But after she had checked the oven she still stood there. The kitchen was very cold. It always smelled of cold fat in spite of all the time she spent cleaning it.

They had been going to have it all modernized. Until Brian lost his job.

The glanced at the pantry door. Perhaps she would just check. There was no harm in checking, was there?

For the last four or five months she had been saving up for the baby. Most of the things she'd got for Kevin were worn out now, and the maternity grant wouldn't cover replacements. At first she saved whatever was left in her purse at the end of the week. But that was usually just a few coppers. Then she made herself save all the 50p pieces. Sometimes when she saw a shopkeeper about to give her a 50p in her change she would pray for him to change his mind. She needed the money now.

But she made herself stick to her self-imposed rule. And was rewarded. The sum quickly mounted up. By now the jar was almost full.

She kept it right at the back of the pantry, behind everything else. Not that she distrusted Brian. More than once she had given him 50p and asked him to put it in the jar for her. She was horrified to find herself suspecting him now, so horrified that she almost closed the pantry door without checking on the jar.

But it was no use. She had come this far. She had to know. The jar was too light. She felt this, even before she saw that the money was gone.

She brought it out into the kitchen, convinced that there must be some mistake. Brian couldn't've done this to her. She even put her hand inside the jar and felt all around it, as though her eyes might be deceiving her and somehow, by some miracle, the money was still there.

She sat down at the kitchen table with the empty jar in her hand. Perhaps she had put the money somewhere else? It had crossed her mind to do that more than once. Yes, that must be it. She had moved the money to another place and then forgotten. She did forget things these days. He was always telling her about it.

She began to search. All the time she knew there was no hope, but the mere act of searching seemed to ward off the moment when she would have to accept what had happened.

At last, though, she was forced to return to the table and the jar. Of course, she told herself, she didn't *know* that it was Brian who had taken the money. Though he was the only one who knew where it was, and she always remembered to lock the door whenever she went out.

She looked at the clock. She would know as soon as he came in. He would not be able to hide it from her.

But she knew already. She had thought he would never be able to hurt her again, but it wasn't true. This hurt.

He was not back by eleven. Lisa sat in the armchair by the fire, with an old woolen dressing gown thrown across her shoulders more for comfort than warmth. She was so exhausted by now that she felt sick.

If only he would come, she thought. She wanted it to be over.

At last she heard his key in the lock. Immediately she became tense, tense almost to breaking point. But I won't say anything, she told herself. I'll wait to see what he does.

He continued to fumble with the lock. To her over-strained nerves he seemed to be making enough noise to wake the dead. If only he doesn't wake the children up, she thought. To have them downstairs and crying on top of everything else would be more than she could bear.

At last he was in the house. He paused outside the living-room door and for a moment she thought he was going upstairs. But no. There he was, swaying slightly, holding on to the edge of the door for support. But she knew him too well. He was not as drunk as he appeared to be. He was using drunkenness as a defense.

"Supper ready, is it?"

"Yes."

He looked at the table in mock surprise.

"In the kitchen."

"In the kitchen."

"If you want it on the table you'd better let me know when you're coming home."

He glowered at her as he went past. She no longer had any doubts. His guilt had made him hate her.

But still she said nothing, though she tensed again as he began banging and clattering in the kitchen. He was picking things up and crashing them down at random. It was a technique he had for making it seem as though the kitchen—neat and tidy as always—was a pigsty in which it was a miracle if you succeeded in finding anything. She stood it as long as she could, then went to stand at the kitchen door.

"Having trouble?"

She knew she sounded aggressive. Not just angry but coldly, bloody-mindedly aggressive. Normally when he came home in this state she humored him. But not tonight. Tonight the words stuck in her throat.

"It's in the oven."

He stood and glowered at her without saying a word. She stared back, and saw a flicker of fear in his eyes. He started to bluster. "Well, aren't you going to get it then?"

"No. It's your supper. Get it yourself."

"It's your job."

"And it's your job to keep the family."

"Oh, yes. I wondered how long it'd take you to throw that up."

"I've never thrown it up. You can't say that."

He bent down to the oven and, with a tea-towel wrapped around his hand, began pulling out the tray. It was stiff and he was jerking on it one-sidely, so that after a few minutes he had succeeded in jamming it completely. He kept his face down, but Lisa could tell by the set of his shoulders that he was painfully, irritably aware of her standing there, watching him. It seemed to drive him to a frenzy. He wrenched at the tray with his full strength. It flew out of the oven, sending the dish toppling over on to the floor. Brown stew splashed and splattered everywhere.

It was too much for Lisa. "Dirty, filthy, drunken bastard. You clean that up yourself. I'm not doing it."

He tried to scoop some of the stew back into the pot, and burnt his hand.

"I'm sick of you, coming in drunk like this. It's bad enough when it's your own money . . ."

He had to silence her somehow. So he stood up and hit her, not very hard, on the side of the head. But the blow liberated something in him, an enormous anger that had been chained up waiting for this moment. He hit her again. And again. It was easier now. She was driven back against the wall.

When it was over he stood and stared at what he had done.

She said, coldly, "Would you pass me the flannel, please?"

He stood and watched while she wiped her mouth. There was nothing much: one smear of blood where his ring had caught her. Regret for what he had done fought with the need to bluster, to keep up a front at any cost. She was too tired to wait for the outcome.

"I'm going to bed."

He looked at the floor.

"Leave it."

"But . . ."

"I said, Leave it."

She lay on her back in bed. The ache that had been with her all day became briefly worse and then vanished completely. She moved her legs about, luxuriating in the space, dreading the moment when her husband must appear to fill it.

Meanwhile her mind played back almost automatically every detail of that scene. She went over every word, every action, until her anger went stale and bitterness took its place.

He had not admitted taking the money. He had hit her rather than face up to what he'd done. But it didn't matter. She knew.

When, finally, she felt him in the room with her, she lay with her eyes closed, pretending to sleep. She heard the soft thud and click of his clothes going off. Then the jingle of money in his trouser pockets.

"If you've got any left I think you might have the decency to put it back."

No reply. She opened her eyes to find him with his trousers half down and an injured expression on his face.

"Put what back?"

"You know what."

"I don't know what you're on about." She turned her head away from him. "It's me own money."

"You know it's not."

He started to bluster. It was intolerable, he wouldn't put up with it a minute longer, she did nothing but go on at him, didn't know what to pick at next. . . .

"So you'd steal from your own child," she said, quietly.

He tried to fight back. "If that's what you think of me all I can say is I've been around too long. I've a bloody good mind to go."

He waited for her to speak, his trousers halfway up his thighs.

"Well, what have I to do?"

She turned away from him again.

"Mind, if I go, that's it. I don't come back." He waited. "I mean it, mind."

She sat up, leant across the bed and in one movement pulled his trousers up around his waist. "Bloody go then!" she cried.

There was nothing left for him to do but to pick up his shirt and sweater and go. At the door he tried again, "I'm not coming back, you know."

"Go. Go."

She listened to him go down the stairs. There was a pause, then the sound of the front door opening and closing. She sat on the edge of the bed, trembling slightly. Suppose he had really gone for good? The baby would be born in a few days. A week at most. How would she manage alone? Then she shrugged. She was managing alone already, wasn't she?

At the back of her mind was the knowledge that he would not go. He depended on her too much.

It was a relief to put the light out and lie in the darkness alone. She ought to sleep. It was midnight now and the baby would be awake before six. "The baby" she called him, forgetting this other that was on the way. So near now. She closed her eyes and tried to sleep. It was useless. As soon as her eyes closed an automatic re-enactment of the row began. And always the resentment, the bitterness that grew and grew until it corroded everything.

That was the worst thing about these rows: each one seemed to arouse not only its own bitterness but the accumulated bitterness of so many previous rows. In between times she would sometimes think she had forgotten, but the next row brought it all to the surface again.

Worse than the row was the day after, when he would sit walled up in silence, trying to pretend that nothing had happened. He would not by any word or gesture acknowledge that he felt remorse. And so the remorse bit into him like acid. This was something that she could never get her mother to see. She couldn't find the right words to express it, though she knew exactly what was happening.

Once she had been sitting in the living room, sewing. It was the day after the worst of their rows, and, although she hadn't realized it, the light from the window was showing up the bruises on her face. Suddenly he had fallen on his knees and crawled towards her, burying his head wordlessly in her lap.

And she was sorry for him. She felt how like a child he had become. Underneath the drink and blustering and violence he was like this all the time.

Sometimes she thought that even if he found work now it would be too late.

And he wasn't looking.

In the mornings if he didn't have to go and sign on, he just sat in the armchair with his face in his hands. On a bad day there was no rousing him at all.

He hadn't always been like this. At first he'd been restless. Up and down, up and down. He seemed as if he didn't know where he wanted to be. He'd even get up in the middle of the night, fancying something to eat.

Mrs. Harrison had said George was just the same when he first retired. It had nearly driven her low, she said, the way he went on. And then, gradually, it started to wear off. It was the shift work, she said. He seemed as if he wouldn't get used to a normal day.

But with Brian it didn't wear off. If anything it got worse. At the finish he was walking around and around the sofa like somebody caged.

One day he'd begun to talk about his work. Slowly at first, then with increasing excitement. She'd never known much about his job. He'd never talked about it before. Now, through his eyes, she saw the blast-furnaces for the first time, bigger than the house they lived in. She heard the roar of flame; she felt the heat on her skin; she watched the molten metal poured out. The whole dark, cavernous building was full of the roar and crackle of heat. "It doesn't matter how often you see it. It's a thing you never get tired of."

She remembered the last talk. He'd laughed a bit, but not as if he thought something was funny. "Them bloody seagulls, they're a real pest. They can't keep away—the heat draws them. There's hundreds of 'em. They always find a way in, specially if the weather's bad. You just look up and there they are. And they've tried everything to stop them. Even broadcast an alarm call—you know, the sound they make when they're frightened? But it was no use. Didn't seem to bother 'em. Drove us mad, but it didn't worry them! And ever so often . . ."

Lisa waited.

"They don't do any harm, you know. Only shit in your eye if you look up at the wrong moment." He was staring into the fire. "Ever so often one of 'em falls. Must be the fumes, I suppose. It can't be they just go to sleep because if they did they'd wake up when they felt themselves falling. And they don't. They fall like stones."

She didn't know how to break the silence. "What happens?" she asked.

"What do you mean, What happens?" He was grinning at her as if he hadn't a care in the world. "They bloody burn, that's what happens."

"They wouldn't feel nothing, though, would they?"

"Wouldn't feel a thing."

He'd never talked about his job again. Or anything else. There were the morning silences. The evening drinking. Rows. Occasionally, violence. Nothing else.

Lisa was afraid. She didn't know how much there was left of the love she'd once felt for him. There were times when she hated him, times when she despised him. There were many, many times when she pitied him. But were there ever any times when she still loved him?

She lay awake for a long time, listening for the sound of his key in the door. But there was nothing, and at last she slept.

The dream woke her. She lay, still half-asleep, trying to

recall the details. Something had been holding her too tight, squeezing her so hard that it hurt. But she couldn't remember what it had been. Nothing pleasant, anyway.

The empty bed didn't surprise her, and at first she thought Brian must have got up early, as he so often did. The early mornings were his worst time. He woke at four o'clock and could not get back to sleep. Then she remembered. Immediately, she pulled a sweater on over her nightdress and hurried downstairs.

He was asleep on the sofa. For a moment relief knocked the breath out of her. She could only stand and stare. A trickle of saliva had run out of the corner of his mouth and down on to the cushions. He looked like a sulky, disappointed boy. She went to pull the curtains back, but then stopped.

She could not bear the squalor of the ashy hearth. And she didn't want him to wake.

She didn't expect him to clear the kitchen up. She had told him to leave it. But she was still angry to find the mess untouched. There was another smell on top of the smells of cold fat and stew: a thin, sour, acid smell. She went closer. He had in fact tried to clear up the stew. Only the effort had proved too much for his stomach. There was vomit there now. On top of everything else.

Tea first. Definitely tea first.

She stood at the sink to fill the kettle, and, as the ancient plumbing groaned and shook, she felt a tightening of her belly, the squeezing she remembered from her dream.

She knew it now for what it was. It was no more than mildly painful yet she held on to the edge of the sink in horror. It couldn't be. Not yet. Though why shouldn't it be? She was already six days late. When it was over she put a hand down between her legs and brought back a string of translucent stuff rather like snot with a plug of dark red blood at the end. Christ.

She felt the baby heave. She thought of Brian on the sofa sleeping it off. She saw the mess of stew and vomit on the floor. The situation was too horrific to be anything but funny.

She sat down at the kitchen table and laughed until her chest ached. She wiped her eyes, made a cup of tea, and carried it through into the living room.

"Hey up," she said. "I think I've started."

She felt almost cheerful.

He woke with a start and stared wildly about him.

"I said, I think I've started." He gaped at her. "The baby—Oh, here, have a cup of tea. I'll talk to you when you're awake."

Halfway up the stairs she yelled over the banister. "And clear that bloody mess up. I'm not doing it."

Darren was cooing in his cot. He turned his head towards her as she came into the room, and wriggled with delight. Kevin was whimpering. Which meant he had wet the bed.

"Never mind, flower. You couldn't help it."

As she picked him up another pain started. She buried her face against the side of his neck until it was over, inhaling his pissy-little-boy smell as eagerly as if it had been gas and air.

They would have to go to their Grandma's while she was in hospital. And, although they drove her to the edge of desperation at times, she dreaded the separation from them.

If only she could have had the baby at home. One thing, she wasn't going to go rushing in. She would hang on at home as long as ever she could.

Iris King looked in that afternoon.

"I hear you've started."

"Aye, and stopped again. Twice."

"Aw, dear. It's awful when it's like that, isn't it?"

"You know, I feel now, if only it would get cracking . . ."

"You'll be having this'n in the new hospital?"

"Yeah."

"Well, it's very nice up there. And one thing I will say, they don't leave you hanging about. If they don't think it's happening as quick as it should, they sharp shove dynamite up yer. I know. Our Lindsey had both hers in there."

"I liked St. Monica's."

"Yes, well it was homely, wasn't it?"

"Oh, and they were good. Sister Richie was smashing. I tell you one thing, I'm not rushing in there."

"No, don't you. Do you know, I had three kids in St. Monica's and they never managed to shave me tash off once. There was never bloody time. I made sure of that. Sister Richie used to play war. She'd come to take the stitches out, you know. 'What am I meant to do with this?' she says. 'It's like hacking your way through the jungle.' "

She shifted her considerable bulk around in the chair. "Bairns gone to your Mam?"

"Yes. Brian took them. I didn't feel like going."

"No. That's a nasty cut on your lip."

Lisa flushed miserably "Yes, I walked into the coalhouse door. Last night, in the dark. Brian will leave it open."

"Sounds a bit like our Ted. He was forever leaving the coalhouse door open when we were first married. Till I fettled him."

Lisa grinned in spite of herself. "And how did you do that?"

"I took the meat chopper to him, love. Aye, you don't believe me, do you? But it's the truth."

"Good afternoon, Mrs. . . . ?"

"Goddard."

"Goddard. Yes. Well, Mrs. Goddard, Nurse tells me you've been having a show?"

"Yes. Since yesterday morning."

"Pains?"

"Off and on."

"Well, let me see." He finished creaming the glove and inserted two fingers into her vagina.

"They were never really regular . . ." She stopped. His eyes had a not-listening look. He was concentrating on whatever his fingers were telling him. She tensed up a little as the probing went on.

"Try to relax. Bear down a little. Yes, yes."

He took off the glove. "Well, Mrs. Goddard. A week over your date. Show. Pains, and I'm afraid . . ." He looked at her card. "I'm *afraid,* another little kick in your blood pressure. I think we'd better have you inside."

She pulled a face.

"Better to get it over with, isn't it?"

"Yes. It's just . . . I've never really been in a hospital. I had the first two in a nursing home."

"Yes, St. Monica's. Well, I think you'll find you prefer the new hospital."

She managed a smile. "Yes. Like you say, it's better to get it over."

They had taken her name and address, her age, her religion and the date of her birth. They had written down details of her previous pregnancies. And of this pregnancy. They had shaved her and poured pints, or what felt like pints, of soapy fluid up her bum. They had draped her in white and green cloths. They had raised her legs high above her head, and fastened them into stirrups.

Now she lay and looked at the doctor, whose head and shoulders were framed by the deep V of her thighs. She couldn't see his face, for he too was draped in white and green, with a cap to cover his forehead, and a mask to cover his mouth. But she decided he looked kind. There were deep wrinkles at the corners of his eyes; they made him look kind.

Beside her, the nurse was getting the instruments ready. She heard the chink of steel. She felt the tightening of fear in her belly and looked up at the lights around the table: huge lights, like the one above the dentist's chair. She could see her reflection in the steel surround, but it was too far away and too distorted by the curve of metal to register anything so messily human as fear.

The doctor approached the table. "Well, Mrs. Goddard? And how are you today?"

"All right."

"Let's see. This is the third. . . . Third?"

"Yes."

"Oh, well, then, you know what it's all about. I'm just going to break the waters. Shouldn't hurt at all. Might be a bit uncomfortable."

He reached for a pad of cotton wool and began swabbing down the skin. Lisa winced and tried to pull away.

"Too hot? Sorry. Nurse!" He waited impatiently. "It always amazes me, you know. In the bad old days when we used to stick a finger in the water to find out how hot it was. I never scalded anybody. Now I've got this marvelous little gadget for keeping the water at blood heat. I scald them all the time. Strange, isn't it? Nurse, wouldn't you say that was strange?"

The nurse obviously didn't know what to say.

"Pay no attention to me, my dear. I'm just an elderly Luddite. There Mrs. Goddard. Is that better?"

His eyes had acquired the familiar unseeing look as his fingers probed and delved.

"Bear down a little. Ah, yes. Not as . . ."

Lisa guessed from his tone that he was about to start. She closed her eyes. There was a fumbling at her skin, the coldness of metal, and then what felt like steel teeth began to nibble at the entrance to her womb.

"Just relax," the nurse said. "Breathe deeply."

Finally the teeth got a hold, and bit. Instantly a warm, thick goo oozed out of her and down on to the bed.

"There." He was already stripping off gloves and mask. "There. Not too bad. Was it?"

"No."

And it wasn't. It had hardly hurt at all.

The nurse gave her a sanitary towel and helped her off the table. One thing *hadn't* changed. You were still expected to keep the towel in position without benefit of pants or belt. She shuffled along the corridor to her room, like an old woman, hanging on to the wall for support.

"This is what I'm going to have when I have a baby," the nurse said, sliding the needle into a vein and taping it down on to the skin. "Speeds things up no end. You set them off at breakfast-time and the babies are here at tea-time. It's far and away better. You never get the cases of real exhaustion now like you used to get. Some poor girls, you know—they used to go days. You'd see them come up into the Consultant Unit and they'd be in a terrible state. You don't get any of that now. No." She watched the clear golden fluid flow along the pipe. "No, this is what I want. Either that or not come in till the head's there."

The nurse waited with her for a few minutes to make sure that the drip was working, then left her alone. She lay and looked out of the window, waiting for the pain to start. But at first there was nothing. She had had no pains at all since she arrived at the hospital, though they had said that labor was about to start. She watched the drops of fluid flow along the plastic and into her arm. She was on the sixth floor. You could see nothing out of the window except clouds, clouds, and a solitary seagull riding the currents of air. The sunlight gleamed bonewhite on its breast and wings.

In the next room a woman who had gone into labor spontaneously the night before started to cry out as her labor advanced. There was an awful, familiar rhythm to her cries. Then came the trundle of wheels, a series of deep gasping breaths, and the "singing" of the gas and air machine. With a preliminary tightening of the womb, Lisa's own labor began. The pains strengthened rapidly. From the beginning they were evenly spaced. This should have made them easier to deal with. But it didn't. They were harder to ride than those varied and unpredictable pains that come at the beginning of a normal labor. It was like trying to swim in a sea of corrugated iron. There was never any time when you could relax and allow the current to carry you.

The pains were stronger too. Very strong. There was something mechanical about their strength, their remorseless regularity. She felt them as extreme heat, as though she were being forced to stand too close to a furnace, to watch the door open, slowly, knowing that the heat would be strong enough to sear her eyeballs and burn her skin. Then as the contraction ebbed, as the door closed, came cold and ashen darkness.

This rhythm went on hour after hour for most of the day until her whole being was subdued to it. People appeared and stood by the bed, taking her temperature, her blood pressure, lifting her on to bedpans, listening to the baby's heart. At first she spoke to them, but as the day wore on speech became too much of an effort.

Dimly she realized that it was dark outside. There was a soft light on in the ceiling above her bed.

The doctor came. The sheets were pulled back. He waited for the current pain to die away, then delved deeply into her. The sister looked at him enquiringly and he answered with a barely perceptible shake of the head.

They changed the drip; the pains doubled and tripled in strength. The peaks were unbearable. Each one tore a cry from her lips.

Between pains, she said to the sister, "I don't think I can stand this."

"No, love. And I don't think you can either. I'll have a word with the doctor."

Another needle; and, for a time, troughs of darkness between the glittering steel peaks.

Somebody pressed the mask down over her face. She tried to tell them she didn't want it, but it was too late. She heard a voice say, "Come on. Make it *sing*. It won't work unless you make it *sing*."

There was a moment of nausea as the room began to bend and shift around her. Then her head was free again.

"I don't really want it," she said. "I'm not in all that much pain."

The worst of the pain was over now. The work had begun.

She lay with her legs in stirrups while they began the elaborate draping of cloths.

"I've got another pain coming," she said.

"Well, push then! And again! Deep breath and hold. That's right. Shoulders back. Chin in."

All the lights above the table were on. When she screwed up her face with the effort they exploded into little chips and splinters of light, so bright they hurt her eyes.

Rest.

Then another pain. She pushed and sweated and grunted, hearing the final shriek of exhaled breath dimly, as though some other woman was making these sounds.

When she opened her eyes again the doctor had arrived. She heard him say, "All right, next time." And saw the scissors. The next pain mounted to a swelling, gasping, bursting climax, in which her flesh was cut open, though she did not feel it.

"I'm going to give you a bit of help."

She wanted to say, Oh no, but she couldn't. The next contraction had already begun. Now she sweated and labored for delivery, bearing down as though the baby had to be forced through a solid wall of flesh. It was no good. She felt the head slide back.

Metal hands entered her, and, as the next pain swelled to a climax and she was told to stop pushing, guided the baby's head into the world. Water gushed out of her. Then a thin trickle of a cry, where only silence had been before.

The crying went on. A purple, howling dwarf appeared in the doctor's hands. Face gray-purple, blood-streaked. Tiny hands clawing at the air.

A girl.

The nurse brought the baby for her to see, but briefly. It had to go to the Intensive Care unit. She craned her head to watch as it was taken away.

"Ten pounds," somebody said. "No wonder you had trouble." The doctor sat between her legs, and sewed.

"How many stitches have I got?"

"Only five."

In the next room somebody had started to groan. They all hurried away, leaving her alone.

Behind her head a clock ticked. She craned her head to see it. It was almost three a.m. The minute had moved, not smoothly, but in a series of jerks. She lay and watched it until her neck was tired.

The lights were still on. They hurt her eyes. One of the drips in her arms had been taken down but the other remained. She found it difficult to move. Gradually, she realized that she wanted to be sick. There was a bowl beside her, but she couldn't reach it. There was a bell, too.

She couldn't reach that, either.

In the next room a woman screamed. There was a murmur of voices soothing her.

"Sister!"

She was afraid that if she vomited like this, lying flat on her back, she would choke.

After she had been shouting for what seemed like hours the Sister appeared. "I'm sorry," she said. "There's nobody to wash you. You'll have to wait."

"I think I'm going to be sick."

The Sister came and moved the bowl closer.

"I'm sorry," she said again. "I'll send somebody in as soon as I can." Her shoes squeaked out of the room.

Lisa lay with her eyes closed.

In the next room the unknown woman screamed again.

She was cold and shivery after she had vomited, and not all of it landed in the bowl. She wanted the lights to be switched off. She wanted somebody to come. Nobody did. She was alone with the whiteness of the walls.

At last a woman came. She was disgruntled because her "dinner hour" had been interrupted. It was now four a.m.

"Where's your towel?"

"I'm sorry. I don't know."

Her teeth were chattering. She could hardly speak.

The woman flounced out in search of it, every inch of an ample behind proclaiming that it wasn't *her* job to look for the patients' towels.

They took her not to the main ward, but to a single room. In spite of her exhaustion she could not sleep. Then, in the morning, they gave her some pills that kept her under for the rest of the day.

In the evening, her mother came. "I've left Brian looking after the bairns. I asked him, Did he want to come, but he said no."

"No, he wouldn't. He doesn't like hospitals."

She could hardly keep awake. At last her mother said, "I'm going now, Lisa. You have a little sleep."

It was a relief to be alone.

Next day was Sunday. She lay with the *News of the World* unopened on her bed and watched the people going to Church. There were not many. After about an hour the doors opened again and they all streamed out. One woman wore a scarlet coat and hat, as bright as holly berries against the gray stone.

Lying there with the blood flowing out of her, she did not feel that she had given birth at all. It might as well have been an operation. There was no baby there. No babies anywhere, though sometimes in the distance she thought she heard one cry. Her room was a long way from the nursery. And the Intensive Care unit was on a different floor.

She had a clear picture of her own child, that howling dwarf who had clawed so desperately at the air, but it was encapsulated in her mind, unchanging, like the last glimpse of a person who has died.

One of the nurses went to see it. It had reddish-brown hair, she said. It looked as though it might be going to curl. Lisa listened dully. *Her* child had black hair, black and straight. She saw it again, wet and bloody from the womb.

No . . .

When she first learned she was pregnant she had asked for an abortion. Darren had been six months old. Kevin, two. The doctor had told her there were no grounds.

It might have died in labor. She knew they had been worried about it. Things had started to go wrong as soon as they strengthened the drip. The heartbeat had been too fast; the water had turned green. It could so easily have died.

Next morning at six the door was thrown open and a cot wheeled in. "Here's your daughter!" the nurse said.

Lisa Goddard

The baby was curled up asleep, mouth and cheek pressed out of shape by the mattress, bottom stuck up in the air. Lisa worked herself across to the side of the bed, grimacing as the stitches pulled, and stared at the child. Her hair *was* reddish, almost auburn, and, yes, it did look as though it might be going to curl. She saw blood pulsing across the opening in its skull. And drew back. There was nothing about this baby she recognized as hers. If she had been an animal she would have rejected it, would have sniffed at it and turned away, at once and finally.

Instead, she read the label on the cot. She read the label on the baby's wrist. Her mind told her that it was hers.

She found herself dreading the moment when it would wake up and demand to be fed.

There was nobody she could talk to. She listened as her mother and the nurses said what a beautiful baby it was. And prayed for the moment when she would be allowed home, when she would no longer have to lie in this little cell of a room, pretending.

When she was well enough, they transferred her to the main ward. Here at least there was the presence of other women to distract her, and by that time, too, she could move about more freely. She spent a lot of time in the dayroom, aimlessly flicking through old copies of *Woman* and *Woman's Own*, talking to the other women, waiting anxiously for the moment when she would have to go back along the corridor to feed the child.

They went together, a whole crowd of women in billowing, shapeless dressing gowns, smelling of milk and blood, walking with that curiously splay-legged, rolling gait that sailors and recently-delivered women share.

After the babies were fed, the women lay on their beds for an hour with curtains closed. There was supposed to be silence, but there never was.

As soon as the nurses had gone, Julie, married ten days and, at seventeen, the youngest woman there, sat up on her bed and looked out of the window. There was a building site immediately below.

"There's some smashing fellas down there."

"You wait. One of these nights she'll be knotting the sheets together. We'll all wake up and find her gone."

"I wouldn't mind. I'm sick of this."

"Give us time to get me stitches out and I'll join you."

This was Sonia, almost forty and the oldest by several years.

Lisa lay and listened. Normally she would have joined in, but the child, asleep in the cot beside her, dampened her spirits. Everything she saw or heard seemed to be taking place on the other side of a dirty window pane. So she lay and listened, passively.

"You've had your stitches out, haven't you, Maureen? What's it like?"

"Oh, just like plucking your eyebrows. It's nothing much."

"You know that girl up the far end, her with the scar on her neck? They say she had it in the bath. Didn't know the head was there."

"Gerraway."

"Oh, I don't know . . . You talk to her."

"My God, I bloody knew."

"My husband's first wife only had a girl. You watch, when she finds out about him she'll be dead jealous."

"Me Mam said if it was a girl I hadn't to bring it home. 'Don't bring it around here if it's got a crack in it,' she says. But I expect she'll come around."

Brian came to see her twice in the first week.

"Well, how are the kids?" Her mother had told her, but she had to find something to say.

"Oh, they're fine. Darren's got a bit of a cough."

"And you're looking after yourself all right?" He had refused to go either to her mother or to his own.

"Oh, yes. I'm all right."

"You're getting your food, aren't you?"

"Yes."

"Because you must, you know. You can't live on . . ."
Beer she had been going to say.

"Your Mam always gives me something when I go over to
see the bairns."

He hardly looked at the child in the cot. She did not expect
it. At this stage the children seemed hardly to exist for him at
all.

She reminded him of what clothes she would need when he
came to collect her. Then they sat in uneasy silence for a
while, before both started to speak, simultaneously, on different subjects. She was restless all the time he was there and,
although she did not know it, tense. Only after he had gone
did she realize how talking to him had tired her.

She lay back in the bed—they always had to be in bed at
visiting time—and closed her eyes. When she opened them
again the baby was awake. It stared at her through the transparent side of its cot. Its eyes were still dark blue, birth-blue.
It seemed to Lisa that somewhere in their depths was the
beginning of pain, a bewilderment that mirrored her own. To
the very depths of her soul she felt guilty. Yet she in no way
neglected the child, was more than once told off for nursing it
too long after a feed. She felt compelled to stare at it, to
stare, and go on staring, as though the thin purple eyelids
with their network of flickering veins was a code that she had
to decipher or die. Afterwards she could not remember what
she thought of at such times, though her mind was certainly
not blank. There seemed to be a great pressure of painful
feelings, aching like matter in a boil, too confused to be
expressed.

She had not wanted this child. If she had had the courage
to express her deepest feelings, her gut reaction, she would
have said to the nurses, "Take it away. It isn't mine." But of
course they would have thought she was mad.

She did not for a second believe that there had been any
actual mix-up in identities. It was simply that she could not
believe the child was hers. There was no point in trying to
talk to anybody about it: she knew she would not be able to

convey the sheer force of her feelings without sounding either deluded or callous. She remembered her grandfather: he had had a stroke, a bad one, though he had lingered on for many months after it. He had not been able to accept that his left arm belonged to him. In the beginning, while he was still very confused, he had actually struggled with it, trying to force it out of the bed. Later, he had lain quietly, apparently accepting what his eyes and his reason told him must be true. But Lisa had seen him, sometimes, when he thought no one was looking, turn on that arm a glance of fear and distaste.

She felt like that now.

She heard the other women talk, counting the days and hours to their release. They were all, without exception, looking forward to going home. Lisa dreaded it. It took her all her time to cope with Kevin and Darren, whom she loved. How would she manage to care for this baby for whom she felt nothing? Its weakness terrified her.

She felt an enormous distance between them, and saw no way of crossing it.

Once and once only she felt a stab of recognition. One of the Sisters asked if she could borrow the baby to give a demonstration bath. Seeing it, red and howling, struggling in the nurse's hands, Lisa thought, Yes. And when it rose from the bath with dark and streaming hair the pain was so extreme that she had to turn aside; she could not bear to look.

The feeling vanished. But it had given her hope. The time she spent simply staring at the baby increased. And then one day, as she was changing its nappy, she found a smear of blood on the cloth. She parted the lips of the vagina and there was more blood. Her heart contracted with fear. She looked at the other women, each of them preoccupied with her own baby, and she could not tell any of them. She was afraid of what they might say. Nor could she put another nappy on the child and ignore the blood. In her heart she knew the baby had some terrible disease. She was to be punished.

At last a nurse came in. Dumbly, Lisa showed her the blood, and was startled when the nurse smiled.

"Oh, that. That's nothing to worry about. It's . . . well, in a way, it's her first period. All the female hormones in your blood get across to her, you see. Then when they stop, she starts to bleed. Just like a period. If she'd had a dirty nappy, you'd've been none the wiser."

"You mean it's all right?" Lisa asked, still afraid to believe it.

"Oh, yes. It happens to every baby, every girl. Only normally, you don't see it. I don't see it all that often. And I change hundreds."

"Then there's nothing to worry about?"

"Nothing at all."

Lisa turned back to her child with a sense of relief, and wonder. She looked down at the baby and remembered that she had planned to call it Katherine if it was a girl. Only somehow, she had never really believed it would be. She had not been ready for a girl.

Now that began to change. She felt a spurt of excitement, the feeling she had had for hours and hours after Kevin was born, so strong that it had kept her awake at night.

That little rounded stomach! The coil of dry and brittle cord! How strange that under that soft flesh there should already be muscles as strong as those which had thrust it into the world.

She picked the baby up, and felt it nuzzle and butt her neck as the automatic search for milk began.

"Greedy. You've just been fed."

The child was warm against her skin, but she was back miles and miles away, back in her own childhood. She remembered how she and her brothers had gone bird nesting. She had always played with the boys, always been the tomboy of the family, in spite of the passion for dolls that had earned her childhood nickname: Doll.

They had climbed a stone wall up above Harrier's farm, right on the edge of the moors. They must have walked miles and miles that day. The boys had run on ahead but she had found a chrysalis clinging to the side of the wall and had stopped to examine it. Then, as she held it on the palm of her hand, it had begun to twist, curving into a crescent and rocking like a little boat. Some clear brown fluid had squirted out of it. Perhaps it was the warmth of her hand or perhaps she had picked it up just as the time came for it to split. She watched and felt it move. There was something wonderful about it; and terrible too. It squirted out more fluid and in a spasm of revulsion she threw it as far as she could across the heather.

Then she ran on to join the boys. Later that day in one of those meaningless orgies of destruction that children go in for, they smashed some of the carefully-gathered eggs, shouting and screaming, trampling on delicate chips of blue and white, smearing each other's faces and hair with yolk.

And she had shouted and screamed and smashed harder than any of them.

Now she held her daughter in her arms. And the thought that inside that tiny body was a womb like hers with eggs waiting to be released, caused the same fear, the same wonder. She walked across to the window holding the child in her arms.

The building site was deserted in the rain. There were puddles scattered over the gouged and rutted ground, looking like patches of trapped sky. Shadows of clouds and birds drifted across them.

My daughter.

IV

Muriel Scaife

It had been raining heavily all day. The clocks had been put back only two days before and people were not yet used to the swift descent of twilight. They grumbled and looked pinched at the abrupt arrival of winter.

There were eight people huddled together in the porch of the doctor's surgery. It was difficult to move about without touching somebody else, a stranger, and so they looked down at their boots, or, vacantly, at the stripping trees.

One man poked his head out into the rain and said, "I don't know. I can't see any sign of it." But he was on the fringes of the group, able to move freely. Those at the center, hemmed in by other people, felt a greater constraint and did not reply.

Muriel Scaife twisted her head round to look at her son. He was breathing on the doctor's brass plate and then rubbing the condensed breath away on his sleeve. Over the past year his nose and ears seemed to have grown out of proportion to his face, giving him a Mickey Mouse appearance that was both funny and pathetic. He didn't know what to do with his hands and feet and you could almost feel the spots pricking their way to the surface of his skin.

She said, "Richard. . . ."

Instantly he looked around at her and smiled. Then, aware of other people watching, blushed. It was an embarrassment to him, being seen to smile at his mother in a public place.

After a few minutes she felt him move closer.

"It won't be so bad," he said.

"At least with Dad out of the way she'll only be able to go on about him behind his back."

She looked at him gratefully. Richard seemed almost able to read her thoughts, to enter into the conflict of loyalties between her mother and her husband that was so painful to her. At times she wished he saw less. They were becoming too close. Too close for *his* good, at any rate. Once or twice recently she had caught herself thinking aloud in front of him, saying things that no twelve-year-old boy should be expected to understand.

"I'll be glad when it's over," she said. "Much as I love her."

The bus arrived at last. Those getting on jostled those getting off and from the confusion an elderly woman emerged wearing a maroon-colored raincoat and a professionally-martyred expression.

After the greetings were over, after the usual comments on Richard's height had been offered and endured, they set off back to the house. Richard had reached the age when to walk with members of his own family, particularly his mother, was torture. He could not bring himself to walk beside her. Muriel, as she talked to her mother, felt her son tagging along behind, and her heart bled for him. But you couldn't say anything. He wouldn't thank you for it.

Richard, scuffing his feet in the gutter, was convinced that everybody who saw them was thinking, "Oh, look, there's Richard Scaife. Funny you never see him with lads his own age. He's always trotting along behind his mother. Bit of a pouf, if you ask me. I mean it's not natural, is it?''

He found a stone and kicked it viciously across the street.

". . . no worse than he usually is, Mam.''

"That's bad enough. Is he still smoking as much?''

"It's the only pleasure he gets. He says it eases the pain.''

"Does it hell! And it must be costing you a pretty penny. But then that's you all over. Too soft to make backsides of.''

Muriel lowered her head. Her mother's opinion of her intelligence had been made clear over many years.

"My stomach's bad 'n' all, you know. Some of us have to carry on.''

"Well, Mam, if you get you can't manage there's a home for you with me. And it's not just me saying it, it's John as well.''

"Don't think I'm not grateful, but it wouldn't work and you know it wouldn't.''

"It's him, isn't it? You'd come to me like a shot if I didn't have him.'' There was a long, dragging silence. Then Muriel said, "Well, Mam, I can't bury me husband to please you.''

They turned into Union Street. It was full of women hurrying home from the shops to get the tea ready before the men came home. Muriel nodded or waved to the ones she knew.

"At least he minds the kids so I can work. I couldn't do the school cleaning if he wasn't there to keep an eye on them.''

"No sign of *him* going back to work, I suppose?''

"No.''

"Dear God.''

"He's bad, Mam. They wouldn't keep giving him the sick notes if he wasn't bad.''

"I blame meself. I should never've called you Muriel. It was always an unlucky name. God knows my mother never had any luck. And you couldn't say I did. And now you. Thank God you didn't lumber Sharon with it.''

"I wanted to. I wanted to call her Sharon Muriel. It was you put a stop to that.''

"She'll live to thank me for it."

"It isn't names that does it, Mam."

"Well, what does, then? Your father never worked. He doesn't work."

"I don't know. Some people have it harder than others. That's all there is to it."

"Well, I hope Sharon gets a husband what'll turn out."

Richard listened to their talk but took no part in it. Everything seemed to be changing: nothing was safe or easy any more. Even his Gran. Once he'd looked forward to her visits. Now she seemed to have shrunk overnight into a silly, superstitious old woman, always going on about what she'd suffered.

Well, she had suffered.

Out of the corner of his eye he saw a gang of boys, two or three years older than he was, standing on the street corner. He cringed inside his coat, waiting for the jeers. They didn't come, because he was walking with his family.

Just as he had got himself safely past his mother turned around and said, "Oh, look, Richard. There's Steve."

"Yes," he said. He hated her, then, because she couldn't see that for him the street was a dangerous place.

"You know, Mam, you forget one thing. John thinks the world of me. That makes up for a lot."

"Gets the bairns here. Doesn't buy their shoes. If he give up smoking it might."

"It's not all that much."

"It's not what you buy him. It's what he sneaks out of you! I've seen him send the bairns out behind your back."

"Not Richard."

"Sharon. *And* she charges him for going. Only one in this family with any sense."

They reached the house, took off their wet coats, and crowded into the back room together. The front room, with the three-piece suite John and Muriel had bought when they were first married, was never used.

"He's not here then?"

"No. He's gone to see their Betty."

Silence.

"It's his sister, Mam."

"Oh, I say nowt about that. She set on and brought them all up after their Mam died. He has a right to go and see her."

So it went on. Tea was eaten and cleared away. Richard started on his homework. He couldn't avoid hearing most of the conversation, though he tried to shut it out.

". . . and the bedsprings creaking. He's always on your bones, our Muriel, you know he is. You'd think when you have to get up and go to work at six o'clock he'd at least let you get your rest."

"I am married to him, Mam."

They'd forgotten he was there. Sometimes in the early morning, or late at night, Richard, too, heard the bedsprings creaking and it made him feel . . . excited, and ashamed at the same time. Sometimes he felt like playing with himself, but of course he couldn't. It would have been too much like joining in.

"That's the real reason you won't come to me, isn't it, Mam?"

"I couldn't stand it. I'd see you getting more and more worn out and I couldn't keep me trap shut. It wouldn't do."

There was a long silence. Muriel stared into the fire wondering why John hadn't come home. He didn't like her mother, any more than her mother liked him, but he had promised to be back before she left.

Her Mam said, "What's that you're studying, pet?"

Instantly, Muriel was on the alert to protect Richard, if he should need it. She saw him go tense. He seemed to dread questions about his school work almost as much as he dreaded comments on his changed appearance.

"Algebra."

"And what might that be when it's all at home?"

Richard looked towards Muriel for help, but she didn't know the answer. He mumbled, "Lettersinsteadofnumbers."

"Oh. What's the point of that?"

"I don't know."

"He has to do it, Mam."

"I don't doubt it. I asked him what the point was that's all. I mean it's not like sums, is it? You can see the point of that. I mean, all this algebra and French and all that, but what's he going to do if he can't add up?"

"He can add up, Mam."

"Not like your Dad, I'll bet. Your Dad could go down a column of figures like greased lightning. That's where he gets his brains from."

"It's not from me."

"You're right there. You stick in at your books, lad. *You'll* never have to work the way your Mam and me have had to work." She lowered her voice. "Pity Sharon's so slow. Still you've got it where you need it. He's the lad."

Muriel listened, saying as little as possible. She was watching the clock, waiting for the moment when she could decently suggest a final cup of tea.

After she had seen her mother off from the bus station, Muriel walked back quickly through the misty October night, fully expecting to find her husband waiting for her when she got back. When he wasn't there, she felt a stab of misgiving, but pushed it to the back of her mind. It was no use worrying Richard, who was still wrestling with his whatever-it-was. She got the ironing board out and started work on a pile of sheets and pillowcases. From time to time as she worked she looked across at her son's bowed head. He ought to be in the street playing, as his sister was, but she had learned not to question him. He became irritable very quickly on the subject of homework and school.

They worked in silence. There was the roar of flames, the regular thump-thump of the iron on the board and an occasional sigh from Muriel as she bent down to pick up another sheet. When she sighed, Richard stirred and looked up. The iron was giving trouble again. She wetted her fingers on her tongue and tapped the base. The sizzle of spit reassured her.

"You can never tell whether this thing's hot or not."

"It's clapped out. You want to get yourself another."

"Oh, yes. I can see meself."

As she ironed, her lips moved. The sight was a familiar one to Richard. It meant, usually, that she was at work on the endless sums of feeding and clothing four people on his father's sick pay. Her school-cleaning job didn't bring in much. The twitching of her mouth hurt him: it belonged to an older woman.

"He should be back by now," she said, peering short-sightedly at the clock. "Good God, is that the time?"

"He'll be all right."

"Oh, he will, will he? He could hardly walk."

"He's just making sure he stays out of Gran's way, that's all." His mother went on standing there, blinking in her short-sighted, vulnerable way. It irritated him. "You worry about him too much."

Muriel opened her mouth to reply. Then shut it again, tightly. Only the heavier thumps of the iron on the board revealed her anger.

Richard went back to his Maths. It was his worst subject. He struggled with the meaningless squiggles on the page, trying to make sense of them. But his mother's uneasiness had communicated itself to him. There was a knot of anxiety in his stomach.

"He's mebbe stopped off for a drink," he said at last, breaking a silence that had become intolerable.

His mother didn't reply at first. There was another silence, less strained now, and then she said, "Oh, I don't think so. He hasn't had a drink for months. He says he can't keep it down."

"There's still plenty of time, Mam. He's been this late before."

"You'll have to stop now, love. I need the table for supper."

"I'll go upstairs."

"Don't be daft, it's like a morgue up there. Surely you've

done enough?'' She looked at him, almost pleadingly. ''You seem to have been on with that for hours.''

''Yeah, O.K. It'll do.''

It wouldn't. But he could do the rest tomorrow morning in the cloakroom at school.

''You notice our Sharon's not back. She's staying out too late.''

Richard cleared away his books. Muriel started to lay the table.

''I wouldn't worry about him if he wasn't so yellow.''

''He's always been yellow.''

''No, he hasn't. You don't remember him when he was well.''

That was true. His father had been ill as long as Richard could remember. There had never been a time when he was not coughing, or holding his stomach, or complaining of this, that, or the other pain. Richard didn't take it very seriously. He had early adopted his grandmother's view of the matter: that there was nothing wrong with his father that hard work wouldn't cure.

The phlegm was the worst thing. Every morning his father brought it up, not in gobs and short, stringy bits as he did during the day, but in one long, sickening stream. Sometimes, when his mother had already left for work, Richard had to empty the bucket. He hated the job. He hated the blue stubble on his father's chin. He hated the foul smell of his breath.

Now, remembering those mornings, he looked down at the fork he held in his hand. Like everything else in the house it dated from the time of his parents' marriage. There were bits of yellow showing through where the chrome had worn away. And suddenly he wanted to sweep it all aside—the little table, the knives and forks, the photos on top of the telly, the whole too-small, too-cosy room. It seemed to have shrunk around him, to fit too tightly, like a garment that might tear if he tried to move.

Half an hour later they were still waiting. Muriel no longer

tried to convince herself that nothing was wrong. John should
have been home hours ago.

"Well," she said. "It's no use just sitting here. I'll go and
look for our Sharon."

"I'll go."

"No. You stop here." She was already tying the scarf
around her head. "And she won't half get a piece of my mind
when I find her. Worrying everybody like this."

She paused on the doorstep of the house, catching her
breath from the shock of wind and darkness. The Browns'
house was opposite. They had still not had the window of the
front bedroom repaired: she thought of the two girls sleeping
in that cold room and her lips tightened. Neither of her two
had anything like that to put up with, or ever would have, and
she had less coming in than Mrs. Brown.

As she looked, the door opened and Kelly Brown came
out. What *does* she look like? Muriel thought, taking in
the child's cropped hair and filthy clothes. "Kelly," she
said.

The girl looked up. For a moment Muriel had the sense of
a startled animal. Then Kelly hunched her shoulders and
blinked. "You haven't seen our Sharon, have you?"

"No." She started to walk away. Then called over her
shoulder, "There's a whole gang of 'em on the corner of
Alice Street. She could be there."

Muriel hurried along the street, her anxiety quickened by
the sight of Kelly and the memory of what had happened to
her. But almost at once she heard the sound of children's
voices and there was Sharon, playing with a group of other
girls.

There was only one lamppost in Alice Street and the children gathered to play beneath it, while the great swoop of rain
and darkness stretched away from them on every side. Muriel
was about to call Sharon, but then she stopped, her imagination kindled by the group of figures in the circle of light. One
girl was poised to enter the rope; the others chanted around
her:

There is a Maid lives on the Mountain.
Who she is I do not know.
All she wants is gold and silver.
All she wants . . .

Their voices, as they sang the ancient words, were quick and passionate; their faces vivid under strands of rain-darkened hair.

When Sharon left the game, red-faced and protesting, Muriel could sympathize. The chanting took her back to her own childhood: the games, the fights, forged and broken friendships, love and betrayal and hate. As they walked home, she tried to take refuge in memories of that past.

But it was no use. She thought of Kelly leaving the house alone.

"I notice Kelly wasn't with you," she said. "Doesn't she play with you any more?"

"She doesn't play with anybody."

Muriel looked down at her daughter's fair hair, still pulled back into childishly fat plaits, and wondered how much the other children knew.

"Your Dad isn't back yet."

"Isn't he?"

She wasn't interested. She was still looking back over her shoulder at the little circle of light, dwindling away into the darkness. The singing had started again. Muriel sighed. Perhaps it was just as well Sharon didn't worry. It was bad enough to have herself and Richard twisted up—probably over nothing. He might be there when they got back. She walked more quickly.

But he wasn't. She swallowed her disappointment, and hurried both children upstairs to bed.

After they had gone, she got together everything they would need for school the following day. She left the house by six o'clock, and John was in no state to deal with an outcry over a missing sock or tie. She picked up Richard's algebra book and put it in his satchel. It was better not to leave books lying round where John was: he hated them so much.

It had taken her a long time to realize why. When they were first married and letters came through the post John had always said to her, "No, you see to it." She hadn't thought anything about it: she took it for granted that she should settle the bills and write whatever had to be written. Then, for the first time, she'd tried to get something on the H.P. And that night she'd said to him, "You'll have to have a look at this, John. I can't make head nor tail of it." And she'd shown him the agreement.

To her surprise, he thrust it roughly away from him. "You shouldn't get the stuff if you can't figure out what to do about it," he said. "I'm tired. A man doesn't want to come in from work and start puzzling his head over that rubbish."

It was the first time she'd had anything from him but gentleness. She went very quiet.

After a long silence, he said, "Well, lass. I suppose you had to know, didn't you? I can't read."

"But . . ."

He looked at her. She went quiet again. He'd sat and read the paper, *seemed* to read it, many a time. She'd seen him stop and buy a paper on his way to work.

"I've never let on to anybody. I've always . . . Ever since we were married, I've dreaded the post."

It dismayed her, that he should have been hiding this fear, when she'd thought they were happy. She said as much.

"But we *were* happy. And we still will be. If you can put up with a thick husband."

" 'Tisn't to say you're thick 'cause you can't read. You can reckon up as good as anybody."

"No, but it's always there. I live in dread of folks finding out."

"Well, it doesn't matter to me."

"That's easy said."

"You don't want to let it bother you."

Later that night, when she was standing at the sink washing

up, he had come up behind her and cupped his hands around her breasts. "I can't be all that thick, can I?" he said. "Or I'd never have married you."

It had never mattered to her that he couldn't read. She read things to him, and they figured it out between them. If anything, it had brought them closer together.

After tidying around the room, she sat down by the fire to wait. The house was peaceful all around her, full of firelight and sleeping children. She was tired after her long day: the warmth and the roar of flames made her drowsy. Yet, beneath the surface of her mind, something that could not be so easily lulled roused itself to keep watch. She had never been able to take happiness for granted, perhaps because she had lost her father while she was still a child. She must always be aware of time passing, of the worm that hides in darkness and feeds upon innocence, beauty and grace. John's hands on her breasts, the children asleep upstairs: nothing was to be taken for granted. Love, security, order: these were achievements painfully wrested from a chaos that was always threatening to take them back. She remembered the children playing in the lamplight. Life was like that. *Her* life was like that. A moment in the light. Then the lamp goes out, the circle is broken, the chanting voices are silenced forever.

She was being morbid. She was letting John's absence prey on her mind. In a moment, she told herself, she would get up and turn the telly on. The room would be full of flickering light, there would be no more pressure of darkness, no more sense that life is threatened, no more feeling that you must stay awake to guard it.

They brought him home shortly after eleven o'clock. Two of his mates had found him clinging to the railings outside the station. Until then everybody had walked past him, taking it for granted that he was drunk.

"It's lucky we happened by," one of the men said. "He could easy been stuck there all night."

They had a struggle to get him up the passage. His

legs buckled underneath him or shot out at extraordinary angles.

"Hey up, Jack!" They lowered him into the armchair, their faces set from the strain, for he was a big man, though the illness had stripped flesh from his bones.

"I'd no idea he were as bad as this."

They stood there, a little shy in the house they had never entered before. The younger man said, "Have we to get the doctor for him, Missus?"

John started to gasp and struggle.

"No, thanks. If he needs the doctor I can easy send our Richard around." Seeing them look doubtful, she said, "I've seen him as bad as this before."

After they had gone, she came back into the room and said, "All the same, they're right. We've got to get the doctor in, John. You can't go on like this."

"What can he tell me I don't know already?"

"It's not what he can tell you. It's what he can do for you."

"Aye. Nowt."

She was kneeling beside him, trying to smile. He mustn't know how much his appearance had shocked her. Perhaps it was only because he was so short of breath, or perhaps it was because she had been away from him all day and so saw him with fresh eyes, but to her he looked like death. His face was the color of old newspaper. The bones of his skull jutted out. When he smiled, his lips stretched out like a band of fraying elastic. He looked as if he would never get his mouth shut again.

"I'm surprised your Betty letting you come home, the state you're in."

"Nay, lass, don't blame our Betty, it was me. I knew you'd be worried. All I could think was, I must get home."

"All the same."

"I know what he'll say. I know before I go, so there's no point going, is there? 'Take it easy.' 'Drink plenty of milk.' "

"I'll go with you."

"Nay, lass, you've got enough to do. More than enough."

They had a cup of tea together. His lips twisted with pain as he drank. Before the cup was finished he was asleep, his head slumped forward on to his chest.

Reluctantly, she shook him awake. "Come on, John. Howay up to bed. You'll feel better once you're lying down."

"You go on up. I won't be a minute."

When she woke, hours later, the space beside her in the bed was still empty. She went downstairs, in darkness, because she was afraid of disturbing the children.

He had built the fire up and was sitting over it, half-asleep.

"John. What *are* you doing? Look at the *time*." She went across to him. "Come on up to bed."

"No!"

He struck out at the arm she tried to put around him. She stepped back, shocked into silence. In all their married life he had never hit her.

"No," he said again. "You go back upstairs. Go on, now. I'm best off where I am."

The following day she came hurrying in from work to find Betty sitting on the arm of his chair. Betty was a big, jolly woman, not unlike Iris King. As a child of twelve she'd been left to bring up a family of younger brothers and sisters. In return they all adored her.

There was a lot of laughter that tea-time. Even Richard, coming in from school with a pile of homework, joined in. Listening to that joyous, yelping laugh of his, Muriel realized how rare a sound it had become. But her eyes were mainly on John. Betty had the rest of them in stitches, taking off people they'd known.

Muriel put on her coat and scarf to see Betty to the bus stop. Normally the two women were suspicious of each other, each a little jealous of the other's relationship with John. But today they set all that aside.

"I had to come. Last night, well, I didn't think he'd get home to tell the truth. But he would go. There was no stopping him. He says two of his mates got him home."

"Yes. He was lucky they happened by. It could've been a lot worse." Muriel paused, looking down towards the High Street. "He didn't go to bed last night."

"I wondered about that." Betty's lips twitched. "That's me Mam all over. She was like that. You couldn't even get her to sit down to begin with. No, she stood. Bolt upright. And all you could get out of her was, 'I'm not going to bed. If I go to bed, I'll die.' And when she lay down we knew that was it. That was the finish. All the Hodgkins go like that."

"He's not going anywhere."

"I never got over it, you know. I was only twelve. Younger than your Richard. Oh, I know, I like a laugh, I don't give a bugger for anybody, but I've never got over it."

"John's not going."

Betty looked at her in silence. And in silence they waited till the bus came.

As she got on, Betty turned and looked back. "You don't want to listen to what he says, you know. You get the doctor in."

"Well, has he been?"

Richard threw his satchel down, and lowered his voice in response to a warning glance from Muriel. "Well, has he been?"

"Yes. He come this morning."

Richard waited for more. Muriel went on laying the table.

"What did he say?"

"Hospital."

"Oh." He took his time absorbing the information. "When does he have to go?"

"He says he's not going."

Her voice was flat, apparently indifferent. Looking closer, Richard saw that she was on the verge of tears.

"But if the doctor says he has to . . ."

"Well, he won't go. And that's that. I can't make him."

He didn't know what to say.

"Here, tek and give him this. I'm late enough as it is."

"You're not going to work?"

"Of course I'm going to bloody work!" The futility of the question made her angry. "We've got to live, haven't we?" She was already knotting the familiar scarf under her chin. "And tell our Sharon not to go too hard at them mince pies. I don't know when I'll be able to bake again."

Richard carried his father's tea through into the living room and put it on his lap. This was the time of day he dreaded most: his mother at work, Sharon out playing, himself and his father cooped up together, silent and ill at ease.

He got out his books and spread them over the table. He sat down, trying not to hear the steady chomp-chomp of his father's jaws, the disgusting way he swilled tea around an already-too-full mouth. He could feel the tension. He could feel how his father hated the books. He wasn't just indifferent to them, he wasn't neutral: he really hated them.

When he sat looking at the newspaper, as he sometimes did, his eyes did not move across the page. Richard had noticed this, but didn't know what it meant. Bills, letters, all that sort of thing, his father passed over to his mother. It was as though anything that involved reading or writing was woman's work.

So it was always like this in the late afternoons.

John Scaife hardly knew how it had come about. He knew only that he hated the books which were almost instruments of torture to him, so keenly did he remember the humiliations of his school days. Once and once only had he dared to show interest and that was because the book his son was reading seemed to be full of pictures.

"What's that you're looking at, son?"

"Nothing."

"Well, it must be something."

"It's nothing to do with school. It's from the library." He stared at his father, defensively. "It's about birds."

"Birds!"

"Yes." Briefly he showed a picture of some long-legged, white bird in flight. "That's a heron."

"Not a lot of use that, around here."

For there were no birds. Only sparrows and starlings. And seagulls of course.

"I like the pictures."

"Ah, well." John rustled his newspaper uneasily. "Only birds I ever fancy are in here." And he showed a picture of a woman with big breasts, smoldering on page three.

As soon as he had done it he was cursing himself. He saw Richard flinch and look away. He was at that awkward stage of early puberty: wincing, hypersensitive, fastidious. It was the last thing he should have said. Crude. Unnecessary. Not even true. What he wanted was to meet the boy on common ground: to share jokes and interests, to introduce him to the world of work, pub, football. But he couldn't do it. Of course the boy was too young, but that was the least of it. His feet were set on a different path.

Out of fear John did all the wrong things. He would hawk phlegm up whenever his son was in the room, or lift one buttock from the chair to fart, or wander around in his underwear with his scraggy chest showing, and the varicose veins in his legs. And when he saw the boy's involuntary recoil it was almost a relief.

Now he was ill and there was very little time left.

Richard heard his father clear his throat several times. Then, almost humbly, John asked, "What's that you're studying, lad?"

Richard looked up, uncertainly.

"Latin."

"Oh. Latin."

There was silence. Each of them searched for something to say. If only it had been something else. Arithmetic. Geography. Even French.

"It's quite easy."

Now he sounded not just unfriendly but stuck-up as well.

There was no doubt about it, the lad had brains. At first, when he'd gone to the big school, John had tried to damp down Muriel's enthusiasm. She had poured her soul into the boy, and John was afraid she was going to be disappointed.

"Don't build on it," he said. "There'll be a lot of clever lads up there. You can't expect him to stand out there, the way he did in Ewbank Street."

But, it seemed, Richard did stand out. He won prizes, he came first or second in nearly everything. But instead of making him relax, it only seemed to make him work harder, as if his whole life was geared to marks and percentages and prizes.

He was jealous. That was what they all thought, even Muriel. And perhaps he was, a little. Of the boy's chances, but also of the school, the part the school played in Richard's life.

"You know, Dad, you'd be a lot more comfortable in bed. Why don't you go up? And I'll make you another cup of tea."

"No. I'll stop where I am." A pause. "Thanks, lad."

Over the next few days, John became worse. Sometimes, particularly if he had had something to eat, he would actually cry out in pain. Muriel tried to persuade him that the doctor was right, that he would be better off in hospital. He didn't argue with her, simply shook his head and waved her away. He needed all his concentration, all his strength, to cope with the pain. It was right what Betty said. He was like a sick animal that will not lie down, but sweats and strains to stay on its feet.

Muriel was worn out by it. After the first night she did not leave him at all, but slept on the sofa with a blanket thrown over her. She never got much sleep, though at six o'clock every morning she got up and went to work as usual.

One day, John, coming into the kitchen on his way to the toilet, found her crying.

"You go to bed tonight, lass. There's no need for you to stop up with me."

"I'm not leaving you."

146

She brushed the tears away, angry with him for finding her like this.

"I can manage on me own, you know."

"Yes, I'm sure."

John slept—if he slept at all—in the armchair, with Muriel's coat over him. She had offered him an eiderdown, which would have been warmer, but no, he wanted the coat. It smelled powerfully of fish and chips, more faintly of scent. The scent was Ashes of Violets. It was what she put on when she went up to Richard's school, that and a dash of lipstick, smeared carefully on to her lips and rubbed into her cheeks.

Muriel lay on the sofa. It was made of leather, cracked in some places, rubbed thin in others, and had not been new even when they bought it. They had made love on this sofa when they were a young married couple. Comfort hadn't mattered so much in them days. In fact she was pretty sure Sharon had been started on it. And she'd lain there in the early stages of labor, putting off the moment when she'd have to give in and go to hospital. It had seen so much of her married life. While she lay on it, nothing terrible could become real.

Though John's breathing rasped in the darkness, with unnervingly long pauses between one breath and the next.

Muriel could not sleep.

Once, John got up to use the bucket. It was too cold for him to make the journey across the yard at night, though he still insisted on doing it by day. Muriel screwed up her eyes against the light and turned to face the wall. The sight of her husband's wasted body frightened her. The light went out again. The night wore on. Muriel didn't think she had slept at all, because there seemed to be no time when she was not aware of the roaring of the fire and her husband's gasping breaths. But she must've done, because when she next looked at the clock hours had gone by.

She got up and tiptoed across to the mantelpiece to check on the time. While she was there, John gasped again, louder than before. Muriel turned to look at him. His face was just visible in the gray light that had begun to seep through the curtains. And for the first time she began to doubt what the doctors told him. Was it just ulcers? Was he going to get better? He looked like death. She waited for the next breath. It came with a shudder that shook every bone in his body. Then his eyelids flickered open, his lips curled back to reveal rows of white teeth, years younger than the surrounding skin. "Not yet," he said, smiling. "Not yet."

Muriel didn't know what to say. Should she go back to the sofa and pretend nothing had happened? Or should she try and respond in some way to what John had now so openly acknowledged? In the end, she did neither. She sat down in the other armchair and said nothing.

"See if you can stir the fire up a bit, lass. It's burning dead."

Muriel poked and battered at the ridge of coal. When she looked around again she could see John's face quite clearly in the leaping flames.

He was trying to say something. It was an effort. There was a crust of some yellow sticky stuff at the corners of his mouth and his lips were so dry they looked cracked. He had to ferret about with his tongue to find a passage for the words.

"Thanks, love. There's nothing beats . . . a good fire."

Muriel waited. John's eyes had closed again. After a while, they flickered open. "You'll be all right, you know, Muriel. There'll be a pension. And if ever you wanted owt you'd only have to ask our Betty."

"It's not the money."

She wanted to fold him in her arms and cover his face with kisses, but she forced herself to sit still. His eyes closed again. Even when they were open, there was a milky bloom over their darkness.

"He's a good lad. You always thought I didn't care as much about him as I do about our Sharon. Go on, be honest, didn't you?"

It was too late for anything but truth.

"Yes," she said.

John smiled again. Struggled for speech. "Nay, lass. I think every bit as much about him. Somehow you can't show it with a lad."

His eyes closed again. Muriel sensed that he had no clear idea of how much time had passed between one flicker of his eyelids and the next. When she was sure he would talk no more, she went back to the sofa and lay down again. Surprisingly, she slept.

In the morning everything was normal again. The fire had burned low. The room was ashen in the early-morning light.

John was asleep at last. Muriel started getting ready for work. She was just putting her tights on when John woke up.

"Muriel?"

"Yes."

"Are you off to work?"

"Yes. Unless you'd like me to stop at home?"

"No, love. You go."

"Is there anything I can get you?"

"I think I'll come on to the sofa. I'll be better lying down."

Muriel came back into the room with a cup of tea. John sat up, cradling the cup in his hands, while the steam rose into his face. He didn't look such a bad color as he had the night before. He'll get better all right, she thought. She was ashamed of the morbid thoughts she'd had during the night. But you got like that at night. Everything looked worse than it was.

"Are you sure there's nowt else you fancy?"

Dimly, from the street outside, came the sound of men's boots tramping up the hill to work.

John smiled. "Do y' know, lass, I think I could fancy a bit of bacon."

He looked surprised, and pleased. Indeed his whole mood seemed to have lightened. He patted his stomach, almost boastfully. "It's a bit easier this morning."

And so, Muriel thought, tilting the frying pan so that the fat ran evenly across it, it's going to be all right. She would have him on his feet again by Spring. There was a thick rind on the bacon, which he didn't like. She reached for the kitchen scissors, and as she did so became aware of a glugging sound, like water hiccuping from a too-narrow pipe. It went on and on. Suddenly, she was afraid. She ran back into the living-room and there was John, blood gargling from his mouth. Above the black hole his eyes rolled about, frenzied and unseeing. The flow of blood seemed to have stopped. It was like nothing she had ever seen before: so black, so foul-smelling, it didn't seem like blood at all.

She cried, "John. Oh my God, John," and bent over him. As she did so, a second eruption began, pumping out thick, black blood all over his chest and neck. His eyes rolled again. He was choking on the blood. She began pulling huge clots of it from his mouth. It seemed the only thing to do, and while she was doing it, she did not have to see those eyes. Her fingers found a thick rope of blood, twined round it, and pulled. The clot slid out of his mouth, with the sound of a sink coming unblocked, and after it flowed a frothy, bright-red stream of blood, looking almost gay against the blackness of the other blood.

John's head fell back against the pillows. White on white. Muriel thought numbly, Shock, and tried to pull the eider-down up around his chest. She was distressed to the point of panic when she could not lift the limp arms to push them inside.

She put her hand over her mouth to stop the twitching of her lips. Then she went to the foot of the stairs and yelled, "Richard!"

He came down, buttoning up his shirt, and grumbling, "Aw, Mam. . . ." He stopped when he saw his father. She watched his face go very blank and smooth. He said, "I'll go for the doctor."

"No. The ambulance. The fish-and-chip shop have a phone. Keep banging on the door till they answer. They won't mind."

She fell on her knees by the sofa, and said, "Don't leave me. I couldn't live without you."

150

A sound came from the open, blood-smeared mouth. But no words.

The ambulance came. He groaned as he was carried along the passage. Then there was the redness of blankets and John's face, ashen, as the men sweated and strained.

A little crowd had gathered. There was Iris King, and Mrs. Harrison, and a couple of girls who had been on their way up to the cake bakery.

Muriel hesitated on the pavement, torn between the desire to go with her husband and the need to stay with her children. Though she did not know it, she was whimpering, her fingers knotted against her teeth. Iris King came running across the road and got hold of her.

"Howay, Missus, you hop up into the ambulance. I'll see to the bairns."

"I've left the gas on!"

"Don't you worry, I'll see to it. Go on."

She remembered nothing of the journey, except the groans that came out of John's mouth whenever the ambulance jolted over a bump in the road. She stared and stared at the red blanket. It must be red so that you didn't notice the blood, she thought dazedly. And got hold of John's hand, reassured by the contact, though the fingers were limp and cold.

Only much later, in the waiting room at the hospital, did she look down at herself, and realize that she was covered with his blood. The front of her cardigan had dried and stiffened. You could bend it like cardboard.

They were bringing him home. Muriel sat in the armchair by the fire, her fingers knotted in her lap. Iris King, who had come across to help scrub out the front room, stood just behind her chair.

Very faintly came the sound of a car, drawing up outside the front door.

"That'll be them now," Iris said.

Muriel looked up. "Then you'd better go and let them in."

The words dropped from her mouth like stones. "Richard, you go."

She wasn't so calm now. Even as she spoke, the flesh of her cheeks twitched and puckered like porridge coming to the boil.

"Come on, love," Iris said.

Muriel didn't even look at her, just jerked her head back like a horse avoiding the bit, and went on staring at the door. "Let them in."

Iris went to open the door. Muriel followed her into the passage and saw a man with a bald head and dark, formal suit. Behind him other men struggled and strained, lifting something heavy out of the van. She could hear a muffled exclamation, a word of warning; then the measured tread of feet. The afternoon was dark. Only the men's hands and faces and the white fronts of their shirts were clearly visible. These patches of whiteness came towards Muriel until suddenly, blocking out the light, there was the coffin, swaying and lurching over the doorstep and into the house.

The coffin lurched, the men staggered, as they tried to turn the corner from the narrow passage into the front room. Muriel's hand held her lips together as the men slowly maneuvered the coffin around. They were bowed beneath the weight. There was a smell of fresh sweat mingling with the heavier smell of lilies.

She backed away. In the doorway behind her, Sharon whimpered and hid her face in her hands. But Muriel had eyes for nothing but the coffin. It tilted dangerously again and the man with the bald head called out, "Mind!" Suddenly, Muriel cried out and started to run, her arms and legs jerking like a puppet. Iris followed, and they ran out of the house, across the yard, and into the back. It was wash day. Sheets and towels and pillowcases were draped and hung out all along the alley. Muriel ducked and dodged between them as she ran, though the wet sheets slapped against her face, and the arms and legs of wet clothes twined themselves around her neck. It was a nightmare. Then Iris caught her, and wrapped her broad arms around her.

"Where you going, love?" she said.

"I don't know."

It was a wail. She would have liked to throw back her head and howl.

"Howay home."

Iris tightened her grip on Muriel's shoulders, and they walked back up the alley together.

She made herself go into the front room to see him in the end. She and Iris had scrubbed and polished that room until it shone. Now she could see nothing in it but the coffin. It was so big. So big. The lid was off now and there was a white cloth over his face.

Betty stood at the head of the coffin and pulled the cloth back for her to look. She felt a great surge of relief, for it wasn't John lying there. It was somebody else. Nothing like John. She thought, They've sent the wrong body. She opened her mouth to tell them, but something stopped her, something that knew this was John.

"Doesn't he look peaceful?" Betty said. She bent over the sunken ivory face. "You'd think he'd just this minute gone to sleep."

Immediately, a mad hope flared in Muriel. Suppose he wasn't dead? Suppose he *was* just asleep? But the yellow cheek was cold and spongy to her touch. It didn't feel like skin at all.

She wouldn't accept what her eyes and hands told her. She said, in an irritated voice, "Come on, now, John, this has gone far enough." Dimly she was aware of startled looks from the other people in the room. She neither knew nor cared who they were. She was beginning to get angry. "Come on, now," she said again. And she began pulling his head and shoulders, to make him get out of the coffin.

Hands pulled her away. And there was Betty, hissing and spitting, "Get a grip on yourself, woman. At least think of the child."

153

She saw Richard's face, stricken, as if he had seen her doing something obscene. She couldn't understand what was happening. She didn't know who all these people were. She turned and walked stiffly out of the room.

One by one the neighbors came in to see him. Muriel could not bring herself to go in with them. Always there was the flare of hope when she saw the face. It wasn't John. Or if it was John, he was only asleep. Hope wore her out, faster than grief.

It was Richard's job to take the neighbors in to see his father. He lifted the cloth back from the dead face, and his own face remained expressionless, though inwardly he was shaking with horror. He had not been afraid before, but he was afraid now.

People talked about sleep and death as if they resembled each other, but it wasn't true. This yellow doll, it didn't look like a man. It didn't look as if it ever had been a man. And, having seen it, he knew, not as some vague generality, but as absolute, inescapable fact that one day he too would die. His father's death left him exposed. There was nobody now to stand between him and that great void. Young though he was, he was the next in line.

His grandmother came to see his father. She stood looking at the old enemy for some time. Then, pursing her lips, said, "Well, he looks lovely. I will say this: you can rely on the Co-op to do a good job. I had the Co-op when your Granddad died."

Afterwards, he heard her talking to his mother.

"I don't know what you're thinking about, our Muriel, letting a child that age do that."

His mother's voice said dully, "He's better with something to do."

"He could've come to me till it was all over. Both of them could. You went to your Auntie May's when your father died."

Later he said to his mother, "I am going to the funeral, aren't I?"

She looked away from him. "No, love, I think it's best you stop here. I need somebody to look after the house."

He didn't argue. It was his grandmother's doing. He knew that.

For Muriel, the funeral passed like an unhappy dream. All the curtains in the street were drawn. Iris King and Mrs. Harrison had gone from door to door collecting money for a wreath. And the church was full of her neighbors, standing a little towards the back, at a respectful distance from the family. Everybody seemed to have a cold. At every pause in the service the church was full of the sound of coughing.

The Vicar, too, had a cold. Once outside, he hurried through the remainder of the service, almost gabbling the words. There were specks of rain on the cellophane sheet he held over the page. The tip of his nose, which he rubbed repeatedly with his handkerchief, was as red, as raw-looking, as the clods of clay he threw into the grave. Muriel looked down at the coffin, and tried to imagine John's face as the earth thudded down on to the lid. And again she thought, He's alive. But the thought was dull and heavy inside her.

She went back to work the following day. The children went back to school. Nothing had changed. Everything had changed.

The numbness that had carried her through the funeral lasted several more days. Then one afternoon—John had been dead just over a week—there was a knock at the door. A young man stood there, a young man with ginger hair, and freckles on a dead-white skin. She stared at the freckles, she might almost have counted them, but it was an effort to concentrate on the words that were coming out of his mouth. He was saying that he had brought the things from the hospital. She remembered that she had promised to collect them: it had slipped her mind till now. She held out her hands for the parcel.

But when she had carried it back into the living room she did not want to open it. Instead she walked restlessly around the room, staring at the brown paper as if it concealed a bomb. At last she said, aloud, Oh, don't be silly, and, fetching the kitchen scissors, cut through the string and tore the paper off. There were his blue and white striped pajamas, his battered leather shaving case, and his slippers. She pushed her face into the pajamas and breathed in: there was the smell of his body, the smell of sickness, and the lingering, foreign smell of rubber sheets. The slippers. She had meant to buy him another pair this Christmas: these were a disgrace. The sole of one of them was actually hanging off. It lolled towards her like a tongue, and immediately she saw John's tongue, trying to clear a passage for the words to get out.

And then she burst. She told Betty about it afterwards. She said, "I just burst. There was this horrible crying and I knew it was me and I couldn't do anything about it. I was telling him I loved him. Stuff like that. I was telling him to come back. And talking to him, and all the time I knew he was gone." She ran down the yard to the lavatory and hung over the bowl to retch.

She was glad it hadn't happened when the kids were at home.

She tried to keep busy and, at work, succeeded. But at home she wandered from room to room, starting on a job only to abandon it half-finished. She seemed to be looking for something, but she didn't know what it was. And she listened all the time for John's voice. Even outside the house she went on searching. She had to look at the face of every man she passed in the street, though she knew that none of them could be John. And it was the same in the supermarket. Every time a man walked past she had to turn and stare after him. Once, she saw a man disappearing around the corner of the street and something in the set of his shoulders reminded her of John. Before she knew what she was doing she had started to run, and was pulling at his sleeve. Then there was the stranger's face, inquiring and concerned, a little embarrassed, perhaps.

And she opened and shut her mouth, but no words would come. In the end she mumbled an apology, and turned away.

But that night, as she sat alone, her cheeks burned with shame. He must've thought she was mad.

She tormented herself going over the past. She shouldn't 've sent him to hospital. He was dying anyway. He wanted to die at home. And she should never 've left him. She had not been there when he died. She had gone to the waiting room to lie down for an hour, because she knew the end was close. And during that time he had died. She blamed herself. He might have recovered consciousness. He might have wanted to say something to her. She would never know.

Her mother came to see her every weekend, but they were often on the point of quarreling. The old lady's conviction that her son-in-law had enjoyed excellent health, though a little shaken by his death, was by no means overcome. She tended to minimize her daughter's loss, to hurry Muriel along the road to recovery long before Muriel was ready. There was no open breach, but the relationship between them was more distant than it had ever been.

Muriel was left alone. People said, Well, at least you've got the children. But the children were no help. At times she felt the additional burden of *their* grief was more than she could bear. Sharon was easy enough. She simply retreated into babyishness, sucked her thumb and followed Muriel around like a young child. It was Richard.

He had caught a cold while his father was ill. It didn't get better but seemed to settle in his throat. He was permanently hoarse and although she took him to the doctor and got some pills, they didn't seem to do him any good. It was difficult to get him to take them. He, who had been so grown-up during his father's illness, such a help, really, was now withdrawn and uncooperative. And he had developed a fascination with fire. On the night of his father's funeral, when she was exhausted and longing for bed, he had insisted on staying up to watch some film; and she had come downstairs to find a fire blazing halfway up the chimney and Richard crouched over it, throwing handfuls of salt into the flames.

She was afraid to leave him alone in the house. Yet twice every day he had to be left alone: in the early morning, and again the evening, when she was cleaning at the school.

Iris King rescued her from this dilemma by offering to have the children in her own house before and after school. But this could only be a temporary solution, because Iris, who would not accept payment, could not be allowed to go on doing it for nothing. Muriel wondered whether she should get a job cleaning in a pub, where the hours would be more convenient. But she dreaded making the change. It was better at the school where she knew all the other women and got on well with them. And there was another thing. John would not have wanted her to work in a pub.

She looked forward to the evenings when the children were in bed, though sometimes she was so tired that she went to bed almost immediately after them. They were all sleeping in the back bedroom: Muriel could not face the double bed alone. She lay and listened to the children's breathing. At least they could sleep. She could not sleep. Or if she did her sleep was disturbed by nightmares. She never dreamed directly of John's death, but always there was a sense of foreboding. And once she saw him in his coffin, and when she bent down his hand came up and stroked her face.

From these dreams she awoke with a cry and lay sweating in darkness, wondering whether she had woken either of the children. She lay and listened to their breathing. When she was sure they were still asleep, she turned over on to her side.

If only the night would pass. At night the line between reality and nightmare was blurred. She convinced herself that he had been alive when they put him into the earth. She saw him, in the darkness, begin to stir and open his eyes. She got up to face the day, most of her energy already spent in a battle with shadows.

Guilt was the hardest thing to bear. She should not have let him go into hospital, not when he was dying anyway. Though they had been able to give him injections. She couldn't've done that. He'd only said one thing to her after he went in. His eyes had opened and he'd said, Oh, Muriel, however are you going to manage? Oh, she'd said, don't you worry about that. Just you think about getting better.

His last thoughts, before he lost consciousness, had been of her.

She heard him moving about the house. Downstairs in the living room, poking the fire. At night, in the other bedroom, beating the pillows into shape. He had been such a restless sleeper. She lay and listened and heard him cough. The cough went on and on. Stop it, she said. Oh, please God, stop it.

It was no use. She had to go. In the door of the front bedroom, she stopped and called his name. Softly, so as not to wake the sleeping children. "John? John?"

Darkness, then silence, answered her. She went into the room and drew back the curtains. Moonlight fell onto the counterpane and quickened the depths of the mirror. She sat on the bed and tried to think small, practical thoughts about changing her job, and Richard's tonsils, and whether she should take him back to the doctor. But gradually, as she continued to sit there, the moonlight peeled all such thoughts away, stripping her to the bone.

She looked at the bed. Once, newly-married, the first shyness over, she had run her hands over his whole body, every inch of it, down to the spaces between his toes, and he had lain and looked up at her, half-delighted, half-afraid.

Where was he now? In your mind. In his children. Mechanically, her brain supplied the answers. They were not enough. Her mother believed in reincarnation. Her father hadn't believed in anything. He'd thought that when you were dead, that was it, you were finished. What did *she* believe? It was such a muddle inside her mind. She didn't know what she believed.

There was a footstep outside on the landing. She looked towards the door, hope flaring up again in defiance of reason. But it was only Richard.

"I heard somebody moving about," he said. "I didn't know who it was."

She saw that he had been frightened. Poor Richard, with his enormous hands and feet, and his voice that squeaked whenever he was trying to sound particularly grown-up: this couldn't've come to him at a worse time. She had been about to answer him, impatiently, she often did now, though it was not what she wanted to do. Instead, she patted the bed beside her. He came and sat down and she put her arm around his shoulders. She could tell from the vibration of his chest that he was crying, though he made no sound.

"We ought to go back to bed, you know. Sharon'll be frightened if she wakes up. And you've got school in the morning."

"Yes, I know."

But they went on sitting side by side.

"By the way, I've got your blazer back from the cleaner's. Do you know what they charged me for it? 70p. They think they can get away with anything."

"Well, it was a mess."

"Even so."

They sat in silence for a while. Then he said the last thing she expected him to say. "I went to the cemetery on my way home from school."

She waited. He looked at her accusingly. "I couldn't find the grave."

"Well, where were you looking?"

"The new bit."

"He's not there. I had him put on top of his mother. Betty wanted it. And I didn't mind."

"Oh."

He bent forward, his big hands clasped between his knees. She said, "I should never've listened to me Mam. I should 've took you with me. It was your place."

He looked up at her. "That's all right. It doesn't matter." He squeezed his hands together. "It's all over now, anyway."

But it had mattered. She could see that.

160

"I was surprised how many people turned out," she said. "There was a lovely wreath from the street. Mrs. King was saying, Everybody gave." The thought made her throat tighten.

"There's no need to talk about it," he said. "Not if you don't want."

He was offering her the means of escape. But even as he said it, he looked at her pleadingly. And she wanted to talk to him about his father.

She said, hesitatingly, "You didn't miss much. The Vicar got through it that fast you'd've thought he was in a race." Her voice was sharp with anger. "Still, I suppose they must get tired of it. I mean, it's just another job to them. But it was what your father wanted. He always said, Don't have me cremated, Muriel."

There was a long silence. Then Richard cleared his throat. He mumbled, "Shouldn't think it matters much. I mean you're gone, aren't you?"

"Yes."

Another long silence. "All the same, I wish I'd been there."

"I wish you had." Her voice shook. There were tears running down her face, though for the boy's sake she would not sob aloud. She said, "You know the night your Dad had the hemorrhage, he was talking about you."

He looked up at her then.

"He said what a fine lad you were. That he wasn't as worried about me as he might've been because he knew I had a good son."

Richard was looking down again, one hand clasping and unclasping the other.

"He said I thought he favored Sharon, but he didn't. He thought every bit as much about you, only it was harder to show it with a lad." As she finished, her voice wobbled. And then she was sobbing openly. She couldn't've held it back any longer, not to save her life.

Richard looked at her almost with dread. He had never seen his mother cry. Even on that terrible day when they had brought his father home and she had tried to drag his body from the coffin, she had not cried. Then she held out her arms, and he started to cry too, pressing his wet cheek into her neck.

Richard was the first to stop. He put an arm round his mother's shoulders. And she started to dry her eyes.

"Well," she said, on a shaky laugh. "I think we both needed that."

"We will be all right, won't we? I mean money and all that."

"We'll manage. We always have done, haven't we?"

"I could get a Saturday job."

"You're not old enough, lov."

"Well, a paper round then. I'm old enough for that."

"We'll see. You go back to bed, now, love. I'll just stop here another few minutes. No, go on, I'll be all right."

After he'd gone, she went on sitting there for a while. The moonlight was stronger now, strong enough to cast shadows over the bed. She stroked the coverlet and said, very quietly, "Oh, John, I loved you."

Then she got up and wandered across to the mirror, but she did not look into it. It could show her only what she most feared to see: a woman, white-faced, sodden and alone. Instead she turned to the window and looked out on to the night. The moon was high and magnificent, ringed by haloes of frost. She was aware of it as another presence, a gaze she was compelled to meet.

And so she stood by the window, alone and not alone, until she heard Richard's voice calling to her from the next room. "All right," she said. "I'm coming." She took one last look, then, bracing her shoulders, went back to her children.

V

Iris King

"What's this money on the mantelpiece then?"
Iris went to the kitchen door to see what her husband was on about.

"Oh, that. That's what we collected for John Scaife. There was a bit left over from the wreath. Mrs. Sullivan and me, we thought we'd have a walk down the town tomorrow and see if we can't get a nice little vase or something to put on the grave."

"Poor sod." Ted put the money down abruptly.

Iris turned to Mrs. Sullivan, who was having a cup of tea with her in the kitchen. "Ted used to work with him, you know."

"Twenty year, nigh on. Up to a year gone March. I've seen him walking up that hill when he should have been at home in bed. And then folks turned around and said he was lazy. I'll tell you one thing, Missus. I wouldn't do it. No, by hell would I. I look at that place and I say to meself, Now then, Ted, don't strain yourself. It'll be there when you're gone.''

As he spoke he was putting on his coat to go out. After he'd gone Iris sat down and lit another cigarette. ''I had a hell of a job getting him to go to the funeral, you know. He's scared bloody stiff of owt like that. Says he wishes he didn't have to go to his own. And hospitals. He hasn't been up to see our Brenda once.''

''How is she?''

''Getting over it. She looked like death yesterday, mind. You know how you do. It upset me. I wished after I hadn't gone, because she wasn't conscious.''

''She's been an unlucky bairn. I mean, a girl of her age, having to go in for scrapes.''

''She's been in for a scrape—I think I'm right—six times.''

''Poor bairn. What is she, fifteen?''

''Sixteen gone August. You know when he said it was her ovary I was pleased because I thought well, at least now they do know what's wrong. She's hardly had a normal period, that kid. She doesn't know what it's like. And pain! It was Ted spotted it, you know. She was bent double and Ted said you know this is happening every month. I said, gerraway. Well, you know she was only eleven. But after I thought about it and it dawned on me he was right.''

A groan from the living room interrupted her.

''That's our Laura back from me Dad's. I wondered why Ted was so keen to get out.''

Iris walked into the living room. Mrs. Sullivan, following her, saw a tall, gaunt woman with hair cut like a child's and thick, brown stockings that drooped in folds around her ankles. She had staring eyes.

''Laura, this is Mrs. Sullivan.''

Laura groaned again.

''They've only just let her out. She's supposed to be better but I'm buggered if I can see it.''

''It'll be her nerves, is it?'' Mrs. Sullivan approached timidly.

"No, it's schizophrenia." Mrs. Sullivan backed away. "She's living in a different world. So *they* say. I have me doubts." She bent down and peered into Laura's eyes, as if through the letter box of an empty house. "Sometimes, I think they're right. Sometimes I thinks she's a lot more with it than she cracks on. Now and then you catch a very funny look in her eye."

"It's a big responsibility, isn't it?"

"Oh, it is. No doubt about it. I don't like leaving her, you see. And Ted won't stop in with her. And there again when I go to work I can't take her with me. The old people don't like it."

"Well, no. . . ."

"Well, it's what she was in for, see. She was cleaning for this old man and one day she just took it into her head to set him on fire. One minute he was sat in his armchair, next he was up in flames. Or rather the chair was. He wasn't badly burned but I mean to say at that age the shock could've killed him. I said when I went to see her, I said, What d'y' want to do that for, Laura? She just turned around and said, Why not? He was no use. That was all you could get out of her: he was no use. I said to her, I said, Laura, that's not the point."

"I'm surprised they let her out."

"Well, to be honest, so am I. And the old people don't take to her, you know. They say she sits and stares at them. Which she does. She stares at me. For all I know she's making up her mind I'm no use."

All this time Laura had stared straight ahead of her, her feet planted side by side on the floor, her back rigid.

"Laura, I'm going to see our Brenda now. Listen, Laura, do you want to come?" Silence. "Talk to a chair leg, you'd get more sense. Laura . . ."

"I'll stop where I am." Her voice boomed out, expressionless as a foghorn, seeming to come from several feet behind her head.

"You'll be all right, won't you? Not do anything silly?" Silence.

"It's the fire I'm frightened of," Iris said in a whisper. "I don't like the way she looks at it."

"I think it's wonderful the way you manage. What with Brenda as well."

And Ted, she might have said.

"Oh, I just carry on."

In fact as she stood in front of the mirror to tie the scarf around her head you could see she wasn't well. She had the dull eyes and permanently gray skin of somebody who keeps going on cups of tea, cigarettes and adrenalin.

When she was ready they left the house together.

"Iris, what is she to you?"

"She's supposed to be me aunt. But if you believe that you'll believe anything." Iris paused, deciding whether or not she should go on. "Me Dad's stepmother had her fifteen months after the old man died. Now she always said it was me Granddad's bairn and she was late. Well. *I* think it belonged to me Dad. He was still living with her, see. But that doesn't matter to me. Whether she's me aunt or whether she's me sister she's still the only relation I've got after me father goes. I've got to see to her."

"You've took a lot on, Iris."

"When haven't I had a lot on? You tell me."

They parted at the corner, Iris went up North Road towards the Hospital. She was thinking, as she walked, about Mrs. Sullivan. Poor woman. Fell for a bairn whenever her husband looked at her. And what a husband. Ted was bad enough but Ernie Sullivan was a real blossom. At least *she'd* made sure there were no more bairns. Not after Brenda. Brenda. When she'd got over it a bit she'd take her away for a few days. Even if it was only as far as Scarborough. Or perhaps they could manage Blackpool: she'd always wanted to see the lights but every time she got saved up for it something happened and put the kibosh on it.

Well, if she could get the money raked together, this time she'd make bloody sure nothing happened.

*　　*　　*

"Pregnant?"

"Five months pregnant." His voice was cold.

Iris stared at him, silhouetted against the window of his room. She heard the rattle of a trolley in the corridor outside, the gurgle of water in the radiator behind his desk. She licked her lips. "She can't be," she said at last.

"She is. And you must've known."

"No."

He smiled faintly.

"I didn't know."

Silence. When he spoke again his tone had softened slightly. "But *she* must've known."

"Yes. No. I suppose so."

"You suppose?"

"She's used to missing periods."

"Five months, Mrs. King. She must've been getting movement."

"You know what it's like with your first. You don't know what's wind and what isn't."

"She *knew*. I've spoken to her."

Silence. After waiting for her to speak he went on, "I rather think she was hoping the operation might bring on a miscarriage without her having to tell anybody. Or perhaps she thought I'd do an abortion automatically when I found a baby there. If she did she was mistaken. And don't ask for one. It would be too dangerous."

"You say you've talked to her?"

"Yesterday. As soon as she came around."

"And she definitely said she knew?"

"Yes."

The little cow. Iris felt the blood rush to her head. For a few seconds she was literally blind with rage.

When her sight cleared she managed to say, "There's just one thing. I don't want you thinking you've been conned. Because you haven't. Not by me. When I brought that girl in here I honestly believed she was ill. I had no idea there was anything else."

"Then I'm sorry to have given you bad news. How old is she?"

"Sixteen."

"I can't do it." He shifted uneasily in his chair. "If she'd told somebody sooner . . ."

"I suppose there's no possibility . . ."

"No. It wouldn't be safe."

"I see. Well, thanks for telling me." Iris stood up. Her hands were trembling. She clasped them together and said, "I'll just go and see her now if you don't mind."

"You can always get in touch with the hospital social worker, you know. She'll know what to advise."

Iris nodded. She was beyond taking in what was said. She walked along the shining corridor, her mind empty except for the single word *"pregnant"* which bounced from wall to wall and refused to make sense.

It began to make sense as soon as she saw her daughter. She was sitting on a chair beside her bed, flicking over the pages of a magazine. Her dark blonde hair hung like two curtains on either side of her face. But Iris was looking at her stomach. I've been a fool, she thought. It's obvious.

And immediately she wondered how many other people knew. Even Mrs. Bell had said something about Brenda always looking tired. She'd thought nothing of it at the time. But now she felt that perhaps the neighbors all knew, that they were laughing, sniggering behind her back.

"Brenda."

The girl looked up and went white when she saw her mother's expression.

"The doctor's just told me something about you." She was gasping for breath, sucking in great lungfuls of air, but they weren't doing her any good. "He says you're pregnant."

Silence.

"Well, are you?"

Brenda mumbled something she couldn't catch.

"I asked you a question."

"I must be if he says I am."

"Oh, I suppose *you* didn't know? I suppose this is all news to you?"

"How was I supposed to know? I'm always missing, you know I am."

"You knew what you'd done. You knew you'd been with a fella. Couldn't you've told me? Did you have to let me turn up here and . . . and get slapped in the face with it?"

"I didn't know."

"Oh, pull the other one it's got bells on."

Brenda glanced miserably from side to side, "I wish you'd shut up, Mam. Everybody's listening."

"Let 'em listen. They'll have a proper lugful by the time I'm finished." She raised her voice. "Enjoying yourself, everybody?"

Instantly, all along the ward, heads darted into the cover of knitting patterns and magazines.

"*Mam!*"

"Now just you listen to me. There's things I've got a right to know. For a kickoff, who was it?"

Silence.

"Brenda . . ."

"I'm not telling you. You'd only go around shouting and screaming and showing us all up. You've done it as long as I can remember. You used to go around the pub and fight me Dad for his wages. I used to get that thrown up at me at school."

"I did. I did fight your Dad for his wages. I'm not ashamed to say it. And think on, Brenda, there was many a week you'd 've gone hungry to shit if I hadn't."

"It's been the same all me life. Well, I'm not having it this time. Fighting and going on."

"Oh, I see. I suppose fucking and going on is all right? I suppose that doesn't show us up? Well, let me tell you when you're waddling down the street with a big belly you'll sharp find out it does. Soppy Lil. I never thought it'd be Soppy Brenda. I thought you had more off."

"It's none of your business. I can take care of meself."

"It looks like it."

There was a pause. Mother and daughter each drew breath.

"Is he in a position to marry you?"

"Not exactly."

"You mean he's married already?"

"I mean he's only fifteen."

"Bloody hell."

"Only just turned fifteen."

"Why won't you tell me who it is?"

"I won't, that's all."

"I know, you're ashamed to say who it is. But you weren't ashamed to get on your back for him. Him and God knows how many more."

"You shut your face!"

"No! You shut yours."

Iris's fist came up and hit the girl on the mouth. It was such a lovely relief that she did it again. "Hey, steady on!" somebody shouted. Further down the ward another woman could be heard summoning the nurse.

By the time they arrived, Iris was dragging Brenda around the ward by her hair. The girl was white-lipped and moaning with fear. She had both hands pressed together over the wound in her belly.

"I'll give you shut your face, you little whore."

"Mrs. King!" The Sister's voice cracked across the ward. "Stop that at once."

"I'll murder the little bitch."

"Not on my ward you won't."

The two women stared at each other.

"Are you going? Or have I to send for the porter?"

"I'll fight you and the bloody porter."

Though in fact the fight had gone out of her. Brenda was sobbing in the middle of the ward with a nurse's arm around her shoulders. Wherever Iris looked there were accusing faces. There was nothing to do but go.

At the door she turned and said, "I wouldn't have you back now, our Brenda, not if you went on your bended knees."

"I'll see you in hell first."
So that was that.

When Iris reached home she stood for a few moments with
her back against the door, helplessly staring along the passage.
Then she called, "Laura?" No reply. That meant nothing.
Iris went to look for her, but no, she was out. Thank God she
was out.

Iris crouched over the fire and began putting lumps of coal
on to it, slowly, piece by piece. For a long time she couldn't
control her thoughts at all. She stared at the fire, and the
scenes she'd just lived through re-enacted themselves in her
mind, certain words, certain looks burning themselves into
her, until at last she was exhausted and could think about it
no more.

Laura had most probably gone around to her father's. That
wouldn't last long. She gave him the creeps, he said. He was
almost as frightened of her as Ted was. An hour, two at the
most, and she'd be back.

Iris got up stiffly and looked around the room. Flames
flickered over china and cut glass and polished wood. Everything in the room shone. There wasn't a speck of dirt anywhere.
It made her feel better to look at it. She was proud of her
reputation as the cleanest woman in the street. Although she
worked full-time as a home help, her own doorstep was
scoured every day. Fresh curtains appeared at the windows
once a week, sometimes twice. It was no hardship to her to
do all this. She loved housework. This house of hers had been
a right mess when she first moved into it, and gradually she'd
got it put right. There was a bathroom, now, and an indoor
lavatory. And it had all come out of her own money; there
was no relying on Ted to do anything. If it'd been left to Ted
they'd be living in a tent.

Her eyes roamed around the room. On the wall opposite
were three plastic shields in a sort of reddy-brown color that
looked like bronze. She was proud of them: they were a
recent acquisition. But the joy of her life was her china

cabinet. Sometimes when she was upset she would touch the wood; it always made her feel better. If she ever left Ted, that would go with her. He could have all the rest, but she would take that.

She hadn't always lived in a nice house. She'd been born and brought up in Wharfe Street, near the river. As a young woman she'd battled her way out of it. But it was no use. She was no longer in Wharfe Street but Wharfe Street was still in her. She remembered it. Knew it. Knew every brick of it.

When she thought of Wharfe Street she remembered Mrs. Biggs. She'd lived in the end house, the one nearest the river, and the wallpaper had peeled away and hung in strips. She'd kept herself to herself. She was a clean-living, even religious woman, respected, if not much liked. Then her son, who was a bit not-all-there, had molested and strangled a little boy and left his body on a rubbish tip. Then nothing that Mrs. Biggs could say or do would save her. On the night before they hanged her son, somebody had gone and smeared dogshit all over her windows and all over her front door. And they'd gone on doing it, too. They never let up. She went loony in the end and had to be taken away.

And she remembered Blonde Dinah, traipsing about the room in a nightdress with bloodstains on the back. There'd been men there, it hadn't been just women, but she hadn't cared.

Animals.

They were going to pull it down now. That was what they said. It was all coming down. Too late. Too late for her.

You could talk about it to people and they would say they understood. But they didn't, not really. Nobody who hadn't lived there could understand.

Her parents had split up a few weeks after her birth. When she was six weeks old her mother took her father to court to claim maintenance. Perhaps they didn't give her enough. At any rate when the case was over she'd picked Iris up and walked across the courtroom with her. "Here," she said.

"It's your bairn. You keep it." And she'd dumped Iris in her father's arms.

That was the last Iris saw of her mother.

Now, whenever she felt bitter against her father, when she couldn't stop remembering some of the things that had happened, she thought, well, what else could he do? What could any man do, left to bring up a bairn on his own? He'd kept her, hadn't he? Many a man'd've put her in a home.

They'd lived in a series of boarding houses and some of them weren't much better than brothels and some of them were brothels. Her father paid a long succession of women to look after her. Some of them did a good job, some didn't. Mainly they didn't. As soon as she could walk, she was shoved out on to the street with a slice of bread and dripping in her hand, lucky to get it too. And on the street she'd learned to survive.

Wednesdays and Saturdays were market days. By the time she was five she was stealing from the food stalls. Course she'd got copped. One day she was just reaching out for a banana when a hand came down on her bare arm. She looked up to see a man like a tower with a red face and eyes that bulged horribly. She'd been so frightened she'd pissed herself. Ever since, whenever she was worried about something, like going into the hospital for an operation, she pissed herself. Sometimes she woke up and the bed was swimming. She blamed it on that day in the market place.

Though in fact they were very kind to her. Somehow they'd realized she was hungry and not just doing it for devilment. God knows how, because she'd been too frightened to get the words out. And then they were always giving her food. They'd save some for her at the end of the day and cut off the bad bits with their penknives. And the men at the banana-packing place down by the river were just the same. Except the bananas there were still green. They all knew her. They'd even give her a carrier bag of stuff to take home. Not that she ever did. Even at five she'd had more off than that. No. She ate it all on the way, cramming it into her mouth till the juice ran down her chin. God, it was good. Nothing had ever tasted the same since. It had been part of her life. Bags of over-ripe fruit, Wednesdays and Saturdays. Thursdays and Sundays, the shits.

When she got to school things looked up a bit. The teachers rummaged around and found her some warmer clothes to wear, because in her first winter in school she'd only had a pair of plimsolls and a raggy cotton dress. Course, the other kids knew she was wearing their cast-offs. Quite often she was wearing a dress that had belonged to somebody else in the same class. They'd given her hell. Well, you couldn't blame them. It was only bairn-like. But fight! She'd had to fight all the way.

Probably it was the school that told the Cruelty Bobby about her. Anyway, there he was. Uncle Harry. When she saw him coming up the street she'd run to him like running home. Except if she had bruises. Then she'd steer clear. He knew it, too. He used to say, "Howay, my bairn. Aren't you gunna give your Uncle Harry a kiss?" But she'd keep out of reach. She knew what he was looking for. And she had to protect her father. From a very early age she'd known that keeping Dad out of trouble was her responsibility.

As she got older, the beatings got worse. Her periods started. They were lodging with Blonde Dinah at the time. She'd taken her out to buy her first sanitary towels and shown her how to fit them on the belt. Iris had had a soft spot for Dinah ever since, though there were those who'd cross the street when they saw her coming. But her father had been terrible when she was in her teens. Course, you could see it from his point of view. A young girl growing up in that area among a lot of old pros. He didn't know what to do about it and finished up beating the hell out of her every time she looked at a lad. At the finish she set her cheek up at him that bad he picked up a pan of boiling soup and poured it over her head. It'd been a hospital job that time, and when she come out she went to stay with her Auntie in Jarrow. And when she come back she got on with Ted, and married him. Course she had to, but by that time she'd've married anybody, just to get out. Irene had said, Don't do it. She'd offered to help her out. Even showed her the things she did it with. But no. No! The sight of the instruments made her shudder, and anyway she was in love with the idea of marriage. A home. She had never had a home.

She was married in white. She waltzed out of the Registry Office without a care in the world. She'd really thought all her troubles were over. Now, when she looked at her wedding photographs, she sometimes thought, You poor, silly little bitch. But it was somebody else. She couldn't feel any connection with that past self.

Three weeks after the wedding, he came in and found her still ironing his shirts when he thought the supper should've been ready. He belted her across the ear, hard enough to make her see stars, and slammed out to the pub.

After he'd gone, she sat down and took stock. Her first thought was to hurry through the ironing and get the dinner on. Then she thought, No, bugger it. Course she knew already about Ted's temper. He thought he had a right to hit you. His father had always belted hell out of his mother, so why not? It was just like God bless you to him. But he was making a big mistake. She wasn't his sodding mother.

When he came back she was waiting for him behind the door with the meat chopper in her hand. The blow glanced off him, though there was enough blood around to scare the pair of them stiff. It didn't stop him hitting her again, but it did free her from fear. She never lost her self-respect. The only times she was frightened of him were when she was pregnant or after she'd had the Big Operation. He was a bugger to her then, dragging her down on to the floor and kicking her in the wound. It was a miracle her stitches hadn't bust.

The first baby, a boy, was born dead. There'd been a mix-up over her dates all the way through. *She* reckoned she was overdue; they would have it she was only seven months, but when they saw the afterbirth they admitted she was right. The baby just hadn't grown properly. It lay on the doctor's hand, curled up and blue-black. "Well, Iris," he said. "After all that time. Is this the best you can do?" He was rough, but it was only his way. She'd been in labor three days before they took her to the hospital.

Over the years her memory of the baby changed. Gradually it became more and more like Ted. Finally it was Ted himself lying in the doctor's hand, shrunken and dead.

It was Ted's father pulled her around from that. It was funny, he was a right bugger with his wife and bairns, knocked hell out of 'em, but speak as you find: he was goodness itself to her. He'd given her wormwood to drink to bring the clots of blood away and bound strips from a torn-up sheet tightly around her stomach, in defiance of the midwife. "Never you mind her," he'd said. "You don't want a great big belly on yer, lass your age."

She'd only been eighteen. And she'd crawled around for two years after that. More. Even the next pregnancy didn't lift the depression: she was too apathetic to care. Only when the pains started she thought, "Dear God, have I got to go through all that again?"

The baby was a girl, very small but healthy. She was a crabby baby. More than once Iris threw up the window intending to toss the baby out; but gradually it became less fractious. She saw the results of her care. The baby gurgled and held out its arms. The layer of dirty cellophane that had shut Iris off from the world was ripped away. She had a purpose again. This child of hers would never be left, never be deserted as she had been. No matter how bad things got, and they were bad, very bad, she would never give in.

And it wasn't going to have plimsolls and cast-offs either. It was going to have the best. She called it Sheila.

Lindsey was born the following year. Then a gap of two years, and Brenda.

They'd got out of Wharfe Street by then, though only as far as Bute Street, which was six and two threes. But the house was kept fanatically clean. Iris looked out at her neighbors: the men in prison, the women spending the social security money at the prize Bingo, kids dragged up anyhow, and her lips tightened. It was the women she despised. On their backs for any bugger what fancied a poke, and the kids left to God and Providence.

It wouldn't happen to hers. She had to get out of Bute Street. By this time her Dad had a fancy woman a lot older than himself, but still, Iris enlisted her help and went out to work, first at the bakery, then on the Home Help. The work suited her. She loved charging around a messy house and setting it all to rights. And she loved the old people too. "We've all got it to come to," she often said. She would sit for hours listening to some old person's rambling memories of the past. And then there was the money. She sat and looked at her first pay packet and burst into tears. Money had been that short. If he was drinking heavily he could go through a big slice of it before he got in from work. And it was right what Brenda said, she had gone out and fought him for it. They'd had one bust-up outside the Station Hotel. The police were called that time. She'd thrown him over the bonnet of a car. She wasn't ashamed. She'd had to do it to survive. But that first pay packet, it was wonderful. They needn't starve, now. Whatever Ted did there would be some money in the house. "You think on," she'd said to her two older girls when they got married. "It's nice to have a good husband but it's a hell of a lot nicer to have your own money. A fiver you've earned is worth ten of anybody else's. You can do what you want with it."

Ted was very bad while the kids were little. Fifty times worse than he'd been since. She'd forgiven him a lot but there was one thing she couldn't forgive.

She was in bed trying to get to sleep. The pubs had closed but he still wasn't home which meant he had gone on somewhere, to one of the nightclubs perhaps. Which meant he had switched to drinking spirits. She wasn't as worried about the money now, but she hated the rows, the violence, the way the children went quiet whenever their father walked into a room. In a way, she still cared about him. She would defend him to other people. "He hasn't a lazy bone in his body," she would say. "And he's never missed a day's work through drink." Which was true. Then.

Suddenly, she heard voices. A muffled male giggle. The sound of a milk bottle rolling into the gutter. She tensed up, resolving to say nothing. But she was surprised. He had never brought anybody back with him before.

They were making a hell of a row. She got up and went to look over the banisters. She expected to see two of his mates but no, the men were strangers. She retreated to the bedroom. She only hoped he wasn't gambling, though the state he was in there couldn't be much left to lose.

Then she heard footsteps on the stairs. They were slow and uncertain but it couldn't be Ted, because whoever it was stopped on the landing, as if not sure of the room. She sat up in bed and switched the light on. As she did so the door opened, and a man stood there. He was obviously pissed. He was swaying on his feet. Worse than that, he was fumbling with his flies. He got it out. She stared at him, dumbfounded. He seemed to be in no doubt that he—and It—were welcome.

She grabbed her dressing gown. "Hey, I think you're making a big mistake, aren't you?"

He gaped at her, too fuddled to take the situation in.

"Did he send you up here?" She saw him glance over his shoulder. "Well, go on, did he?"

There was another step on the stairs. "Hey up, Jock," another man's voice called cheerfully. "Don't take all night."

There were two of them. He'd brought two complete strangers home and sent them up here. "Get out," she said. She advanced on the first man. He backed away until brought up hard against the banisters. There was time to notice the little bubbles of spit between his rather prominent front teeth. Then he was tipping slowly, slowly backwards. The blue eyes opened wide and he was gone. Then the silence that had surrounded her ended, the world rushed back. There was a crash, and a cry from Brenda's bedroom.

She thought afterward, she could have broken the man's

back. At the time she wouldn't've cared if she had. He staggered to his feet. The other man grabbed him by the arm and they fell over each other to get out of the front door.

She went downstairs to find Ted. He was curled up on the floor like a fetus, retching. The final stages of his drunkenness were always like this. She bent over him and said, "I ought to kill you. But I won't. You're not worth doing time for."

When she went back upstairs she found Brenda on the landing in her nightgown. She was too frightened to cry. Iris swept her up in her arms and carried her to the big bed for a cuddle. She might as well sleep there. Ted wouldn't be making it that far tonight.

She never willingly had sex with him again. Perhaps once or twice a year when he got too bad, to shut him up; never more than that.

As for other men, well, the bairns came first. Had to. Even if she'd lost Ted, she didn't think she'd've married again. Live tally, her name on the rent book, yes. But marriage . . . no. She'd had enough.

When her children were very small she adored them. My little princesses, she said. As babies they had the biggest pram the street had seen, with all the trimmings: sunshade and broderie anglaise pillowslips. Later they took their first steps in Clarks' Start-rite shoes. No plimsolls for them. They were cherished, coddled, over-protected, overfed, overweight, forced to wear vests on even the warmest day.

As they grew older things changed. Iris would have given her teenage daughters anything, but they were separate people now. There was a conflict in her mind. Sometimes they were still her little girls who must have everything that she had lacked. But increasingly, too, they appeared as rivals who might be resented for having more. Brenda's "tash" started growing. At the same time gray hairs appeared in her mother's head. Iris, for the first time in many years, spent some money selfishly on herself. She went out and bought some bleach and dyed her hair blond.

Iris, in these later years, was often depressed. A blackness would come over her, a blackness she linked in her mind with those early years in Wharfe Street. They were living in Union Street now, a big step up. And yet the past had never seemed so close. She would look around her at the home she had toiled and sweated to create and it meant nothing. She wanted to destroy something. Anything. Herself, if nothing else offered. She would go out and walk the streets for hours, aware only of the blood squeezing through the veins in her head.

The blackness lifted as suddenly as it came. But she knew as she got older that it would always return.

She was just coming out of one of these spells when Joss moved into the street. She hadn't seen him for years. He had lived opposite her in Wharfe Street, and had always been kind. His was one of the few faces from those days that she remembered with affection. They used to talk for hours when she was young. Perhaps he'd fancied her. He'd never said anything, perhaps his legs had held him back. And it hadn't really entered her head. She'd been too busy going out with every good-looking shit on the block. After a while, Joss came to her house like going home. At weekends she gave him his meals. And stuck up for him when anybody laughed at his legs, which they were inclined to do. She'd clocked one girl for doing that. Everybody thought he was her fancy man. But there was nothing like that. All that was over and done with for her. She was glad to see the back of it.

There were long spells when she was entirely well. Then she mothered half the street. Kelly Brown and the Scaife children, Lisa Goddard's little lads—they all knew and loved their Iris. Oh, my Iris, Kelly used to say when she was little. Oh, my Iris. And she sat with women in labor. Even laid out the dead, though there wasn't as much call for that now. They died in hospital and came back neatly packaged. Sometimes only as far as the front door, before setting off on the final journey. She thought that was disgusting; but it was the new way.

All this was meat and drink to her. She loved life. She

loved to feel life bubbling and quickening all around her, and took it for granted that life included old age, suffering and death.

The girls grew up. The two older girls married, both very young but neither because she had to. Lindsey was settled away from home, but Sheila, after her marriage, was closer to her mother than before. They would sit and laugh about the old times. The time Iris had picked the carving knife up and threatened to kill the lot of them; the time she set the house on fire. When she was well these events seemed to have happened in another life. She could sit and have a laugh about them.

She valued her reputation in the street. She knew she was respected and her family was respected. Her reputation mattered more to her than anything else. It was the measure of her distance from Wharfe Street, the guarantee that the blackness that came from her past would never finally return.

It was this that Brenda threatened to destroy. Well, she wouldn't be allowed to. As Iris wandered around and around her living room, straightening ornaments and cushions that were straight already, she felt her anger grow. She would not have Brenda back in this house. Would not, would not, would not. She didn't care where she went. Her or the baby. She should've thought of all that before she got on her back. She'd learn. She'd grow up bloody fast. She'd sharp find out what having a bairn was like.

This resolve held firm to the end of the week. She did not go back to the hospital, but was kept informed of Brenda's progress by her eldest daughter, Sheila, who visited every day. This had come as a surprise. Iris expected unquestioning obedience even from her married daughters. She had not actually forbidden Sheila to visit, but she had assumed that she would not go. So it was something of a shock when every day Sheila came in with fresh news.

"She says she's made up her mind to keep it, Mam," Sheila said, retrieving her own child from the coal scuttle in which he took a compulsive interest.

"She doesn't know what she's on about. It's bad enough when you've got a man bringing the money in."

"She says everything's changed now."

"Oh, aye. You mean, they've invented a bairn what wipes its own arse? I *have* missed out."

"She says she'll get the Social Security."

"She'll get a long way on that, the way she spends."

"Oh, I know. She talks big, but underneath she's scared stiff. You can see she is." Mixed in with Sheila's sympathy was a certain satisfaction. As a child she'd always got the blame when things went wrong. "But she's bound to be scared, isn't she? I mean, she's only a kid herself."

"If only she'd been honest about it. It could all have been over and done with months ago. He'd 've done her if she'd gone to him straight away. And told the truth."

"She was frightened."

"What of?"

"Mam!"

"Well, I'm asking you. What of?"

"Of you leathering her. Which you would've done, so don't say you wouldn't."

"I'd 've took the skin off her back."

"Well, then."

"She didn't half want something to do. Five minutes pleasure and a lifetime of misery. How often have I said that to you?"

"I don't know, Mam. I've lost count."

"But it's the truth, isn't it?"

"For her it will be."

Iris was silent. There was a lot in Sheila's attitude that she didn't like.

"You see, Mam, mebbe with her not having proper periods and that she's been running away with the idea she couldn't get pregnant. And that was bound to make her . . ."

"She knew what she was doing was wrong. Didn't she?"

"Granted she did, yes."

"She knew enough to keep her knees together. That's all you need to know."

"Yes, Mam. But . . ." Sheila paused, wrestling with the child on her knee. "Oh, go on, then, get mucky. You never got much pleasure out of it, did you, Mam?"

"I got none."

"Well, it's not like that for everybody. You can't just . . . What I'm trying to say is, it's natural, isn't it?"

"I'm bloody sure it's not."

The two women retreated into silence. Iris had always assumed that Sheila shared her attitude to sex. Now, suddenly, she was forced to see her daughter as a woman who apparently enjoyed "it." And wasn't afraid to look you in the face and say so! A thought struck her.

"Our Sheila, are you on the pill?"

"I've been on it a year."

"You're as bad as she is. Rotting your guts out for a man."

"The doctor said . . ."

"Doctors!"

"A lot of men wouldn't put up with what me Dad puts up with. Twice a year if he's lucky."

"A lot of women wouldn't put up with your Dad. Keep it out, right?" She tapped the end of her nose. "Anyway, she can't 've got much pleasure out of him. If it's owt like the rest of him she'd need a winkle-picker to find it."

Sheila looked guilty. "We don't know who it is."

"Don't we?"

"She's never said owt to me about it."

"No. But you'll have seen that Sally Almond there, haven't you? Brenda was always around their house. And Billy Almond's fifteen."

"I honestly don't know, Mam."

"That's who it belongs to. And he goes to the daft school, and so does Sally, and so does the other brother. I used to know their Mam. She never had much on top. And what there was he belted out of her. He drinks, doesn't he? Loud-mouthed git. Well, I can tell you one thing, our Sheila, if she was nine months gone with triplets I wouldn't let her marry into that lot."

"I can't see our Brenda going with somebody daft. She was always the brainy one."

"Aye. And she was always the one that wouldn't be told. I used to say to her, you've got a head on you like a forty-shilling piss-pot, my girl, but I'll see you brought low. And I have."

"Mam, if she wouldn't be told, whose fault was it?" Silence. "Yours. She could do no wrong. She only had to ask and she got."

"I didn't just ruin her, I ruined the lot of you."

"She got more than we ever got."

"I had more! I was working then."

"Anyway, it doesn't matter whose fault it was. She's the one that's paying for it."

"Aye, now she is. And later? Who do you think's going to bring it up? She can't. She doesn't earn enough to keep herself."

"I thought you were having nowt to do with it."

"Oh, that's likely, isn't it? Turn me back on me own flesh and blood. If I could do that, I wouldn't be sat here. I'd 've left the whole sodding lot of yer, years ago."

"They say she can go into a hostel."

"She going into no hostel. She's coming home."

"She's frightened, Mam."

"She has no need to be. I'll keep me hands off her. I don't know how, mind, but I will."

Sheila looked at her mother suspiciously. "You've got something up your sleeve."

"Mebbe I have."

"You're not going to go around their house?"

"No. Though I might be doing some other poor lass a favor if I did. I'll tangle with that lot later."

"So what are you going to do?"

"None of your business. I've got a lot more on my mind

than you think. Do you know what I'm really frightened of?"

"No."

Silently, Iris pointed towards Laura, who was sitting in the far corner paying, apparently, no attention to what was going on. "You see Brenda as she is now—you see Laura when she was young."

It took a moment to sink in.

Sheila drew back. "Oh, no, Mam, I don't think so."

"Don't you?" Iris stared at Laura, expressionlessly. "I do."

"I don't mind stopping in with her, you know. If you were wanting to go out."

Ted came and stood over her, waiting for a reply.

"She's all right," Iris said irritably. "She doesn't need anybody stopping in with her. And anyway, I'm not going out."

"It's your Bingo night."

"I've told Joss I'm not going."

Still he hesitated. Iris fumed with impatience, spooning hot fat over the eggs in the frying pan. She tried to look as if his going to the pub, or not, was a matter of complete indifference to her, and was glad when an egg broke because it gave her a chance to say, Sod it.

"You sure you'll be all right, now?"

"Of course I'll be all right."

He looked back again before he opened the door. Then with an odd, ducking, evasive movement of his head he was gone.

That was something they could all do, every last one of 'em. She'd always tried to drill it into her girls: a man can put his cap on, you can't, you're stuck with it. And it isn't months, it's years. Sixteen years. They don't do as much as that for murder. She loved her bairns, she wouldn't have been without them. But she had no illusions left.

Ted knew the girl was pregnant. Oh, nobody had actually

told him, but he knew all right. He'd heard them talking. But he never mentioned it. Worrying about that was her job.

She shovelled the other egg on to a plate, and called into the living room, "Your tea's ready. Will you have it in there?"

"Yes, please."

She carried the plate through. Brenda was lying on the sofa, her bronze hair loose and falling almost to her waist. When she pushed it back from her face her eyes were so black you'd 've thought somebody had belted her one.

Which they had not, thought Iris virtuously, amazed by her own restraint.

They ate in silence. Once Brenda looked up from her plate to say, "Where's Auntie Laura?"

"Round me Dad's. I've got enough on."

"Oh." She was obviously not looking forward to a whole evening of her mother's company. Her face had dropped when her Dad went out.

"Did they feed you all right in there?"

"It wasn't bad."

"You're not feeling sick?"

"Oh, no. That's wore off."

So she had been sick. No periods, morning sickness, and she knew she'd been with that lad. And she still turned around and said she didn't know she was pregnant. You'd need to be a bloody imbecile to believe that.

When the meal was over—Iris had to force the fried bread down, it stuck in her mouth like concrete—Brenda switched the telly on.

"You can put that off. You and me have a lot to talk about."

"I'll just put the plates in the sink."

She was bent double when she walked.

"You should be standing straighter than that, our Brenda. When d' y' say you had the stitches out?"

"Yesterday morning."

"You should straighten up after that."

"Yes, well. I was smashing this morning. I think I'm a bit tired."

She was gray with pain.

"Yeah, well, you're bound to be." Iris was not going to show too much sympathy. To give Brenda her due she hadn't asked for any. She looked at her daughter, sourly acknowledging a stoicism equal to her own. She wasn't impressed. She'd rather the girl had shown some sense.

They sat in silence; the tension between them tightened.

"Well, Brenda?"

"It's no use going on at me. I've said I won't tell you and I won't." The silence frightened her. "I don't care what you do."

"I'd only need to blow on you!" Silence again. "I suppose you do know?"

"Of course I do. I don't get on me back for just anybody, you know."

"No, Brenda, I don't know."

"He's not old enough to do anything."

"He was old enough to get you like it." Iris forced herself to swallow the bitterness. "Anyway," she went on, "I wasn't going to ask you who it was because I already know. There, that surprises you, doesn't it? I'll deal with that lot later. No, what I was going to ask you was, What are you going to do? That's more to the point, isn't it?"

"Have it."

"That's true! And then what? What about when it starts yelling and you're up all night and you still have to turn out to work in the morning? Because don't think your father's going to keep it, my girl, he isn't. And don't run away with the idea I'm giving my job up to look after it because I'm bloody not. I've done my share."

"I haven't thought."

"Well, think then."

"I can go in a hostel."

"No, you can't. You're not showing me up."

"I thought mebbe our Sheila . . ."

187

"Don't you think she's got enough on?"

"One more doesn't make much difference."

"Oh, doesn't it!"

"I can get another job. They might have me back at the bakery."

"They might. And who's going to look after it while you work?"

Brenda's tongue flicked across her lips. "Auntie Laura's in all day."

"You must be desperate! She'd fry the poor little sod."

"Well, the only other thing I can think of is the Day Nursery."

"Waiting list a mile long."

Brenda said nothing. She had turned her face away.

"And don't think you'll be going out much in the evenings either. I'm not stopping in with it while you're off gallivanting. For all I know, falling for another. You can forget that. I stopped in years with you lot. And I'm not stopping in no more."

"I'll manage."

"You don't know what you're taking on. It's not like baby-sitting, you know. You can't hand this one back when it screams."

"I'll manage."

It had gone on too long; she was hardening again. Iris said quickly, "I saw him the other day. He was stood outside the Chippy with his mates." She watched her daughter's reactions closely. "Laughing his bloody head off."

Silence.

"Well, Brenda, was it worth it?"

"You know it wasn't, so why ask?"

"Because you mightn't have to go through with it, after all." She saw Brenda flinch. After all this time hope was like a slap in the face. "I was talking to a friend of mine the other day—I say friend, she's a woman I wouldn't piss on if I had the choice. I used to know her, oh, a long time ago. When I

188

was young." Her mouth folded bitterly around the words. "She used to live opposite us. In Wharfe Street."

Brenda waited for her to go on.

"Big Irene. That's what we used to call her. She hasn't half gone down. I wouldn't 've known her."

Brenda waited again, impatiently.

"She used to help girls out of a jam."

"You mean get rid of it?"

"Yes."

"Did you mention me?"

"Of course. I wasn't looking her up for old times' sake."

Brenda would never know what it had cost her to go back to Wharfe Street, cap in hand to a woman like Irene. "She said she'd look at you."

"You mean . . ."

"I mean nothing. She said she'd look at you."

Brenda sat and thought. Her hand went down to her stomach. "The doctor said I was too far on."

"It's a question of what *you* want, Brenda. Nobody else can make your mind up for you."

"He said it was too dangerous."

"He said that because he was mad. And who wouldn't 've been? You took him for a trot, didn't you? Him and me."

Brenda sat there, leaden.

"He'd 've done yer, if you'd been open and above board. It was nowt to do with your ovary. It was the daft way you carried on."

"Oh, Mam, do you really think so?"

"I'm positive." She had told herself all this so often that in fact her voice did sound confident. Confident enough to take Brenda in.

There was a rush of color to her face that drained away as quickly as it came, leaving her even whiter than before. She said in a trembling voice, "Well, what are we sat here for?"

"You couldn't go like that."

"Couldn't I? Mam, I could walk over hot coals."

Iris breathed out, letting herself relax for the first time

since they'd started to talk. "Mind, it's your decision, Brenda. It's got to be. It's your bairn."

"I just want it out of me."

"Then you'd better get dressed."

Brenda stood up and started to hobble towards the door. Halfway there, she laughed and said, "This is no use." She straightened up, biting her lip. "I can't walk down the street like that."

"You sure you're all right?"

"We can't wait, Mam." At the door she turned. "It's going to be bad, isn't it? The pain."

"You're going to have pain no matter what you do."

Brenda started to say something else, then shut her mouth tight.

"Leaving it there another four months won't make it any easier."

"No, Mam, it's all right, I know."

Iris left her alone for a few minutes, then followed her upstairs to her room. Brenda was just pulling a dress over her head.

"I'm trying to think of what I've got that's loose," she said. "Anything tight rubs on the scar."

Scar was the wrong word. It didn't look anywhere near healed. There was a red part near the bottom of the wound that looked as if it might have pus behind it.

"Didn't they say anything about this, Brenda?"

"No. He seemed to think it was all right."

"Well, if he thinks so, it must be."

But she was frightened. She tried to think back to her own operation. When they'd took everything away from her, had it looked like that? Perhaps it had. She could only remember what it looked like after Ted kicked it.

"I'm not building up me hopes, Mam," Brenda said, after Iris had helped her do up the zip. "She could easy take one look at that and chuck us out."

"She might."

If she wasn't so desperate to get her hands on the money.

"After all, it's not the end of the world, is it?"

Brenda's self-control was slipping away. She had got herself so tightly screwed up to face the worst. Now there was a chance of escape . . . She could hardly cope with it.

"You put a bit of make-up on, flower, I'll just go and get me coat."

Iris went into her own room. Her hands were shaking. She thought, God forgive me if I'm doing wrong. She's only a bairn.

She opened the second drawer of her dressing-table and groped underneath a pile of clean underwear. Her fingers closed on a roll of notes. Nobody else knew about this money. She'd got it raked together in case Ted was made redundant, and she'd promised herself she wouldn't break into it for anything. Well, she was going to have to. She didn't know what Irene would charge. She'd been too flustered to go into all that. But she didn't expect it to be cheap.

As she withdrew the notes, her eye fell on a plastic crucifix she kept on top of her dressing-table. She wasn't what you could call religious, in fact she couldn't remember the last time she'd been in a church. The crucifix had been bought on a trip to the seaside in the sort of shop that sells souvenirs. But it wasn't just an ornament. It stood for the things she believed in, for what she felt about life. Whenever the problems of her own life threatened to overwhelm her she would get down on her knees in front of it and pray. But now this had happened and she couldn't pray. She couldn't justify what she was doing. What was kicking in Brenda's belly was a human being and try as she might she couldn't pretend it was anything else.

But there was no other way.

With a last furtive glance at her reflection in the mirror, she shoved the roll of notes into her handbag, and fled.

They walked past the Bingo queue on their way down the High Street. Iris was cursing herself: if she'd left it a bit later they'd 've missed all that.

"Aren't you coming tonight?" one woman shouted.

"No, I'm giving it a miss."

Several of the other women waved.

After they had passed, Iris said, "You're doing fine." Brenda's reply was to squeeze her mother's arm. She was in too much pain to speak.

They turned into Wharfe Street. Iris lifted her face to the drizzling rain. She could smell the river.

"Here we are."

They were quite big houses, some of them. Steps led up to them from the street.

"Doesn't look as if there's anybody in," said Brenda. "I hope she's not gone out."

"Perhaps she's at the Bingo!"

"Yeah. We probably just walked past her."

They giggled together like a pair of conspirators. Brenda, who was feeling light-headed with pain, sat down abruptly on the step. "I'll have to stop here, Mam. I don't think I could walk back."

"I'll see what's going on," said Iris, and climbed the steps. There were ten milk bottles on the top step, unwashed and turning green. Inside, dingy lino, and a table with uncollected mail: mainly postcards and circulars. It was a boarding house, sort of. Very sort of, if she knew Irene.

"What d' y' want?" a voice asked from the blackness at the top of the stairs.

Iris squinted into the darkness. "I'm looking for Big Irene."

"Who? Oh, Irene. She's on the top floor. Just go on up."

Big Irene had shrunk inside her skin, which was now as baggy as an old balloon. But she was still making an effort. There was blue irridescent eyeshadow on one wrinkled eyelid: she'd given up or got pissed before she reached the other. Her legs were bare and scaly, mottled with Granny's tartan. She'd always been one for sitting over the fire.

"Why didn't you ring, love? I'd 've come down."

"The woman said to come up."

Brenda fell into the nearest chair.

"What's the matter with her?"

"You know what's the matter."

"What else?"

"She's just come out of hospital. She's had her ovary out. At least I think they took it out." Iris realized she didn't know whether they had found anything wrong with the ovary or not. Perhaps it had all been put on. She licked her lips nervously. "Of course she's had the stitches out. They seemed to think at the hospital she was going on all right."

Irene was bending over the chair to peer into Brenda's face. "She's a funny color," she said, straightening up.

"Oh, she never has much color."

Irene pulled her thumb and forefinger together along her sunken jaw. Iris turned away so as not to see the struggle between fear and greed. And pity. Give the woman her due. It wasn't just the money.

When she could bear it no longer, she said, "Will it make a difference, the ovary and all that?"

"Oh, I shouldn't think so," said Irene. She didn't know what an ovary was but she wasn't going to admit ignorance. She'd always taken a pride in what she did. There wasn't a lot you could take a pride in these days. "No, I shouldn't think so. But I'll have a look at her. Make sure she's no further on than she says she is."

"Oh, I don't think . . ."

"One thing they all lie about, love, is that. It's bad enough if she's telling the truth." She looked sharply at Iris. Then turned to Brenda. "Howay, then, love, let's have a feel." Her fingers poked and prodded the white mound. "Yes. She's about as far on as she says. Well, love, it's not exactly a tiddler you've got in there, is it? You should've told yer Mam."

"I know I should. I just kept on hoping and praying I'd come all right. And then when I started getting the pains I thought it was coming away."

"How old are you?"

"Sixteen."

"Sixteen gone August," Iris said.

"Why won't they do her? I've known married women get them as easy as wink."

Iris swallowed hard. "He says he can't do her. But he's only saying that out of spite. She didn't tell him, you see. And of course he was livid."

"He should've known. You can practically see looking at her."

"Well, I can't say anything, 'cause I didn't know."

Irene looked down at Brenda, who seemed almost too tired to care what decision was reached.

"Well, you'd better lie down," Irene said at last. "It's not getting any smaller while we're stood here gassing."

"You're not going to do her now?" Iris said, forgetting that this was what she had hoped for when she came.

"Better get it over with," Irene said, in a loud, confident voice. Then whispered, "She'll not sleep for thinking about it."

"I'd rather get it over, Mam."

Iris made as if to open her handbag.

"Give it us later, pet."

There was a cup of tea on the table with cigarette butts floating on the dregs. She was a mucky cow. Iris twisted her hands together.

"You're not stopping, are you?"

"Oh, I couldn't leave her," Iris said, though she knew she would not be able to bear Brenda's pain.

"You go, Mam," Brenda said. "There's no sense us both suffering."

"Well, if you're sure you'll be all right. . . ."

Brenda grabbed hold of her hand and squeezed it hard. "I'll be all right."

"Course she will. That's a grand lass you've got there."

"I could kill the bastard."

"Aye, I know. It's an old saying, 'The sins they do by two, by two, they pay for one by one.' It's true, is that."

She touched Iris tentatively on the arm for a moment;

across the years that divided them, there was a flicker of friendship. "Give us half an hour," she said.

Brenda gave her mother one last, stricken look, then Iris staggered down the unlit staircase and out into the street.

It was still raining. She walked towards the river, past rows of houses boarded-up and waiting for demolition. She passed the place where in the last war a bomb had fallen and saw herself as a small child wandering across the blitzed ground. The tide was out, the river shrunken. She leant against the wall and gripped the iron spikes that ran along the top. They were wet and rusty: streaks of orange rain trickled on to her wrists.

Brenda might die. Iris wanted to run back, to stop it happening: the child would grow up as thousands before it had done. But she didn't. Instead she went on clinging to the spikes, pulling on them as if she was in pain.

Brenda got on to the bed. It sagged alarmingly under her weight. There was the sweetish smell of stale urine from the bucket underneath. It was full to overflowing: she couldn't 've emptied it for days.

Irene was busy in the room behind her. She couldn't see what she was doing, though she heard the chink of metal in a bowl. It was a bit like the dentist. You just had to lie back and look up at the light and listen to the sound of things being got ready. Except at the dentist you knew it was all right really. Even if you were frightened, you still knew. The pain wouldn't be unbearable, nothing would go wrong, you certainly wouldn't die. Here there were no limits. Pain stretched ahead of her like a tunnel that she was afraid, and compelled, to enter. Any amount of pain.

She closed her eyes briefly, and opened them to find Irene's face between her and the light.

"I'll just have another look," she said.

Her fingers prodded the white belly, digging in deep around the navel. She looked frightened. But she only said, "You've got a good little figure on you." Her eyes were all over, breasts as well as stomach. She was jealous to death. It was written all over her face.

If only she'd start.

"Right, then. Knees up. Let's be having you."

Brenda spread her legs and shut her eyes, shuddering as the old woman's fingers opened the lips of her cunt and started to probe inside.

Iris waited outside the door, afraid of what she might see when she opened it. Then she drew a deep breath and went in.

Brenda was sitting up in a chair, drinking a mug of hot tea, laced with whisky. She looked white and sweaty but managed a wobbly smile.

"How are you, love?" Iris asked.

"Oh, I'm all right. It wasn't as bad as what I thought it was going to be."

Iris turned to Irene, who was rinsing a bowl out at the sink. "How much do I owe you?"

"Oh, just give us ten quid."

It was cheaper than she had thought. Irene came towards her, drying her hands on a dirty tea towel. Iris handed the money over and as she did so Irene whispered, "If she doesn't start within the twenty-four hours you bring her back."

"But . . ." Iris looked at the girl and lowered her voice. "What do you mean?"

"It's not over, you know. She's got it all to come."

"I know that. But I thought you could more or less guarantee it starting?"

"No, I've known them come back nine, ten times before anything happened."

"My God, don't tell her that."

"She's like you, isn't she, Iris?"

"I don't think so."

"I do. She puts me very much in mind of you as a girl."

"Can I phone for a taxi?"

"I'd rather you didn't. I don't want her seen leaving."

In case anything happened. "All right. Brenda, have you finished your tea?"

Brenda stood up, and swayed. The two older women hurried across to support her. "Howay, love," said Irene. "Your Mam'll soon have you home."

They half dragged, half carried her to the door.

"Put a hot-water bottle in the bed, Iris. And get a bit of something in. Brandy."

The passed an off-license on the way to the taxi rank in the middle of the High Street. Iris went in and came out with a full bottle of brandy. Brenda looked at it, but she didn't say anything.

Curtains twitched all along the street as the taxi drew up outside their house. You didn't see many taxis. It was like an ambulance, almost. Iris thought, Nosey buggers. Still, I suppose I'd do the same.

She put Brenda to bed, filled the hot-water bottle, and sat down to wait.

Ted was home before closing time— a rare event.

"How is she?" he asked nervously, poking his head around the door.

"Bit restless. I'm stopping up with her."

"Is she all right?"

"Course she's all right. You go on to bed."

He stood there in his stockinged feet, holding his shoes in his hand.

"Goodnight, flower."

"Night, Dad."

Then he padded across the landing and shut the door.

He seemed to have shrunk since she married him. It wasn't just her imagination: there was a photograph of them on their wedding day and she hardly came up to his shoulder. Whereas now . . . Perhaps it was with his chest, perhaps it was just he hunched himself up. And she'd put on weight. They'd ranted and raved at her up at the hospital to lose weight. But she couldn't. It wasn't that she couldn't stop stuffing herself; she ate very little. She seemed to need the weight. She wouldn't 've known how to go on if she'd been thin.

Brenda moaned. Instantly, Iris was on her feet. "Is it starting?" she asked.

"I don't know. I think it might be." She looked up at her mother. "It doesn't hurt much," she said.

Not yet. Iris held on to her hand. She thought, It's funny—yesterday I could've killed her. Now if I could bear the pain for her I would.

By two a.m. Brenda's hair was stringy with sweat. She sat on the blue plastic bucket which sagged and pouched beneath her weight and tried to pee. Iris stood behind her, her hands on the girl's sides, and helped support her.

Brenda twisted round to look up at her mother. "How much longer, Mam?"

"I don't know, love. I don't know." She was almost sobbing herself.

"Can't even bloody well pee," Brenda said. And laughed.

"Let's have you back on the bed. Piss on the sheets, for Christ's sake! I've got the mattress well padded."

She heaved the girl back on to the bed. Brenda flopped back against the pillows, as white as they were, her face glistening with sweat. Iris offered her a swig of brandy, but she waved the bottle away.

"Is me Dad asleep?" She'd been moaning a bit earlier on, hadn't been able to stop herself.

"I think so, I don't know. Don't you worry about your Dad. Worry about getting that out of you."

The baby was born, alive, shortly after dawn. It was a boy.

For the final minutes, Brenda gripped the head of the bed, mouth wide open, lips stretched to splitting, like the other lips between her legs. At the last moment she looked down and—

"Eyes!" Iris said, putting a hand over her daughter's face, as the bag of membranes bulged out and burst.

"I didn't see it, Mam," Brenda said. "I mean I just caught a glimpse . . ." She stopped. "I didn't see it."

"Didn't you, love?"

"No. No, I didn't see it."

The baby clenched his fist feebly, lying on the floor of the lavatory with the *News of the World* spread over him.

Iris pulled back the sheets.

"It's all right, isn't it?" Brenda opened her eyes. She'd been drifting off to sleep.

"Oh, yes, it's all right."

"I'm not getting blood on the sheets, am I? I seem to be losing quite a bit."

"Oh, don't worry about the sheets. They'll wash."

"I'm not losing too much, am I?"

"Why no! Don't worry about it. I've had four bairns. I ought to know."

There had never been as much blood as this. Never.

Brenda's eyes closed. When she spoke again it was in a whisper. Iris had to bend down to hear what she said.

"It *was* dead, Mam, wasn't it?"

"It was never alive, flower. It's not a *baby*, you know."

A few yards away, on the floor of the lavatory, the rustling of the newspaper ceased.

Brenda was asleep. Iris knotted a scarf around her head and went to find her shopping basket. The worst was still to come.

She took the child and wrapped him in newspaper and laid him in the basket. Then she slipped out of the house and down the street to the row of derelict houses at the end. The door of one of the houses was loose. She had seen children playing inside it the other day on her way home from work. At the back, where the yard had been, was a heap of rubble.

It was raining. Still, mercifully, dark. She took the roll of sodden newspaper and began digging a grave in the rubble.

She hardly thought at all of what she was doing. Her mind was bound in by horror. Only her blood seemed to cry out against it. This was her own flesh and blood. She was burying her own flesh and blood.

When the last brick was heaped on top, when not a scrap of newspaper remained, she stood up and wiped away the dampness from her face, and never knew if it was tears or sweat or rain.

By the time she returned Ted had got himself up and off to work. She checked that Brenda was still asleep and that the flow of blood was no heavier. Then she went downstairs, slowly, like an old woman, and started to light the fire.

She thought of nothing; her whole being was preoccupied with the task of getting warm. As soon as the fire was lit she huddled over it, staring into the flames.

She felt rather than heard Laura come in. Rousing herself, she said, "Hello, cock. How are you?"

Laura didn't reply. Perhaps she was sulking. She hadn't wanted to stay with Iris's father. Iris forced herself to try again. "There's a cup of tea in the pot. Do you want one?"

Still no reply. Laura sat down in the far corner and fixed Iris with her stare.

Oh, God, keep me sane, thought Iris. This lot'd drive any bugger mad.

She turned back to the fire, resolving to pay no more attention to Laura. If the bleeding didn't slow down soon she'd have to get the doctor in. Of course he'd be nasty, but after all, what could he do? They'd got it out of her. That was all that mattered.

She did not hear Laura get up. She did not see her go across to the sideboard and pick up the heavy, cut glass vase. She huddled over the fire and thought about her daughter while Laura, with the solemnity of an executioner, lifted the vase high in the air and brought it crashing down on to her skull.

". . . and I wouldn't care, you know, but I still had me

rollers in. I've been picking bits of plastic out of me head ever since.'' Iris laughed heartily, patting the bump on her head. She was enjoying life again.

"She can't 've known what she was doing," Joss said. He had come rushing round as soon as he knew what had happened.

"Gerraway. She knew. We went to see her, didn't we, Ted? And she was sat up in bed, cool as a bloody cucumber. Wasn't she, Ted?"

"Never blinked."

"There you are. And she cracked on she didn't know who I was. Didn't she, Ted? But I could see it in her eyes. She knew. Mind you, what a carry-on. Two doctors come out to section her, you know. It's their fault for letting her out. She wasn't fit to be out. I said at the time, didn't I, Ted? I said, she's not fit to be out. Didn't I?"

"Aye."

"The doctor said, mind, if I hadn't turned me head that would've been it. It's a heavy vase. Well, you can see it is."

They all turned to stare at the vase.

"Anyway, Ted says he's not having her back. Not without a very big improvement. I told them that. It was a lady doctor and she looked at me and I said it's no use, that's what he says, it's his house. It's his decision. I believe in a man being master in his own house. Told her that, didn't I, Ted?"

"Yes," said Ted, not without irony.

Brenda came in, yawning. "Is me tea ready?"

"It's in the oven."

She trailed through in her dressing gown. The two men avoided looking at her. They were slightly shy with her still. There was a groan from the kitchen.

"Not liver again, Mam."

"You'll eat liver till you look like it," Iris said. "I want to see the roses back in your cheeks."

"Aw, Mam."

"Never mind, 'Aw, Mam'. And when you've eat it you can get dressed and give your bloody mucky face a wipe." She whispered to Joss. "She's playing the old soldier a bit now."

Ted stood up.

"Where you off to?"

"I thought I'd have a pint."

"Aye, and the other seven. Don't come back here drunk. I've had enough."

"A man isn't drunk till he's on the floor. You've never seen me drunk."

"Bloody hell." She turned her face away.

Ted nodded to Joss as he went out. Some people said Joss and Iris were having it off. He knew better. You'd need an ice pick.

"He's drinking heavy again," said Iris. "And he's picked a damn bad time. He wants to think on I don't have the bairns to see to now. If it gets too bad I can just up and off."

"But you wouldn't do that, would you?" Joss was alarmed more for himself than Ted. He came here like coming home.

"Wouldn't I!"

There was silence. Joss stretched his legs out and said, "I see Joanne Wilson's married."

"Aye, I saw. Big wedding."

"That was his Mam."

"It's often the case, isn't it?"

"She was in two minds, you know. Right up till the end."

"I know. I met her mother in the street. She said, Iris, we're doing all this, and do you know when it comes to the point I don't think she'll go."

"Poor kid."

"Oh, you don't want to worry about Joanne. She'll give as good as she gets."

"Aye, but it's no life, is it?" He stood up. "Will you be going to see your Laura?"

"Oh, yes."

"Well, you know, if you want a lift . . ."

"It'd be a big help. I couldn't just leave her stuck in there. You look at some of them poor buggers and my God you wonder."

Sheila came in with her husband and the baby and the

conversation became general, light-hearted even. After they had all gone Iris carried the baby to the sofa and put the lights out. Then she crooned to him, softly, while the flames flickered over his face. He was flushed: the blood bloomed in him. Iris pressed her face into his little chest and his hands came up and tangled in her hair.

She thought of Sheila and Bobbie. She'd been scared stiff when they got married, Sheila had been so young. But they were happy: Sheila would never have to put up with what she'd had to put up with. And they'd got this boy. She slid her hand underneath him, feeling the curve of his bottom warm against her palm.

Unbidden came the memory of the other child, red as raw meat, gasping its life out on the lavatory floor.

She banished the image which always, in her rare moments of silence and solitude, returned to haunt her. She turned to the living child. Looking down at him, she saw his mother in the curve of his cheek and brow. It was almost like having Sheila a baby again. She nuzzled into his chest, hearing his heart beat, and the warmth consoled her. Her breath mingled with his breath.

VI

Blonde Dinah

George Harrison never hurried on the way home. He lingered by the river, leaning over the stone wall. He lit a pipe, the last of the day, and revelled in it. Beneath him the oily river slabbed against the wall, briefly irridescent where the light of a street lamp fell on it. He was alone, but he was not lonely. "Lonely" was watching Crossroads because you couldn't think of anything to say. "Lonely," was the other body in the bed.

"What the bloody hell are you going to do?" One of the blokes had asked him that his last week at work.

"Me?" he'd asked, rather nettled by the question. "Me? Nowt. After forty year I reckon I've done my stint."

He couldn't remember now whether he meant what he said, for retirement had produced such a division in his life that everything on the other side of it seemed dim. They weighed on him now, those forty years. He spoke of them with bitterness, where once he spoke with pride.

204

They gave him a clock. Well, they gave everybody a clock. And for a few months he had sat and looked at it. There were afternoons when the time went so slowly that he was sure it had stopped. Time and time again he would get up and put it to his ear, but he could never hear it ticking: the blast-furnaces had seen to that. Only after a while he would notice that the minute hand had moved. So that was all right: he was still alive.

His wife hated having him in the house. She would bang and clatter the pots in the kitchen, and he found himself listening tensely to this, unable to read the paper. When she cleaned the living room, the vacuum cleaner was thrust aggressively between his legs. Well, you could understand that. She was used to having the place to herself. She was used to being able to get on with her jobs.

But even when the family came it wasn't much different. It was, "Hello, Dad. How are you, Dad?" But it was their Mam they came to see. He didn't begrudge it her. She'd been a good mother, none better. But at times he envied her, she seemed so secure, with her children and grandchildren around her.

He spent as little time at home as he could. Though finding somewhere else to go was a problem. He tipped his pension up to Gladys and relied on her to give him what pocket money she thought he should have. Well, he couldn't do any other: there was little enough to keep them on as it was. Though he suspected the kids helped her out a bit, now and then. But his pocket money went nowhere. A couple of pints, a tin of tobacco, and that was it. Finish.

At first he'd tried to keep up with his mates from work. Not for long. It was too uncomfortable, sitting there trying to work out whether he could afford to stand his turn. Not that they expected it of him: they didn't. He expected it of himself.

And after a while the talk left him behind. The names, even some of the processes, were new. There was talk of new contracts, which didn't materialize, and of further redundancies, which did. None of it affected him. He gradually saw less and less of his mates. Eventually the meetings in the pub stopped altogether. He told himself bitterly that nobody wanted you when you were old, that everybody seemed to think you were after something—money, or a drink. But in fact they were not avoiding him. He was avoiding them.

Then there was only the park. In good weather. He sat on a bench at some distance from the other old men who tended to congregate together and sun themselves, wrinkled necks thrust out of knotted scarves, cautiously, like tortoises peering out of their shells.

In bad weather there was the reading room of the library. If the park had depressed him, the library terrified him. For there the real derelicts ended up, sitting at the benches muttering to themselves, pretending to read the *Freethinker*, or *Country Life*, or the *Christian Science Monitor*. They were dirty. They picked their noses and rolled the results between thumb and forefinger, making a pellet hard enough to be flicked away on to the floor. They made noises. They made smells. They were afraid. For the assistants in the library, lads and lasses in their late teens, had power over them and they knew it. They had the power of banning people from the library, of withholding warmth. So sandwiches were consumed furtively, a bit at a time. And those who were compelled to talk to themselves, thrashing out some unending internal feud, tried to do so quietly, though they did not always succeed.

One of the assistants had the habit of walking round the benches. He did so once when George was there and George was horrified to realize that the fear on everybody else's face was reflected in his own. He left at once and never went back.

He was not like that, he told himself. No, definitely not. Though it was hard to maintain any sense of dignity.

Then Gladys got herself a job: nothing much, just a part-time job in the canteen at the local school. But it was enough. He was up the labor exchange like a bolt from a gun.

Give me anything, he said. I don't care what it is. Just as long as it's work.

It was a job in a lavatory. He had to mop the floors and generally keep things clean. It didn't take long, and the rest of the time he just sat. Still, it was work. Money in his pocket. Independence.

Once he came back from work a bit early and heard Gladys and the two girls laughing. He stood outside the kitchen door and listened. The idea of him cleaning out a lavatory was a huge joke, it seemed. He never let on he'd heard, just went back to the front door and staged a second, noisier, entrance. But it hurt all right.

Though there was still the money in his pocket for a drink or a smoke. He jingled the coins now. Money in your pocket. It was everything. You never knew how important it was, till you hadn't got any.

He drifted along, thinking of nothing. Then he became aware of other steps shuffling along some distance behind, on the other side of the road. His stomach tightened. There were said to be people still living in the derelict houses by the river: down-and-outers, no goods, people what'd cut your throat for a tanner and think nothing of it. He was an old man. The days when he could have tackled anybody were finished.

But a second later he was reassured. It was a woman's step. She staggered out into the light of a street lamp and he knew her at once by the brassy blonde halo of hair. Now there was somebody *ought* to think about retirement. In that job forty year was enough!

And she couldn't 've been at it much less. For as long as he could remember she had been a legend. Blonde Dinah: sitting in the pubs all along the High Street, waiting for some man or other to walk into the trap. She never gave up. Sometimes for a few evenings she might be missing, and they thought perhaps she'd packed it in at last. But no. The next night, or the night after, she was back, perched on a bar stool, sweat breaking through the layers of make-up.

He turned back to the river, hardly sparing her a glance. Soon he would have to go home, get undressed in the kitchenette so as not to wake Gladys, and carry his shoes up the stairs to bed avoiding the second and the seventh step, which creaked.

He went on leaning against the wall. After a while he became aware that Dinah was staggering towards him. He was irritated. There was enough room surely to God, there was the whole width of the bloody road for her to get past. Unless . . .

"Least it's stopped raining," she said.

He didn't reply.

"This afternoon I thought it was never going to stop."

She waiting for him to speak. "What's wrong with you, then? Cat got your tongue?"

"Not tonight," he said, hearing the words rasp in his throat. He sounded as awkward as a boy. "Thanks all the same."

"What do you mean, 'Thanks all the same'? Far as I know there's nowt been bloody offered. All I said was, it's stopped raining. It has stopped raining, hasn't it?"

"Yes!"

"Well, then."

She muttered to herself for a few minutes. He heard, "Dear God, if you can't say . . ."

He let her talk. She was hugging her grievance as if for warmth. He felt sorry for her. She must be sixty. At least. Same age as Gladys. No age to be hawking it around the pubs. He wondered what she charged now. Must be giving it away.

"I used to live around here, you know. Bit further down. Wharfe Street." She stood with her back to the river, looking at the row of derelict houses opposite. "Good houses, you know. Some of 'em."

"Car parks."

She glanced at him. "Oh, so you can talk. Yes, car parks. Can't build flats because of the chemicals in the air. Not fit to breathe. My God, they took their time finding that out."

She cleared her throat. The cough got out of hand. Soon she was bent double, clinging to the wall. When, finally, she straightened up there was a blue-black tear running down the side of her nose. She brushed it away carefully with the tip of one gloved finger. The gloves were made of pale gray suede: they added an incongruous note of gentility to her appearance. As though taking her cue from them, she went on in a distinctly refined tone, "And whereabouts do you live?"

"Union Street."

"Oh, yes. Behind the Bluebell."

"That's right."

"Is it coming down around there?"

"No. Not Union Street anyway. Just the bit at the end, and Ewbank Street. And the little streets near the railway line."

"I think it's a crying shame. I don't like to see them come down."

Well, she wouldn't, would she? Her old stalking grounds. But he listened to her talk. The cracked and seamed face lit up, her voice came out warm and spluttery between badly fitting teeth, and her hands, shaping the darkness, re-created a community, as she talked about the past, about the people she had known.

He found himself wondering about her, about what she was like, like . . . well, like. She must get sick of it surely, not to mention sore. Gladys . . . but then Gladys was different. He doubted if they did it twice a year. He left her alone as much as he could, and he believed she understood that and was grateful to him. So that when finally he had to go to her she didn't mind so much because she knew he'd been doing without. Women, decent women that was—well, anyway, Gladys, didn't go too much on that sort of thing.

But perhaps Dinah didn't either? Perhaps it was just a job, like cleaning out lavatories was just a job?

"Course there was no telly then or owt like that, was there?" she added, after a short pause. "People had to make their own amusement."

"Aye, and they were the better for it, 'n' all."

"They were."

"There's over much on tap these days. Nobody has to try for anything."

There was silence again, a companionable silence this time. He sniffed the air: sometimes, standing by the river, you could smell the dawn, hours and hours before the light in the sky changed. It was a marvelous time: all the tension, all the bitterness dissolved away and you were left waiting, waiting for whatever life turned up.

"Do you fancy a walk around my place, then?"

The question ought to have jarred on him. It ought to have been answered at once by a brusque "No". But it wasn't. And by the time he opened his mouth to say "No", he'd realized it wasn't what he wanted to say.

He turned and walked along the river path beside her.

"What do they call you?" she asked.

"George."

"Oh, that's nice. George George is it, or George summat else?"

"Harrison," he admitted. He was reluctant to let her know too much. He was wondering what he'd let himself in for. The clap, most like.

"I'm Dinah," she said.

He wondered whether to say "I know" and decided against it. She was drunk enough to think he was getting at her if he cracked on he knew who she was.

He was dragging his feet. He couldn't remember how this had happened. But he didn't have to go through with it. He could turn and walk away. A smell of beer and cheap scent decided him. He was off.

"Howay, then," she said, tugging at his sleeve like a little girl.

"Look," he said. "I'm not as flush as I was."

"A quid. Or whatever you can manage."

A quid. It should have been disgusting. His mind supplied the word "sordid". Only it wasn't. The raw, cheap scent caught at his throat.

"Go on," she said. "Give yourself a treat. You never know, you might enjoy it."

"No . . ."

But he had given in. They both knew it.

"It's not far. Just round the next turning, in fact."

Though the houses on either side of them now were boarded-up and derelict. Their footsteps echoed along the empty street.

"More to life than money, isn't there?"

"You're drunk," he said.

"Be thankful. Mightn't fancy you if I was sober."

He was beginning to have visions of a dirty mattress on the floor of an uninhabited house. But no. They turned into another street, where the houses had glass in the windows and curtains up.

"This is it," she announced. "We're here."

A strip of sooty grass. Steps leading down into the street. She fumbled for the key.

Then they were inside. Postcards lined up on a table, a creeping smell of drains, and . . .

"Mind them milk bottles. Knock that lot over and we'll have the whole house awake."

They staggered up the stairs together, she making exaggerated shushing sounds, he stumbling and leaning against her as though he was the one who was drunk. But it produced a sort of intimacy, a feeling of being conspirators. He was beginning to enjoy himself.

The light at the top of the stairs changed all that. The bed was gray, unmade. It seemed to fill the room. She kicked off her shoes. "Thank God for that," she said.

It was what Gladys always said at the end of the day. The tingling in his groin stopped. He sat down on a chair near the door and started to take off his shoes. Slowly.

There were photographs on the table beside the bed. Old ones. Yellow with age. An unshaded light bulb swung in the draught from the door. Not in a million years. He started to say something, but her hands were already on him.

"I don't seem . . ."

"Oh, it'll do all right, will this." She pressed his cock into the valley between her wrinkled breasts. "Why, man, it's like a steel rod!"

It wasn't. As a matter of fact it was nowt like. Her shammy-leather breasts enclosed him. He had never sat astride a woman like this before or even imagined it to be possible. Almost in spite of himself he started to thrust, but it was no good. Then her hand went down between her legs and came up again. She smeared cunt-juice all over his nose and mouth.

He was shocked. But then the smell started to get to him. People said fish, but it wasn't fish. It was wet seaweed, and rock pools and the sand shifting in between your toes.

"Nowt wrong with that, is there?" She had rolled his foreskin back. When he didn't speak she laughed and said, "Here, give us a lick."

She took him into her mouth.

It was morning when he woke. He lay for a moment, dazed, looking at the clothes and shoes scattered on the floor, wondering how the bedroom came to be in such a mess. Then, remembering, he got up and started to hunt for his clothes.

They had taken everything off. Both of them. He didn't know, now, whether he was shocked or pleased.

He looked down at her. She looked like Gladys lying there, her mouth open, a wisp of hair shaken with every breath. It disturbed him. She ought not to look like Gladys. He had always believed there were two sorts of women: the decent ones and the rest. He felt they should look different, for how could you tell them apart, how could you remember they were different, if every sag, every wrinkle of their used bodies proclaimed that they were one flesh? There was even a dark line down her belly, stretching from navel to groin. At some stage she must have borne a child. Though he had never heard of her having any family.

He looked down at his own body, at his limp cock, and

212

gave the knob a friendly squeeze before he pulled up his pants.

He was in a hurry to be gone. He counted out some money, quietly, so that she should not wake. He put it down on the bedside table by the photographs. After a moment's reflection he took one two-bob bit back again: there was no need to go overboard. He thought, I could walk out without paying. But no, he didn't want to do that. And besides she might wake. Sleeping like that with her mouth open, thirst would wake her before long.

She was lying with her legs apart. The mound of hair was going thin on top, as though frequent shaving had made it lose heart. He had never actually seen it before. It was funny in a way. You spend your whole boyhood thinking about it, wondering what it's like; but when you finally get it you don't really *see* it. He had never seen Gladys naked. Not with everything off.

Almost against his will, he knelt down until it was on a level with his face. The lips gaped, still dribbling a little milky fluid. And there it was. A gash? A wound? Red fruit bitten to the core: It was impossible to say what it was like.

She stirred in her sleep, tightening her thighs as though aware of some need to protect herself. He took one last look and went. He almost ran down the stairs, unloading guilt behind him at every step.

The sun was shining. He stood on the steps and breathed deeply before setting off in the direction of the river. His step was jaunty. He was on the way to being his old self again: the self that would look back on this night's work with a mixture of pride, amusement, and shame.

Through the few remaining chinks in his perception, the morning struck at him. Seagulls screamed and dived in the air above the river. And one detached itself from the rest to fly under the steel bridge; wings, briefly shadowed, gleamed in the restored light.

The air made his lungs hurt. He remembered John Scaife who had died two months back, not much more than half his age. He was sorry for it but, remembering, stood taller. He thought of how much life there was still to live, of how much life there was inside him. You're not dead, no, not till they nail down the lid.

He did not think of Dinah, who stirred in her sleep and woke, aware of the empty bed.

A tom cat with tattered ears crossed his path. Though he did not normally care for cats, he exchanged a glance with this one: cynical and accepting. The cat stared back at him. Their paths converged, crossed, separated. He went on his way, whistling now. God knows what he would find to say when he got there, but he was glad to be going home.

VII

Alice Bell

It was January now. Alice Bell spent her days in bed: it was her solution to the price of coal. Whenever she moved newspapers stirred and rustled all around her. The bed was full of them. She had read somewhere that newspapers were as good as blankets, and the house was cold.

There wasn't a lot of fat on her to keep her warm. Her thighs were folds of creased skin, hanging from the bone. Yet beside her on the bed was a black handbag with £100 inside. She had saved it out of her social security money: the "pancrack" as she contemptuously called it. What she got was barely adequate for heating and food. To save out of it, as she was determined to do, meant hunger and cold. Though she didn't usually feel hungry: she had been depriving herself of food too long for that.

She liked the feel of the notes, especially if she was lucky enough to get a new one, though the old, crumpled ones also had their charm. But she liked best to crisp the new ones through her fingers. When she was alone she would often take them out and count them. And yet she was not in the usual sense of the word a miser. This was no meaningless accumulation of money for its own sake. She was saving up for her funeral.

As a little girl, more than seventy years ago, she had witnessed the funerals of paupers. And she still remembered the old rhyme:

> *Rattle his bones*
> *Over the stones.*
> *He's only a pauper*
> *Whom nobody owns.*

Children followed the coffins, jeering sometimes, and throwing stones. Perhaps she'd been one of them, she didn't remember. But the horror of that final rejection had stayed with her all her life. The death grant would not bury her. Inflation had made her small insurance policy useless. And there had to be a proper funeral, paid for out of her own money. Her self-respect, her dignity as a human being, required it. And so she had to save. And starve.

Her other dread was the Workhouse. As a small child on her way to school she had walked past its gates, never without a shudder. It was still in use, though they called it something different now. But to her it would always be the Workhouse: the place paupers' funerals started from.

The "pancrack" she had to submit to: there was no choice. She was entitled to nothing else. You could get what they called a seventy pension, but the man had explained to her that it was really the same thing. Her second husband had been self-employed and too mean to pay a stamp. Every six months she received a visit from the social security people, to find out if her circumstances had changed. The humiliation of these visits, the posh voices, the questions, the eyes everywhere, only strengthened her determination to preserve her independence at all costs. To hang on to her house, to save up for her funeral, and never, never to ask them for a penny more than she was forced. She wasn't going to lie in a pauper's coffin, and she would never, while she had breath in her body, let them talk her into the Workhouse.

"Them buggers have been here again," she would say to Iris King.

"Well, and you shouldn't let them upset you."

"Asking bloody questions. Begrudging you every penny you get."

"T'isn't coming out of their pockets."

"You'd think it was, but."

"Ah, well. You want to think: they'll be old themselves one day."

And so Iris soothed her. And she let herself be soothed.

A stranger coming into the room would hardly have noticed, at first, that there was a body in the bed, for Alice's emaciated frame scarcely raised the covers, and her skin, over the years, had yellowed to the same shade as the pillowcases and the wall: smoke-cured. The room was always full of smoke because the chimney backs were broken and the smoke from her neighbor's fire poured into the house. When she was still well enough to leave the house, she had always carried with her the smell of smoke. The smoke formed layers of soot on all the furniture. You could dust it one minute, and it would be there again the next.

Still she loved the house. Over the years it had become a refuge. Finally, almost an extension of her own body. ·

It hadn't always been so. For Iris King, Union Street was a move up. For Mrs. Bell, it was down. At first she hated it. The house was dark and drab, and it needed so many repairs. The kitchen tap shook and juddered whenever you turned it on, producing a thin trickle of brown water and a shower of plaster from the walls.

Iris King had tried to decorate the kitchen for her, but she'd had to give up in the end.

"I'm sorry, Mrs. Bell," she'd said. "I just daren't mess on with this paper. It's holding up the wall."

And they'd both had a good laugh because incredibly the old music-hall joke was true.

But afterwards Mrs. Bell had felt a bit depressed. She was used to better. Her last house had had a bathroom and an indoor lavatory, with a little strip of green out the back. She'd had a bay window in the front room, too.

You take these things for granted till you haven't got them. The descent to Union Street was bitter.

More than anything else she hated the steam hammer. At first she hadn't known what it was. She thought the neighbors were banging. When it went on and on, she even began to think they might be doing it deliberately to persecute her.

Her nerves were very bad that first winter in the street. She'd just had an operation on her eyes and it'd gone wrong. She came out of hospital so low that for the first time in her life she thought about suicide. The depression went on and on. Sometimes, driven to desperation by the rhythmic banging, she would switch on the vacuum cleaner and leave it running for hours. Anything to get her own back.

Then she became afraid. Nobody else seemed to hear the banging. Perhaps it was inside her head? She didn't trust herself, not since the operation. And it was the first winter alone after her husband's death. Anything seemed possible. Gradually, by trying to trace the sound from street to street, she realized it was coming from the engineering works on the other side of the railway line. The fear loosened its grip. The other women in the street didn't hear it because they had lived with it so long. Only when it stopped there was an odd, uneasy, waking expression on their faces. They were short-tempered, and at odds with everything until it started again.

She avoided the other women as much as she could. She would even go to the shops along the back alley, "arch" they called it round here, to avoid meeting them. She was ashamed of her poverty, and of the changes that sickness and pain had wrought in her appearance. She hardly knew her own reflection in the glass. And to meet other people, to present to them this transformed, deformed self, was more than she could bear.

Gradually over the years her health got worse, until she was confined to the house and almost bedridden. Immediately the neighbors she had ignored began coming to the door to offer help, tentatively at first, alert for the least sign of a rebuff; then as a matter of course. They shopped, made tea, lit the fire.

"You rely on them too much, Mam," her son said, whenever he came to see her. She was a worry to him. He was horrified by the confinement of her life, which seemed to him an almost vegetable form of existence. And he foresaw a time when she would not be able to manage in her own home, even with the neighbors' help.

"I've got good neighbors," was all she would say.

"But there's limits to what you can expect neighbors to do."

At the back of his mind was the fear that he might one day have to offer her a home. And it would be the end between him and his wife.

"They've no need to do anything."

"Oh, don't talk so daft."

The situation improved when Iris King became her home help, for Iris came in far oftener than she was officially supposed to do, even calling in late at night to make sure that all was well. And, through Iris, Alice was bonded into the street in a way she had never been before.

There would be silence until Iris got the fire going, then she would start on her news. "Well, we had a bit of luck last night. Ted did, rather. You know how he never goes to the Bingo? Says he'd rather have a drink? Well, last night his stomach was a bit upset so he said he'd have a walk down with us. Bugger me if he didn't shout on the last house. Didn't even know he was sweating. Hundred and twenty quid. And I wouldn't care but he only gets one book. He can't manage any more. And there's me sat there, four books and not even a line. Anyway he give Joss and me a fiver and then off he went around the Buffs. It had cured his stomach, see. Well, I thought he'd come back in a right state, but no, give him his due, he didn't. Then just as he was getting into bed, no warning, out it comes. He's gunna buy a horse.''

Mrs. Bell thought bitterly that they had won more at Bingo in one night than she had saved from years of starvation. She said, ''Where's he going to keep it?''

''Well, that's just it. First off he said he was going to rent one of them garages up at the end. I said, Ted, you can't keep a horse in a garage, it's cruel, and besides who's going to muck it out?'' She paused, whisking a sheet of newspaper away from the fire in a cloud of smoke. ''So now he's on about tethering it up on the Moor. I said to him I said, What about winter? You can't leave it stuck out there all year.''

There were times when, much as Mrs. Bell loved Iris, she found herself counting the minutes until she left. Her life seemed to be lived at too fast a pace and on too large a scale. Even vicariously, it was exhausting.

''He's always wanted a horse. That's what he says. First I knew of it. But there you are, you see. You think you know people, you think you've got them summed up, but you haven't. There's always summat. There's always summat they come out with and you say, My God.''

''I don't know how she stays sane,'' said Mrs. Harrison, who lived directly opposite.

''She gets very low.''

''She's always seemed cheerful whenever I've had owt to do with her.''

''She puts a good face on it. What else can you do?''

Mrs. Harrison had her own problems, and they'd got worse since her husband retired. ''It's no use, I can't be doing with him stuck under me feet all day. I'm used to being able to get on and get done. And he's not cheerful company. There's hardly a word out of him and when he does speak it's nothing pleasant. I wish he'd die or go and stay with their Freda. Give me a rest.''

The long marital battle was over. There was nothing much left, now, whether of love or hate. Only a weak vindictiveness remained. She remembered all the nights in the first years of their marriage when he'd turned her out of doors in her nightdress, sometimes with a baby in her arms. "And I was stuck in the coal hole all night, because I was too ashamed to go and knock the neighbors up and it was too far to walk to me Mam's. Oh, I know he's changed, he can be as nice as pie when it suits him. But I don't forget."

Dimly, through the years of bitterness and struggle, glowed memories of a happier time. "You'll think me stuck up for saying this, but I was a lovely lass. The lads used to fight over who was going to walk me home from Chapel I was, I was beautiful." She sat with her head bowed, contemplating a past so distant that no vanity could be involved. "When I think: I could've had me pick. They were all after me, you know. Not that they got anywhere. Not an inch above the knee. Well, it was like that then, wasn't it? We just didn't think of anything like that."

Mrs. Bell, who had, to her cost, remained silent.

"And then I had to go and get stuck with him."

"Now then, he must've been the one you wanted."

"He was the one I got stuck with." Her face softened slightly. "He was a handsome fella. What me Mam would've called a good-looking nowt."

"She gives me the creeps does that old bugger," said Iris. "Always praying and singing hymns and telling everybody what a clean-living woman she is. Bad-minded old cow."

Mrs. Bell did her best to keep the peace. She relied on her neighbors, it was true. But she gave back more than her son ever understood. To the younger women, particularly Iris, she was almost a mother. And to the older women, like Mrs. Harrison, she was a friend they could rely upon not to gossip behind their backs. But there was a certain amount of jealousy.

"It's her hats that get me," said Iris. "Where on earth does she find them?"

"Jumble sales."

"There's no need for that. Well, is there?"

"Don't ask me. I don't know how much she has coming in."

Iris had to be content with that. "Have I to light the fire?" she asked. There were rumors of a miners' strike and Mrs. Bell was trying to economize on coal.

"Yes, you'd better."

"I was raking through the kitchen drawer the other night. I've got some candles left over from the last lot, I know I have, but I'm blowed if I can put me hands on them."

"Do you remember how short they got?"

"Do I? I swore I'd never be caught like that again."

"He'll go to the country this time. He'll have to. He's got himself into such a bloody hole."

"I wouldn't care if he was the only one in it."

There was a cold spell towards the end of January. The women of Union Street had to cope with the problem of keeping themselves and their families warm. There were continued reports that the miners were about to go on strike.

Mrs. Bell had a final look at the deaths, muttering the names under her breath as her magnifying glass moved down the page. The list was longer now. After making sure there were no familiar names she pushed the blankets back and added the newspaper to those already in the bed. She tried to do without a fire in the afternoon, so that she could have heat at night when the temperature dropped. Though she had a lot of faith in the newspaper, too. Tramps covered themselves with it, didn't they, and they should know.

Iris had discovered some coal in one of the corner shops and was carrying it home on her back. At the corner of the street she paused to get her breath. Further along, bending down, was the large black-clad arse of Mrs. Harrison. Out gathering again. George Harrison'd drop dead if he ever found out.

As Iris drew level Mrs. Harrison straightened up.

"Now then."

"Now then!"

Iris watched as Mrs. Harrison picked up another french letter and transferred it to the Co-op carrier bag she always

222

carried on these expeditions. Iris was outraged, but said nothing. She was in a hurry to get to one of her old men.

Later they met in Mrs. Bell's house, where Iris had gone to light the fire.

'Well, Missis, did you get a good haul?"

"Only eight."

"Only, she says. That's eight cold bums clagged against somebody's back yard wall. Buggered if I know what they see in it this weather."

"I could never see what they saw in it any weather," Mrs. Bell said.

"Aye, but last night! Freeze anything off. You want to watch yourself, Missis. One of these days you'll pick one up and It'll still be inside!"

Mrs. Harrison didn't like Iris King, who was loud-mouthed, vulgar and irreligious. She turned away slightly and stared at the empty grate.

"I wonder how long it'll be before they settle this lot."

"As long as it takes," said Mrs. Bell.

"There's a lot of greed in it if you ask me. What is it they're asking? Eighty quid?"

"No more than a face-worker's worth. They risk their lives."

"Aye, and there'll be a few lives risked if they go on strike. Old people."

"They'll see the old people don't suffer."

"Oh, aye? Seems to me the more people suffer the better they're pleased. That's what it's about isn't it? Blackmail."

"Shut your face, woman. You don't know what you're on about."

"I know what I get to keep him and me on. And it's a bloody sight short of eighty quid." Mrs. Harrison had carried her own extra coal home earlier in the day and her mouth was still blue from the strain. She looked as if she'd grown a moustache. "Once this is over the price of coal'll rocket. And you know what that means." She lowered her head stubbornly: her political opinions were no less passionately held than

Mrs. Bell's. They linked her with her country childhood. She'd had a pig's bladder hanging up in her back kitchen for years after she married George. And bunches of herbs.

But Mrs. Bell was struggling to sit up. Socialism was more than politics to her. It was almost a religion, a way of life.

Iris hurried in with a change of subject.

"I see it says in the paper Alice Street's to come down. And Walker Street. All along there."

"Bloody good houses, some of them," Mrs. Bell said. "That's your Tory government."

"You mean, that's your Labor Council. Government has nowt to do with it."

No topic brought peace. Shortly afterwards they parted, and for once they did not part friends.

"Lock the door as you go out," Mrs. Bell shouted to Iris. She lay in the darkness, trying to get her breath and her temper back.

She remembered her youth: the meetings, the speeches, heckling, canvassing, marching. There wasn't much she'd learned in the Depression that still made sense in the seventies. And yet. She was poorer now than she'd been then. And worse housed. Then, she'd had a lovely little Council house in Briar Road, with a garden and a window at either end of the living room. It had been a lovely house. When she looked back that was what she regretted most: leaving Briar Road. She didn't regret the meetings, or the marches. She'd 've done all that again.

Oh, but it was cold. She pulled her aching feet up the bed and tried to tuck her nightdress round them. And then she realized. No fire. They'd gone out without lighting it. Bugger it. Well, she couldn't go knocking on people's doors this hour, even if she could get that far. She'd just have to fend for herself. And she'd have to do something. The living room was like an ice-box.

She sat up. There was no coal in the bucket, or not much. Not enough anyway. That meant a trip across the yard. Probably several trips: she couldn't carry much at a time. So much for bloody politics. No, it was no use—she couldn't go. She only had a nightie on and a dressing gown, and the air outside was freezing. She would just have to make the best of it.

Half an hour later a hand rattled her doorknob. It might be Iris. She shouted as loudly as she could, but it was no use. She heard the footsteps go away. Even if it was Iris she could easily think somebody else had come in to light the fire. That was the trouble. It wasn't anybody's job. She had to rely on people doing it out of kindness.

The sound of her voice crying out in the night told her how frightened she was. They were always on at you to keep warm. You couldn't open the paper without somebody going on about hyper-whatever-it-was. There was nothing else for it: she would have to go and get the coal.

She put the light on. The floor near the hearth was covered with silverfish, millions of them, all scurrying for cover. They only came out in the dark. It was better than blackclocks though. They'd had them at home when she was a bairn. But even the silverfish . . . You didn't fancy walking over them in your bare feet. She waited till they were all gone before hobbling across to find her slippers.

She stood on the back-kitchen doorstep, bucket in one hand, stick in the other, nerving herself to face the trip across the yard. The air was so cold it seared her lungs. She pulled the scarf up round her mouth and set off.

Frost glittered on the surface of the yard. An emaciated moon looked down. She began slithering and clanking her way across to the coalhouse. The rubber tip of her stick slipped on the ice and her heart bulged into her throat with fear. Halfway across she stopped to get her breath. There was a waterfall of icicles near the drainpipe where the gutter had overflowed. She'd have to see about getting that fixed.

Then on again.

Snow had blown in through the open door of the coalhouse. She raked about looking for the smaller pieces that might burn more easily. She was very tired. She had to stop when the bucket was only half-full: she could not carry more than that, not with the stick to manage as well.

She set off back. But haste and growing exhaustion led her to take the nearest way, across the center of the yard, forgetting that the drain as well as the gutter overflowed. There was a sheet of black ice and no time to feel fear before she was falling, falling, the world tilting above her head. Then there were stars like pinpoints of frost and the black wires of a telegraph pole cutting into the sky.

She felt no pain, though the fall had knocked the breath out of her. After a while she thought she ought to move her legs, and that was all right, they did move.

The coal had fallen out of her bucket. It lay scattered across the ice.

There was still an orange glow in one of the windows next door. But they had the telly on too loud. Bursts of music and laughter came out and fractured themselves on the ice. She would never be able to make them hear. Even if she could manage to shout. She wasn't sure she could. Her tongue seemed to be very big inside her mouth. She tried to shout, but only a whisper came out. It was no use. Anyway, she needed all her breath to get back on her feet.

She tried to push herself up, but her fingers slid across the ice enclosing a mess of coal dust and frozen snow. The shock had worn off. She was afraid now, and in pain. Her back hurt. But fear was the worst thing. She couldn't get up and if she went on lying there she would die.

Then she thought of using her stick. Not to lean on: the rubber tip got even less purchase on the ice than her hands had done. No, but if she could manage to hook it around the drainpipe she might be able to pull herself towards the wall where there was no ice, like an angler landing a fish. But the handle wouldn't hook around the pipe. And her outstretched hand trembled so much that she dropped the stick and had to start all over again. Finally, she managed to hook the handle round the pipe, but now there was a new terror because the pipe creaked and shifted when she started to pull. It was eaten away with rust, fastened to the wall with a single screw that might give at any moment.

But it held. Slowly, she dragged herself towards the wall, her heels scrabbling on the ice, until she reached a place where the ground was clear and she could stand upright again.

Sobbing, muttering under her breath, she limped back into the living room and rattled the poker at the back of the grate, hoping the neighbors might hear. But nobody came. She was shaking all over from cold and shock. After a few minutes she climbed on to the bed and pulled the blankets up over her wet dressing gown.

Her mind was clear and cold as ice. She went back over what had happened, reliving the moment when the world had turned. She listened for the sound of footsteps in the street outside. Somehow, when the sound of men's boots signalled the first shift of the day, she must get up and go to the door.

Then, after she did not know how long, confusion, darkness, pain. And suddenly there were people too many people pressing round her bed and a bright light that hurt her eyes and she wanted to say Get back and they all pressed in around her and their faces loomed up towards her with the fish-eyed distorted look of faces in curved glass and she tried to say again Get back but the words glugged out of her mouth like water.

Sheets. Tight and cool. The bed narrow. Too narrow for home, and high up. She forced her eyes open. Ice-green light splintered on a water jug. She moved her head: the light was green because of curtains round her bed.

There was a vase of flowers. Red. Familiar. But she could not find the name.

The curtains split around a head.

"Returned to the land of the living, have we?" And so, it seemed, she had.

When the sounds that glugged out of her mouth bore some resemblance to speech, when she could shuffle more than a few feet along the wall, they said she could go home.

At first she had thought they would never let her go. Who would look after her? they asked.

"I can look after myself."

But this would not do. They did not even answer.

"I've got good neighbors."

But you can't rely on the neighbors for everything. They told her so.

They were kind, but they didn't understand. They suggested a convalescent home. She refused, fearing that if she once agreed to enter a Home of any kind they would find some way of keeping her there, or else transfer her to another Home.

They were kind, but she didn't trust them. The need to get back to her own house was very strong now, like a physical pain.

In the end they gave in, though she could tell they disapproved. Old ladies are many, hospital beds are few. They needed the bed.

Her son came to collect her in his car.

"My son's coming to collect me in his car," she told the nurses proudly.

They smiled, though they hadn't understood a word she said. She was excited. When she was excited her speech went altogether.

She sat perched nervously on the edge of the front seat. She didn't like cars, though she liked her son having one. And she looked out of the window at all the changes that had taken place. She hadn't been into the town for many years.

There were whole streets of derelict houses, rows and rows of them, waiting to be pulled down. She pointed at them.

"Yes," her son said. "Worse than the Blitz, isn't it? Council's done more in one year than Hitler did in five."

She tried to answer, but abandoned the attempt when she heard the sounds that came out. The words clotted on the end of her tongue. Sometimes in her excitement and frustration she felt herself start to slobber. She did not want her son to see that.

He was saying, "You know, Mam, you could've come to us if it wasn't for Doreen being at work all day. Only it wouldn't be much fun for you, would it? Stuck in the house on your own."

She might have pointed out that she was stuck in the house all day on her own anyway, but she didn't. She didn't want to hear him making excuses. She didn't want to see him humiliate himself. She didn't blame him. It was Doreen. And he couldn't go against her after all. He had her to live with.

"Oh, don't you worry . . ." she began. But "worry" came out as "worrah", and she couldn't go on. She wanted to cry with frustration. She did cry often now, couldn't seem to stop herself, and the tears dripped down her cheek on to her chest.

Getting out of the car was a right performance. She felt people watching her and that made her worse. Half her body was useless, dragged along by the rest. She had to cradle her dead hand in her living hand, and then how the hell could you manage a stick?

But she got herself out in the end and shuffled the few steps across the pavement and into her house. Her eyes lingered lovingly on every detail of dingy wallpaper and falling plaster. The passage was full of smoke. That meant they'd lit a fire for her in the living room. And so they had. There it was, banked up and blazing in celebration of her return, and the bedclothes aired and turned back. Iris. That's who that would be.

"I'll put the kettle on," her son said.

She lay on the bed and looked at the fire. The wireless, the table, the armchair: everything. She would never be able to look her fill.

They drank the tea. Her son lingered, fussing over the fire, and getting her biscuits and a slice of cake to keep in a tin by the bed. She loved him but she wanted him to go. He wearied her.

"Now are you sure you'll be all right?"

"Yes." Yes, yes, yes!

At last he was gone and she was alone. A few minutes' peace. The neighbors would be in later. All of them.

But now she was alone. She burrowed down into her house, savoring its various textures and smells, an old fox that had reached its earth at last.

She had hoped that everything would be the same. But it never was, quite.

Her doctor came to see her, a dry Scot with a badly repaired harelip, carrying his professional kindness from house to house like a charm against mortality. There was nothing he could do. Her speech would improve with time, he said. As indeed would all the after-effects of her stroke.

Meanwhile, they were hard to bear. Her right side was weak, almost paralyzed. But not numb. There was a constant prickling sensation all over, like pins and needles. It exhausted her. Other people obviously believed that what was devoid of use must also be devoid of feeling. They handled the paralyzed limbs quite roughly at times. But looking down at the dead-white, useless leg Mrs. Bell could not blame them. It looked like some root vegetable, a turnip or a parsnip, that had never seen the light of day. And yet with such a rain of electric sparks it amazed her that other people could touch it and not draw back.

She turned the right side of her body away from people so that all her movements became crab-like. She could not wash and dress herself. She could not get around very well.

Words still clotted on her tongue whenever she became confused, though after the first few weeks her speech was generally easier to understand. Only she still had difficulty with the endings of words. They tended to get left off or to turn up attached to other words. Still more disconcertingly, she found herself thinking one thing and saying another, not realizing, until she heard herself, that she was talking nonsense. People, seeing that she found speech difficult, behaved as if she was deaf. Since, in fact, her hearing had become abnormally acute, their braying voices exploded inside her head, sending splinters of pain to every part.

But she did not give in. No, would not, not if she was brought down to the gutter.

Only she withdrew into herself. She had to search through the wreckage of her mind, to find out what she had left worth saving.

And other people withdrew from her. They were sorry for her, but she made them uncomfortable. It was difficult for them to believe that this slobbering, glugging thing that could not make its wants known was a human being. They took care of her, but they left her alone.

She didn't mind much. She didn't want their pity anyway. When she cried it was not from misery, but from the frustration she was too weak to express in any other way.

Only Iris King still had the patience to sit and listen. And after a while Mrs. Bell began to talk.

Something was happening to her, something strange. As her life drew to its end—and she knew that it was ending— she returned in spirit to her first beginnings. To her first home. Above all, as life ebbed, she returned to her mother.

Sometimes Iris was there to listen. Sometimes she was almost sure she was alone. Then there was only the sound of her own voice, threading the maze of the past.

"She used to send me for the meat in the morning before I went to school. It was really only the men got meat in them days. You just got the gravy. But me Dad used to give me a bite of meat from his plate. I was his favorite, see. Perhaps that's why she never liked me. Oh and if it was tough she used to leather me. I used to say to the butcher, Give it a good bashing, will you, Mister? She'll murder me if it's tough. And she did! She was hard. After our May was born she never walked properly again. She had what they called the white leg. And she had a crutch. She used to drop it on the floor and when you went to pick it up she hit you with it. My God. Still. Looking back on it now I can see she had a rotten life. She lost three out of the first four kids in an epidemic. And I think after that she must've gone a bit low because she used to hide our Annie in the blanket box with all the blankets on top of her. Well, she could've suffocated, you know. Me Dad used to come home from work and hear her crying and he used to say to her, What do you want to do that for? And she'd say summat about, They're coming to get her. Her mind had gone, see. But she got over it. Well, you had to. There was always another bairn on the way. At the finish her womb was fallen that bad she had to wear a big ring and when it slipped out she used to have to lie on the floor and wait till the doctor come to put it in again. You could see her womb, sticking out between her legs. And he used to say Oh, poor Mrs. Stott. And I'm sure sometimes there were tears in his eyes he felt that sorry for her. That was later, after the twins. They both died. And then our little Eddie died. I think I felt that more than she did. He used to bite on her breast and she'd yell and slap him. So I used to have him in my bed. I can still see him sat on his potty. Our Galla, he used to say. Doesn't sound much like Alice, does it? He was only two when he died. I was fourteen. It was like I'd lost me own bairn.

"But you were never told anything. When me periods started I didn't know what it was. I ran in shouting and screaming, Mam, Mam, I've busted. And she had a man with her. I think it must've been the Curate. And she fetched me such a swipe across the face I went from one end of the kitchen to the other. And she said, Don't be so daft, you haven't busted. That was it. That was as much as you got. When our Winnie started I did me best to tell her what it was. But I didn't know. I was married. I still didn't know! And she was just the same when I was pregnant. Not so much as a bloody word. You won't believe this. I was walking down Jubilee Road five months pregnant. I still didn't know where it had to come out. I thought they got it out of your belly button. And I met a girl I'd been at work with and she was a bit more fly than the rest of us. She says, Why, it comes out the same place it went in. And she says, there's no need to be frightened, you know. It's just like having a good shit. Well, it wasn't! But still, it was good of her. I always remembered her for that. And after, when I didn't see me periods, I weaned him on to the bottle and when I went to see me mother she said, Well you daft little bugger you don't see when you're feeding. But how was I to know? You were never told.

"Me Dad was the only one made anything of me. He used to take me out with him on a Sunday and carry me on his shoulders and show me off to his mates. He had this gold sovereign on a chain and he'd hold it up against me hair. It was the same shade of gold.

"But me Mam. I judged her too harshly. Now I look back I see things more her way. She was a hard woman but she had enough to make her hard. Eighteen kids. And we never went without shoes and there was always enough to eat. It might only be broth but there was plenty of it. She was a strong woman. She lived to be eighty and do you know when she died there wasn't a gray hair in her head."

She slept more during the day now. Day and night were running into each other. And she had extraordinary dreams. Once she stood by an open coffin and there was her first husband inside only in the dream she knew it wasn't her first husband it was God and his hand came up and stroked her right side. And she woke up and lay in the darkness knowing that she had been stroked by God.

Physically she deteriorated. The worst thing was that she sometimes lost control of her bowels. The first time it happened she told herself it was just an accident. It could've happened to anybody at any age. But then it happened again. And again.

Half the time she was constipated. Egg bound. She practically lived on raw eggs beaten up in milk. Then suddenly without warning she would overflow into the bed. And she had to lie in it until her son arrived to change the sheets. Because obviously this was something that couldn't be left to the neighbors. It shouldn't really have fallen to her son. She had to grit her teeth to face it, lying there in her own stench. But she had to accept his help. There was nobody else. Once, Doreen came with him. She had taken on the job of washing the sheets.

Her face would've curdled milk.

By now it was obvious that the situation could not continue. Obvious even to Mrs. Bell herself, though she would not admit it. Instead she lay in stubborn silence, waiting for somebody else to speak.

Then she had flu, badly. The doctor was called in. And that was it.

"He says he can put me in a Home whether I want to go or not. Some section or other. If you can't take care of yourself."

Iris hesitated for a long time before replying. Then she said gently, "Well, you know, it's all different nowadays. It's not like it used to be. I mean, the Workhouse. That was the end, wasn't it? It's not like that now."

"St. Anne's."

"Doesn't have to be there. Could be one of the new ones. They're lovely. And even St. Anne's. They've done it up, you know. It's all different inside."

They all thought she was cracked. She'd been to St. Anne's to see Jim's wife. Great big rooms. Thirty to forty beds. And the windows frosted so you couldn't see out. And some of 'em lying in bed with the sides up like a cot.

Rubber pants and nappies on and their minds gone. It'd need more than a coat of paint to change that.

None of this could she get out. Her tongue knotted up. She slobbered a bit, and lapsed into silence.

"Anyway, what did you say to him?" Iris asked, after another pause.

"I said I'd see the fella. What else could I say?"

She brooded about it bitterly. Whichever way you looked at it, it was the end. Defeat. As the time for the visit got nearer she started to get confused. Not by day. By day the issue was clear, if bleak. By night. The darkness, once barren, spawned unspeakable forms of life. Voices whispered in the corners. And although she could never hear a word that was said, she knew they were talking about her. There were heads on the walls, high up, looking down. And they talked in distorted voices, like speech under water.

One night she woke up and there was her husband by the fire. She asked him to put on some more coal and he wouldn't although the fire had burned right down.

Oh, the mean old man, she thought. The mean the mean the mean old man.

And found she had said the words aloud. It was morning.

"Who's a mean old man?" Iris wanted to know.

"Bill. Me husband."

"Your second this is?"

"Yes."

They had both been called Bill. Come to think of it, they'd both been mean.

"I used to get him his beer in a jug. And I'd allus crack on it cost a penny more than it did. And I'd buy meself a pound of apples and eat them on the way home. Well, we didn't have much. And I was carrying our Tom."

"This is your first husband."

"Yes. I wasn't having our Tom to me second, was I?"

"Go on, I'm with you now."

"Do you know, I've never tasted anything as good as them apples. I used to worry at them. Like a dog at a bone. And they were only cookers. He never found out."

She was already drifting off to sleep. The boundaries between sleep and waking were blurred now. She would fall asleep sometimes in the middle of a sentence. Slipping into silence.

If only they would let her be! But they wouldn't. They were too kind.

And besides she made them uncomfortable, lying there under layers of newspaper, emaciated and dirty. They wanted her clean, tidy, bound in white sheets.

On the morning of the visit she asked Iris to wash and set her hair. Then, when she was alone again, she hobbled across to the mirror and looked hopefully into it. My God.

The stroke was there for all to see. One side of her mouth was drawn down in a permanent leer. Of course she knew that. But something—some remaining shred of vanity perhaps—had prevented her realizing how bad it was. She looked to herself like a madwoman. The kind of person who gets put away.

Her hands came up. She hid herself from the mirror. For years she had avoided looking into it: the hag it showed bore no relation to the person she thought she was. Inside herself, she was still sixteen. She had all the passion, all the silliness. Still there behind the gray hair and wrinkled skin. Now the dislocation between what the mirror showed and what she knew herself to be, was absolute. She would have liked to break the glass.

Instead she lay down on the bed and began to work on the down-drawn mouth, trying to mold it into some semblance of normality. She was afraid of her speech going. If she got upset she would mouth and slobber. Better keep quiet altogether than open her mouth and confirm their worst suspicions.

Doreen and Tom turned up an hour before the man was due. They *were* keen.

"I don't now," Doreen grumbled as she tidied the room, "that home help of yours doesn't seem to have done much."

"I asked her to do me hair. Anyway, what can you do in an hour?"

"More than this."

When she'd finished they all sat down. It was like a dentist's waiting room. Everybody nervous and stuck for something to say.

At last a knock on the door. And a small man came into the room, his scalp showing pink through sandy hair. His name, he said, was Wilks.

"So this is the old lady?" He looked at Mrs. Bell but addressed himself to the younger woman. "Well, we'll soon have things sorted out."

His eyes took in the layers of newspaper in the bed.

"She's how old? Seventy-six?"

Tom cleared his throat. "Yes, about that."

"Ah, yes." He was sitting close to her now though still looking the other way. The backs of his hands had red hair on them. She wondered if all his hair was that color. "And she has no income apart from the social security?" Pity his poor bloody wife. "I'm sorry to have to ask you all these personal questions. It is necessary."

The apology was not addressed to her.

Tom said, "As far as I know that's all she gets."

"I'll need to see the book." He raised his voice in the direction of the bed, though he was sitting almost on top of her. *"I'll need to see the book."*

He took a form from the file and began filling it in, taking evident pride in his speed and efficiency. She watched the pen fly over the page.

"You see," Tom was saying, "we can't offer to take her ourselves. I mean Doreen goes out to work now and . . ."

The pen never paused.

"There's really nobody to see to her."

"No. Quite."

He wasn't listening. He'd heard it all before.

They all three watched mesmerized as his pen skimmed over the page.

"We'll find her a place all right. It's just a question of where. I suppose she can manage the toilet all right?" He looked at Mrs. Bell for the first time and yelled, "How are your waterworks, dear?"

Doreen spared her the need to answer. "Oh, we don't have that problem. It's more a matter of . . ." She lowered her eyes modestly, "the other."

He pursed his lips. "Often?"

"Well. More than once."

He ticked a box on the form.

"Now then , Mother," he said. "The doctor says you've been seeing things. Is that right?" He peered at a scribbled note. "Men's heads. Just the heads? Dear me, that's a bit rough." He looked at the daughter-in-law and winked. She wasn't bad if you overlooked the teeth. "How often does that happen?"

If he had been looking at her he might have seen her flinch.

"Do you know how often it happens?"

"No. She's only mentioned it once or twice. And that was to me husband."

He turned back to her. "Well, I don't know about that. Can't have gentlemen friends in the Home, you know. Matron'll have a fit." He enjoyed his little joke. "Now can I have a look at your pension book?"

She got it out of the bag herself, though it took time. Her dead hand seemed to be deader than ever. He glanced at the weekly amount, jotted down the number of the book, and handed it back.

"There. They won't take it all off her, you know. She'll still get pocket money. And if she gets she can't manage the Matron'll take care of it for her, buy her any little thing she wants."

He turned back to the bed.

"Now then, Mother, all you've got to do is sign."

Her glasses, which had broken two years before and had been stuck together with elastoplast, kept slipping off the end of her nose.

"Just make your mark," Mr. Wilks suggested.

Then she spoke for the first time. She said, very clearly, "No. I can write." And slowly she wrote her name on the form: Alice Bell.

"Where are you going to put me?" Now that she had spoken once it was easier to do so again.

"St. Anne's."

"But I don't want to go there."

"Oh, you'll soon settle in." In a more normal voice, he said, "It's the toilet, you know. And she's virtually bedridden. She needs nursing. You can't get that in the smaller Homes."

"The Workhouse."

"It's not the Workhouse now. In your day it was. But it's all changed now."

He had actually spoken to her in a normal voice. Evidently the experiment frightened him, because he didn't repeat it. "The food's lovely. For your dinner you get your meat and two veg, and there's always a choice of pudding."

He was getting his things together as he spoke.

Tom said, "How long is it likely to be?"

"Oh, very quick. Coupla days." He snapped his briefcase shut. "They'll send an ambulance of course."

"No. I think I'd rather take her in meself. If you don't mind."

After he'd gone Tom and Doreen sat on. And on. They seemed afraid to leave her. As if they thought she might put her head in the gas oven like poor old Mrs. Bailes had done.

Well, they needn't worry about that. She hated the smell of gas. Always had done.

She made herself talk. It was the only way to get rid of them. She said she was coming round to the idea, that she could see it was for the best. She would soon make friends, she said. And anyway in a place that size there'd probably be people she already knew. And they'd come to see her. And the neighbors'ld come to see her. In fact it would be no different really, except she'd be better looked after.

By the time they were ready to go she had smiled so much that her mouth felt like a fraying elastic band. Her cheeks sagged with the weight of the lies she had told.

She heard them in the passage congratulating each other on the way she had taken it. Then, at last, she was alone.

For a long time she lay still, her eyes closed, her mind—not blank, worse than blank. Soon the night would come; with whispering and laughter and talking heads staring at her from the walls.

But not yet. It wasn't dark yet. She could. Could something. No. Only wait for death.

And yet why should death appear so promptly? She had had long enough to wait for birth. Standing at the upstairs window in Walker Street listening to men's boots going up the hill and back again, while the midwife came and went, and the pain dragged on all that day and half the following night. Oh but it was worth it, to lie with the child in your arms and know that you had brought life into the world. There was nothing to equal that.

Even the memory of it strengthened her. She was able to sit up and look about the room. Because it had recently contained a stranger, she was able to see it through a stranger's eyes. Even to see herself, sitting up in bed, through a stranger's eyes. No wonder they wanted her put away. She could almost agree with them, especially when saliva dribbled from her loosened mouth and had to be wiped away on the back of her hand. Rubbish. Ready for the tip.

Iris had promised to look in. And the others would soon be round. She did not want to see them. Their sympathy would sap her energy, divert her from what had to be done. She hobbled along the passage and locked the front door. Then she sat down in her armchair and stared into the fire.

She was finished and she made no bones about it. Her body: she squinted at it down the neck of her nightdress. Black dugs, belly silver-streaked from the child-bearing of half a century ago. Gone. And her mind. Her mind crumbled by the hour. She searched among the wreckage for some fragment of hope, but there was none. Her life would not renew.

She understood now the full indignity of rape. That man, the expression in his eyes when he looked at her. The not-seeing. And she could see no way out, except to submit, to accept herself at his evaluation. To give in.

She sat in silence and waited, all hope gone.

And then something stirred. In the ruins of her mind, something so new and unused that it could only be spirit was struggling to stand up. Oh, but it was hard. She could not sustain the effort. She fell back, she dwindled, became again a heap of old garbage waiting for the pit. She preferred it like that. She turned to darkness and away from light.

And yet the growth once started was not so easily stopped.

It made her restless. She began to wander about the house, opening and shutting drawers, caressing each battered object that had accompanied her through life. Everything was steeped in memory. The smell of mothballs from the drawers where she stored her bedlinen. The crack in the fireplace where she had dropped the iron. Gradually she came to herself. That new thing that had started to grow in her pulled itself up on tables and chairs as naturally as a toddler starting to walk.

Her home. They were taking it away from her. The dirt and disorder, the signs of malnutrition and neglect which to them were reasons for putting her away were, to her, independence. She had fought to keep for herself the conditions of a human life.

She was calm again. What she wanted was simple. She wanted to die with dignity. She wanted to die in her own home. And if that was no longer possible, she would go away. She would not be here waiting for them when they came.

She knelt down beside the chest of drawers and began pulling out clothes. Then she slipped off her nightdress and was naked, shivering and goose-pimply in spite of the fire. Normally she would have hurried over such a moment, not liking to see this body that had been fastened to her by time. But today she let herself look. Silver branches spread out across her belly, springing from the sparsely-rooted hair. A tree in winter.

She remembered her mother's body washed and laid out for the grave. How remote it had been, how shocking in its nakedness. Her body was like that now.

At the end her mother called for her and said, "Alice. Alice." Forty years ago. "You always thought I didn't care as much about you as I did the rest. But, you know, I did." Forty years. And it could still bring tears to her eyes.

Getting her stockings on was a struggle. It was hard to bend and still harder to straighten up again. This body that seemed to have less and less to do with her, demanded more attention now than ever it had done in youth, when the spirit suffused it so vigorously that there had seemed to be no possibility of division.

At last, though, the stockings were on, the garters snapped into place around the wasted thighs. At intervals questions bubbled to the surface of her mind. What am I doing? Where am I going? But more faintly now as the unnamed and unadmitted purpose gathered strength.

Finally, before she left, she got her black handbag from under the pillows and set it squarely in the middle of the bed. There was no need to hide it now. She stroked it. There would be enough.

And so she accepted what she was about to do.

She hobbled across the icy yard, remembering her fall but remembering it as something that had happened a long time ago in another life. From the yard door she looked back at the house. Everything known and loved, everything trusted and relied upon, had to be abandoned now. She was committing herself to an act of faith which, if it was ever known at all, would appear to others as folly or madness or mere senile confusion.

She was almost too weak to walk. Her mouth, her skin, even her veins seemed to have dried up, to be cracked and parched as the bed of an ancient river. She wanted. Wanted. The chaos of cold and emptiness was reflected in the darkness of her eyes.

She did not know how she could walk, but walk she did. The weak side dragged, but she had her sticks. She moved slowly, pushing one foot out in front of the other. Then a pause while she brought the stick on the other side into line. Then the other foot, the weak one, could be dragged level.

From the outside it must have looked like a triumph of the will. She alone knew that it was nothing of the kind. Will-power could not have moved her crumbling body from the bed, let alone have driven it out into this cold. She who had lived all her life by willpower alone had ended by setting it aside, to wait passively, to wait in darkness, for deliverance or for grace.

There was washing hung out across the alley, white sheets, frozen and stiff. She had no hand free to lift them aside, and so had to walk through, head lowered, while the hard cotton scraped against her face. And a bubble broke in her mind, releasing the memory of another day. A younger woman, running, running away. And the wet sheets stinging and slapping her face.

Then she was leaving the alley and entering the railway tunnel. Other memories rose to the surface, tugging at the corners of her mind like the mouths of tiny fish. There were more footsteps running, a child's this time, and the child stopped and looked behind her as if afraid of being pursued. And a young girl stood just inside the entrance to the tunnel, with a young man's arms around her. Flakes of plaster drifted down and landed in her hair.

She stopped in confusion as the memories threatened to overwhelm her. These fragments. Were they the debris of her own or other lives? She had been so many women in her time.

She passed the Bluebell. She moved from familiar to unfamiliar streets. Now there were park railings on the left. A steep hill led up to the gates. So steep that after the first few steps she doubted if she would ever make it to the top. But she hooked her sticks around her wrists and began hauling her needled flesh from railing to railing. It was darker now, though not yet dark. And all around her was a web of voices.

At first she thought the ordeal of her nights had spilled over into the day. But no, this was not the sterile torment of the talking heads. This was something different. This was something else again. At first the voices were soft but they grew louder and clearer as she toiled up the hill: a child shouting, a young girl laughing, a woman crooning over her child. She carried the web of voices with her up the hill.

And at last she reached the gates. There was the sky, and pools of clear water, and silence. And her own mind again, simple and clean as a rinsed plate.

Oh but it was cold. And the body stupid. It did not seem to

understand that this cold, for so long an enemy, was now a friend, but must be rubbing its hands and turning up the collar of its coat and looking for a sheltered bench.

The pools of water reflected light into the sky and the light did not disperse but gathered to a radiance that beat down again upon the earth. The light was bewildering because it seemed to come as much from the earth as the sky. She was confused. And the cold seemed to have got into her bones. The small bones of her face and ears vibrated like struck tuning forks, or like a bell after the sound has died away.

A bench. Dead horse chestnut leaves starred the ground. She noticed that one had drifted down and lay on the bench beside her, brown, discolored, the flesh wasting away between raised veins. She moved her hand and the leaf moved. It didn't surprise her. The membrane that had divided her from the world was permeable now, self and not-self no longer an absolute division.

The sky was a clear eggshell blue fading towards the horizon through turquoise, rose-pink and yellow to a somber, glowing red.

At first there was total silence, except for the beating of her heart, quickened by the long walk up the hill. Then a murmuring began, as of the wind through summer trees or waves unfurling on the shore, only darker and more secret: the sound of the sea in an underground cave or blood coursing through the hidden channels of the ear. Then, mixed in with the murmuring, a series of sharp, electric clicks as if a group of women were talking and brushing their hair at once. The noise became louder. And now when she looked at the sky-line she saw that one tree stood out from the rest, its branches fanned out, black and delicate, against the red furnace of sky.

Nothing could now have moved her dying flesh from the bench where it had taken refuge, but she began in spirit to walk towards the tree. At first it seemed to be bare like all the others, though with a jaggedness of outline that suggested not winter but death. By now the murmur had become a shout, a fierce, ecstatic trilling; and when she looked more closely she saw that the tree was full of birds, clustering along its branches, as thick and bright as leaves. And all singing. But then, as she came closer still, as her white hair and skin took on the colors of blood and fire, she saw more clearly, and in a moment of vision cried. It isn't the birds, it's the tree. The tree is singing.

The light was unbearably bright, bubbling in every vein, shaking her heart. She could not bear it. She shrank, she fell back. The world dwindled to a park bench and a litter of dead leaves in the grass.

But there was a child there, now, a girl, who, standing with the sun behind her, seemed almost to be a gift of the light. At first she was afraid, the child had come so suddenly. Then—not afraid. They sat beside each other; they talked. The girl held out her hand. The withered hand and the strong young hand met and joined. There was silence. Then it was time for them both to go.

So that in the end there were only the birds, soaring, swooping, gliding, moving in a never-ending spiral about the withered and unwithering tree.

About the Author

Pat Barker was born in Thornaby-on-Tees in 1943. She was educated at the local grammar school and at the London School of Economics where she studied economics, politics and history. She is married to the Professor of Zoology at the University of Durham, and has two children.